OPHELIA'S WAR

RUBIES OF RUIN

OPHELIA'S WAR

THE SECRET STORY OF A MORMON TURNED MADAM

ALISON L. MCLENNAN

FIVE STAR
A part of Gale, Cengage Learning

GALE
CENGAGE Learning·

Farmington Hills, Mich • San Francisco • New York • Waterville, Maine
Meriden, Conn • Mason, Ohio • Chicago

LIBRARY OF CONGRESS CATALOGING-IN-PUBLICATION DATA

Names: McLennan, Alison L., author.
Title: Ophelia's war : The secret story of a Mormon turned madam Rubies of Ruin #1 / Alison L. McLennan.
Other titles: Mormon turned madam
Description: Waterville, Maine : Five Star Publishing, 2016.
Identifiers: LCCN 2015047689 (print) | LCCN 2016009176 (ebook) | ISBN 9781432831882 (hardback) | ISBN 1432831887 (hardcover) | ISBN 9781432831868 (ebook) | ISBN 1432831860 (ebook)
Subjects: LCSH: Women—Utah—19th century—Fiction. | Mormon women—Fiction. | Frontier and pioneer life—Utah—Fiction. | Choice (Psychology)—Fiction. | Coming of age—Fiction. | BISAC: FICTION / Historical. | FICTION / Coming of Age. | GSAFD: Western stories. | Historical fiction.
Classification: LCC PS3613.C57855 O64 2016 (print) | LCC PS3613.C57855 (ebook) | DDC 813/.6—dc23
LC record available at http://lccn.loc.gov/2015047689

Find us on Facebook– https://www.facebook.com/FiveStarCengage
Visit our website– http://www.gale.cengage.com/fivestar/
Contact Five Star™ Publishing at FiveStar@cengage.com

Printed in the United States of America
2 3 4 5 6 7 20 19 18 17 16

To all the women of the American frontier whose secret wars and stories have gone untold. And to all women everywhere who have ever believed they are *damaged goods.*

ACKNOWLEDGMENTS

To Sterling Watson, Steve Huff, Venise Berry, Randall Kenan, Robert Lopez, James Anderson, and other members of the Solstice MFA community who supported and encouraged this work. And to Alice Duncan and Five Star for publication and editorial support. Also, thanks to my patient family and the broken knee that forced me to begin this story.

men were dead because of me, and only one of them had deserved it. Had I incurred the wrath of God? I didn't believe the Heavenly Father wanted me to end up in the hands of a devil like Uncle Luther. Yet he had given man dominion over all things, over the land, and the beasts—even woman.

I spoke in a hushed but stern tone. "Samuel, we were tired and we took a wrong turn somewhere. We probably got mixed up when we stopped at the creek and let the horses drink." He was silent and his mouth formed a hard thin line. I tried to alleviate his foul mood with a chipper response. "Think about it this way, if anyone is trying to track us they'll be as vexed as we are." He stared at me, squinted, and waited.

I dismounted from my horse and pointed at a big rock near. "Look, I will just scurry up to top of that rock there and see where we lost our way. Don't fret. We'll be back on the main trail in no time."

He looked at the rock mesa with skepticism. "That's a fine idea, but how do you propose to get up there, Ophea?"

"Easy, I'll climb."

"Climb?"

I pointed to the rock mesa, which rose up next to another rock formation. "See how those two rocks form a chimney? I can climb up there and squeeze myself in till I get higher, then the angle eases off, and I can just creep catlike to the top. From there I'll get a bird's-eye view of this rock maze."

Samuel shook his head and looked at the tall rocks. He'd been shifting his body in the saddle but now he was dead still. "I don't like it," he said. "What if you fall? What then?"

I laughed. "My brother, Zeke, and I have been climbing rocks like these for years. I'm sure-footed as a mountain goat. Don't worry. I won't fall."

At first, I'd felt confident. But the mention of falling made me tremble with dread and panic. I'd never been afraid of

Palmyra, New York, 1820

They felt the Lord in their bodies. During the Second Great Awakening preachers roamed upstate New York, spread across the land like herds of proselytizing buffalo, and erected pulpits in meadows. Thousands of people broke from the toils of frontier life and traveled for days to hear sermons.

In the wilderness of the American frontier, spiritual seekers gathered in open-air cathedrals and sat on benches cut from freshly felled pines. They sang improvised hymns, listened to passionate sermons, and exclaimed "Hallelujah." The shackles of the old religions couldn't keep them down. Tired farm wives and their hardened husbands raised their hands to the heavens and praised the Lord. Their bodies shook. They hugged one another and collapsed onto the ground. In a new world, they converted to a new version of God.

A handsome young man walked amongst the preachers' rickety pulpits. Although not yet fully grown, he towered above all others. His high cheekbones and head of loose, blond curls turned many a gaze upon him. The ladies smiled and he smiled back. Even the men couldn't help staring. He fingered the seer stones in his pocket. From these he made his living hunting treasure. Folk magic had been passed down through his family for generations. In the evenings by the dim flicker of candlelight, his mother read the Tarot. She knew her son was destined for greatness and a violent end. The Sun and the Hanged Man appeared every time she drew his cards. But they were always ac-companied by Death.

He listened for a while. Sometimes he liked what he heard and for a brief moment thought he'd found the one true religion. Then something would irritate him, and he would notice a shadow of avarice or lust fall across the preacher's face. He moved on to the next one and then the next, until he tired of the camp-town meetings.

He was a mystic. The wind often whispered to him and the stones spoke. Revelations came from the babbling brook. The tall creaking trees were his prophets. The preachers marched to their own tunes of salvation in a competitive discordant jumble. None of their sermons moved him like the ancient stones, or the trees whose leaves were fed by eternal matter—air, water, and sun.

A powerful dark force cast him into despair. He went into the woods to make his peace with the Lord. He prayed to be forgiven for his sins and transgressions: for laying the black-smith's daughter, and pleasuring himself while conjuring the miller's daughter, and brushing the buttocks of several young ladies in camp town while they were listening to sermons.

Blinding light, brighter than sunlit snow, descended from the heavens in a great spiral and saved him. Two beautiful angels appeared and granted him forgiveness. One golden angel called him son. The angel told the handsome young man that he was chosen to bring a lost religion to the world. The angel spoke of ancient tablets and sacred stones.

Later, the young man had a revelation that his love of divina-tion and copulation were also divine, for they had been bestowed upon him as ways to reveal and spread the one true message. His name was Joseph Smith.

ONE

My parents were both followers of Joseph Smith. A long time ago in Vermont, my father and Joseph had been childhood friends. After my father's first wife and infant died in labor, he was a lost soul. When he caught wind of the news that his childhood companion, Joseph Smith, had been lynched at a jailhouse in Carthage, Illinois, he packed up, and traveled west to join the Saints. They became his brethren in the outrage of injustice and the exaltation of new faith.

Society had cast aside my disgraced, dishonored, and disowned mother. Only the Saints offered to save her from ruin. When she met my father, a bastard swelled her womb. But my father was a brave, practical, smitten man, and he married her despite her condition. Adding insult to injury, my brother, Ezekiel, was born half savage. I don't know how it happened. I don't even know if my father knew. It was just one of Mother's many secrets.

In May of 1858, Father sold our household belongings and bought the necessities for our eleven-hundred-mile pilgrimage to the Promised Land. Among the things he purchased were a covered wagon, a pair of oxen, a tent, bedding, food, and a flat-bottomed iron pot with a tight-fitting lid. We couldn't bring anything extra, but Mother allowed me to carry my dear rag-doll, Dolly, even though she wasn't a necessity.

After my father secured our tickets to paradise, we departed Winter Quarters, Nebraska, the jumping-off place, via the

Overland Trail as part of the John S. Brown Company. I was seven years old and the journey was treacherous. We froze during a freak June snowstorm, nearly drowned fording rivers, were constantly hungry, and feared both Indian attacks and the U.S. Cavalry. But I was a Saint, one of the Lord's chosen people, and I believed he would protect me. Each day I walked beside the wagon until I collapsed from exhaustion. Then my brother, Ezekiel, carried me piggyback. When my small grimy fingers slipped from their clasp around his thin brown neck, he did not have the strength to hold me. The earth beckoned our weary bodies with all the allure of a goose-feather mattress and we collapsed upon it together.

Grafton, Utah, 1867

Not long after we arrived in the Great Salt Lake Territory, we were sent to the desert settlement of Grafton by Joseph Smith's successor, Brigham Young, to grow cotton for the Mormon Church. But while America's Dixie was green and lush, Utah's Dixie was dry and barren. My pa had always said, "Trying to grow cotton, or anything for that matter, in the desert, is like trying to put stockings on a chicken." He had not been a good Mormon because he'd only taken one wife and he questioned everything, including Joseph's death, which he always referred to as suspicious.

The Saints put up with Pa on account of his skills. He was a blacksmith, a handyman, an inventor—a fixer of all things broken and a lover of all things mechanical. Although he was a skilled hunter, he had neither talent for farming nor patience for the mysterious ways of women. He certainly had no desire to have more than one wife. My mother understood him, and over the years she became a hardened practical woman herself. She had always been shunned by society because of my brother, Ezekiel, and so the desolation of Grafton had matched her inner isolation.

The Virgin River that ran through Grafton could not be tamed. Sometimes she was calm and peaceful. At other times her waters boiled and foamed. Then she would rise up and the reckless abundance of her sudden swelling would destroy our dinner basket gardens. She'd carry away the soil, farm tools, and all manner of things we'd thoughtlessly left on her banks. She'd even carry away the careless cow that, while quenching her thirst, ignored the river's thunderous roar. Floods came mostly in spring and early summer, when the mountain snow melted. Soil dropped from the banks and the land was transformed in a mad flash. Sometimes I thought the Virgin was laughing at us. Everything we'd worked for, everything she had given life to, she could take away—and she did.

The first houses in Grafton had been constructed of pine and built by the banks of the Virgin. In 1862, a flash flood destroyed them. The dwellings were hastily rebuilt on higher ground. About twenty modest log homes surrounded by split-rail fences were scattered about on the hillsides. Town center consisted of three adobe brick houses, a meeting and dance hall, and a big tent down near the river.

The cemetery was a half mile west of town and occupied the last bit of level ground before the land turned rough and rocky. Sand filled the graveyard and made it easy to bury the dead, of which there were many on account of sickness, Indian attacks, and even starvation. Farther south the earth hardened to salmon-colored clay.

After about a month without rain, even the hardy sagebrush looked withered. I wandered through the small cemetery and admired the large ornate headstone of the Berry brothers, killed by Ute Indians. Then I stopped and hovered over a small, smooth white rock and said a brief prayer for poor Mary York, who had died of consumption.

Shovels full of orange sand flew from a hole. It was probably deep enough by now, but my brother, Ezekiel, kept digging. The morning wind blew grit into my eyes, which were already full of tears. I cried, not only for the wasted body of our father lying in the flimsy pine box, but also because I was afraid.

"How deep does it need to be, Zeke?" I called. The effort burned my throat. I couldn't dig anymore. I meant no disrespect to Pa, but I hated being in the burial ground and I feared that gaping hole. I wanted to take my shovel, go down to the river, and tend my small garden—focus my hands on life—set them to making things grow in the cantankerous soil of sand and silt.

"Only suitable for growing spiky plants, nothing fit for eatin'." That's what Momma always said, but she never gave up trying—until the sickness took her.

The dirt stopped flying. Zeke's hat was flush with the ground. It looked like his head was growing out of the sand. I didn't like to see him that way because I feared he would be next. The Saints claimed that Zeke was cursed because his real father was a Lamanite savage. They said his people were a cursed tribe who would never enter the heavenly kingdom unless they repented and converted to our ways. Even so, they had buried the bodies of fallen Indian warriors at the edge of the cemetery.

With the sandy earth crumbling under his hands, Zeke struggled to hoist himself out of the grave.

"Deep enough," he said and brushed the dirt from his pants. He looked to the sand and rock mesas that bordered the burial ground. "Deep enough so no coyotes or mountain lions will dig him up."

After we lowered Pa into the ground and filled the hole, Zeke marked his grave with a small wooden cross. We stood back, clasped our hands, and bowed our heads. Two thin crosses—my mother's and father's—now lined up perfectly. Wind stirred my skirt. The crosses were so flimsy and insubstantial, they moved with every breeze. The movement unsettled me. How could the souls of our parents rest in peace while something on top of them flapped and fluttered every time the wind blew? They deserved a better headstone.

Zeke wiped tears from my cheeks and patted my head. He bent over and whispered in my ear, "Later this evening when it cools down we'll go fetch a big stone from the Garden of the Gods. I'll carve their names real nice, make 'em a right proper headstone." He glanced around at some of the large, elaborate burial markers.

I wanted to drape the sparkling ruby necklace over Momma's cross. If she couldn't wear it in life, let her wear it in death. But the ruby necklace, sewn inside my ragdoll, Dolly, was a secret between us, and could only be sold in the most desperate circumstances. Besides, even if someone from the settlement didn't steal the rubies from her grave, one of the ravens surely would.

Ma and Pa would be together now in their own heavenly kingdom. But Zeke and I were alone. I leaned my head against his chest and felt his strong arm embrace me. He was filling out, becoming more man than boy. Zeke had known I was thinking about the flimsy grave-markers. We hardly had to speak. It had always been that way with us.

We had set to burying Pa early in the morning for two reasons. First, it was cool, and we knew too well what digging a grave in the heat was like. We'd done it for Ma, on a hot September day in company with a flock of squawking ravens. Flies had buzzed round her coffin, even though Pa had built it out of some of the best oak—the oak he'd been saving to build her a new table before she became afflicted.

The other reason we got up early to bury Pa was marching down the road toward the burial ground. The men slung shovels over their shoulders, and the skirts of the bonnet-clad women swung like bells as they marched toward us. The women carried goods: bread, dried meat, and fruit, to see us through the hard days of grief and toil. I figured they were just well-wishers coming to pay their respects. After all, we were supposed to be a family, a family of Saints, children of God following the divine teachings of Joseph Smith, working together to build a heavenly kingdom on earth in the land we called Zion.

But Zeke didn't trust them. And they didn't trust him. He looked different from the rest of us. He had raven hair, and his skin was dark—not the dark, chocolate color of a Negro; he had the dark copper color of a Lamanite. My skin was pale and white, covered with orange freckles the same color as my hair, which matched the color of the giant sandstone cliffs that rose up like cathedrals beyond the Virgin River. But no matter how different we looked from each other, no one could tell me that Zeke was not my blood.

Zeke and I had at least three things in common. One was the way our hair formed a widow's peak. My hairline and Zeke's had the same V that our mother once had. The people who spread rumors that my parents had bought Zeke from the Spanish slave traders had obviously never compared our hairlines.

The second thing was that we both had eyes the color of blueberries. Mine stood out against my pale face, but to see the blue in Zeke's eyes you had to look real close. From a distance they could appear hard and black like marbles. The third thing was a connection. We were as connected as two people can be without becoming one. Zeke was my brother. And he was definitely my mother's son.

Zeke looked over his shoulder and saw the Saints coming. He narrowed his eyes and shook his head. "I'm gonna go on toward home, Little O. See if you can stop them from coming around." He hoisted his shovel over his shoulder and started toward our place, about a half mile away, up on a little hill, not far from the river.

"Sure thing. I'll be right along," I called to his back as he went down the footpath.

The Saints had never been kind to Zeke, but things had become a lot worse since the Ute leader, Black Hawk, started making regular cattle raids. Last year, the Berry boys had been killed about twenty miles from town. Two Saints from Rockville had found them scalped, with their hearts cut out. They recognized them as the Berry brothers and carried their corpses to Grafton. Bishop Marley had made sure anyone who wanted to could have a good look before they were buried. After that, the men met in the council tent and made plans for protection and retaliation.

The sun wasn't high, but it was already hot. I took off my bonnet, wiped sweat from my brow, and put it back on, as much to hide as to shade myself. I tilted my head back and looked at the sky. A lone vulture had been circling all morning. Five or six dark shapes now made intertwining circles overhead. The Saints kicked up a cloud of dust as they approached. With pursed lips and narrowed eyes, they watched Zeke disappear over the hill. Brother Thompson stepped forward and spoke to me.

He was a tall, toothless man who had to wear suspenders or else his pants would fall down. He stood too close and I took a step back.

"I guess we're too late. You young'uns must have been up before the crack of dawn to get your pa buried this early." He knelt down, looked into my eyes, and stroked my hair. "Don't worry, Ophelia, you won't be on your own. I'll always have a place for you at my table." He looked square at my bosom then. My cheeks burned. I wished I had run off with Zeke toward home.

Brother Thompson's first wife, Mary, came over, put her

hands on her hips, and glared down at him. "Martin Thompson, we got a big enough brood already." She stood between us, turned her back to me, and scolded him in a harsh whisper. "You leave that girl alone. She's too young for you."

He stood up and towered over her. "Woman—"

"In the name of the Lord! Not now, Martin. Have some respect for the dead."

He shook his head while walking over to stand with the others who had gathered around my parents' graves with their heads bowed.

Sister Mary turned to me and clutched my head to her bosom. It smelled like sweat and curdled milk. I tried not to cry. "Don't fret, child. You're gonna be just fine. We brought you some provisions."

Bishop Marley cleared his throat and eyed us. "I think it's time we all bowed our heads and prayed to the Lord."

I stood by the others with my head down. The bishop took off his hat and held it in his hands. The other men followed suit. A ring of white hair made the bishop's baldness a halo. His low solemn voice made the words sound more like a condemnation than a prayer. The Lord and his will had failed me—again.

After the prayer, the men put their hats back on and the crowd dispersed. Some people went and stood by the graves of their dearly departed—heads bowed and silent. A group of men gathered and discussed their plans to build the schoolhouse.

The bishop walked over to me with his usual air of purpose and self-importance. He stroked his beard and said, "I don't suppose a fourteen-year-old girl and an Indian boy ought to run your pa's place alone. I'll have to take this issue to the council."

I could tell he was thinking about our livestock and how he'd disperse our land and belongings to the community while keeping the lion's share for himself. "With all due respect, sir, I'm almost sixteen, and my brother, Zeke, and I are perfectly capable of looking after things until our Uncle Luther arrives."

The bishop's snow-white, overgrown brows rose so high they almost touched the brim of his hat. "Uncle who?"

I licked my dry lips and squinted into the sun, which was rising behind him. "When Ma and Pa first got sick, my ma sent word to her brother back east. My uncle should be arriving here any day, sir. We'll be in his care."

The bishop looked at the horizon, furrowed his brows, and grimaced. "That's a long way, my girl. We'll wait a few weeks—see if he makes it. In the meantime, you let me know if you need anything." He gazed in the direction of our homestead. "Stay out of trouble now, you hear."

"Appreciate that, sir. I reckon we'll be fine though. Pa was sick for a while, and me and Zeke got along just fine."

The bishop tipped his hat to me, turned, and walked toward the group of men who were now waving their hands and drawing lines in the dirt where the schoolhouse would stand.

I tried to make a quick getaway, but Sister May Belle Hopkins spied me and called, "Ophelia, we brought some things that will see you through. Come on over in the shade! Sit for a spell." She waved me over to a cottonwood tree where four women sat and passed a canteen.

The shade felt cool, but my blood was hot under Sister May Belle's stony glare. She would be the schoolmarm come fall when they finally made enough adobe bricks to raise the schoolhouse. She had a sharp nose and a pinched face, but she wouldn't have been all that unattractive if she'd smiled once in a while. She was known as a prudish shrew who could hear someone cuss from a mile away.

When she called me, I prepared to hang my head and get a chiding. She put a hand on my shoulder. But her look was different from usual, sweet and full of concern. It almost broke my heart to see a woman so hard look at me so soft. I had to concentrate so I wouldn't cry again. Who would have thought that May Belle Hopkins had a tender spot in her cold heart? She looped her arm through mine and walked me out of earshot of the other women. She handed me a burlap sack and said, "There's a fruitcake, some bread, dried elk, a little sugar, and this—" She held up a black book with gold embossed letters. "You be careful with this. I'm going to want it back when you're done."

My spirits lifted. "What is it?" Besides *The Bible* and *The Book of Mormon,* we only had a few books at home and I'd read them all more than once.

"Ophelia, this is *Hamlet,* by Mr. William Shakespeare. Don't show it to anyone." She shook her head and gave me a conspiratorial smile. "The Prophet has not approved it. Before she died, your mother told me she wanted to get a copy of this for you. Did you know she saw *Hamlet* at Ford's Theatre, the very same playhouse where Abraham Lincoln was shot? That's how you come by the name Ophelia. Read this book, child, and know your momma is smiling down on you." She handed me the book and the burlap sack.

I held my shovel in one hand and the book and sack in the other. "Thank you, ma'am. I'll take good care of it." Ma had told me that same story a hundred times. A suitor had taken her to that playhouse, and I think she always wondered what her life would have been like if she'd married that man. I smiled and turned to go. May Belle grabbed my elbow, pulled me close, and spoke low. "Now tell me, dear, has Aunt Ruby been to see you?"

"Pardon?" I didn't know I had an Aunt Ruby or that she was supposed to come. Could she be Uncle Luther's wife?

"Your blood, dear." Her voice was low and she looked around to make sure no one was listening. "Are you a woman yet?"

"Oh! No," I lied. "Not yet, ma'am."

"Well, you be sure to tell me when it happens. I'll help you through. And then you can think about marriage."

The heat and the talk of marriage made me queasy. I wished I had let the bishop think I was fourteen. I pulled my elbow from May Belle's clutch. "I got to go now, ma'am—lots of chores to do." Carrying the goods in one hand with the shovel slung over my other shoulder, I walked through the willows and felt the Saints watching me. I was strung like a bow until I was out of their sight and climbing the hill to our homestead. At least I could look forward to a new book.

Two

It was a dry year. As June turned into July, the days grew hotter. The pink, yellow, orange, and red prickly pear blossoms faded and shriveled under the scorching sun. Swarms of red ants carried the dead blossoms away—to where and for what purpose I did not know. I watered the garden with buckets from the river three times a day. I'd already harvested spinach, lettuce, carrots, beets, and potatoes. The ox, chickens, mules, horses, and cow all needed extra care so they wouldn't become sickly. Since I didn't have to tend Pa anymore, I had more time. My mind wandered to Uncle Luther's arrival. I found myself watching the road near town and the rutted tracks covered with willow grass that led up to our place.

Some Saints acted kind but were not. Others acted stern, but when it came down to it they were kind. I knew who was trustworthy, not just from my own watching, but also from the hushed conversations of Ma and Pa, spoken low in the evenings when they thought I was asleep. Most information, most stuff worth knowing, I learned from eavesdropping. I'd been whipped once or twice. Pa didn't want to do it, but he'd had no choice, as I'd been caught listening to men's talk outside the tent during one of their council meetings. Word got around that I was both prideful and rebellious. They'd said I needed a good hiding to put me in my place. Pa didn't like that talk. He didn't like the community interfering with how he ran his family. This and all the fuss about Zeke caused us to withdraw and spend more time at our own place, raising our own livestock and crops, trying to be independent of the settlement. Most of the other Saints had given up on the idea of growing cotton and were just trying to survive. But they had depended on Pa. He was a skilled blacksmith and could fix just about anything that broke.

I hoped that when Uncle Luther arrived, he'd set Bishop Marley straight about taking over our land and marrying me off to some toothless codger old enough to be my grandpa. Surely Uncle Luther would see to all that. Zeke and I could work the land and take care of the livestock, but we had no experience in what Pa had called "Grafton politics." Since the Grafton Saints had depended on Pa, his word had carried weight.

On Sundays when we'd finished all our work, or sometimes even if we hadn't, Zeke and I would ride out to the waterfalls and cold emerald pools past the big rock cathedrals. Zeke had stopped going to church a long time ago on account of the way the people stared at him. I stopped after Ma died, and I sure didn't miss it. Surrounded by the giant rock walls in the place north of town we called the Garden of the Gods, I felt the presence of the Lord. Those rock walls were masterpieces carved by the hand of the Lord himself. It was a place of purity, unsullied by the hands of holy men getting too big for their britches, saying that the Lord spoke to them. My pa was as good a man as any other, and he never claimed the Lord spoke to him.

I missed Pa. I missed his big sunburned hands, his hard arms covered with soft, yellow hair. I missed the way he was always fixing something with his wet, silly tongue hanging out to the side looking like a dog figuring a sum. I knew Zeke missed Pa too, although he never said it. I also knew the sadness Zeke felt because Pa never called him son—not once. Zeke had waited his whole life for a man to call him son. Pa had taught Zeke how to hunt and shoot. He let him use his tools and showed him how to make things. He taught him all kinds of skills. Even though Zeke wasn't sown from my father's seed, I believe Pa loved Zeke. But he never did call him son, or Zeke, or Ezekiel—only boy.

Zeke taught me to hunt, shoot, and fish. He showed me everything he had learned that Pa never bothered to teach me on account of me being a girl. Every time Ma had seen us coming across the field with me wearing Zeke's old trousers and rifles slung over our shoulders, she would shake her head, try not to smile, and scold Zeke for making me a boy. She loved Zeke fiercely. As he grew, she gazed upon him in such a way that I felt she must have loved his father.

Even after my parents passed, those Sundays at the emerald pools with Zeke were some of the best times of my life—jumping off rocks into deep black pools of water so cold you'd think your head was going to split open. After swimming, we lay on the warm rocks and felt the heat relax our tired muscles. My breasts were swelling and I had a small tuft of orange hair between my legs, so I kept my bloomers on to cover those embarrassing reminders of my emerging womanhood.

We'd kill whatever we could: rabbits, grouse, woodcocks, even squirrels, and cook the meat on a metal skewer over an open fire before we headed back. In the evenings back at home, Zeke played his guitar, and I'd sing along, or read *Hamlet* by candlelight till the moon came up. When the moon was full and the sky clear, I could sometimes read outside. We'd sit on a bench in front of the house, or sometimes we'd just lie back on the ground and watch the stars. Under the sparkling heavens, all our problems were small, and I would think that even if the Lord didn't have a plan, what did it matter? The splendor and the glory of his creations were enough to sustain me. Soon, Uncle Luther would come. He'd ride into town and all our problems would be solved.

★ ★ ★ ★ ★

I never saw Uncle Luther ride into town. One afternoon, he appeared in the doorway, a dark, unfamiliar shape. When I turned around, he scared the living daylights out of me. Zeke was sitting on a bench at the table, chewing on some jerky and trying to untangle some fishing line because we both had a hankering for trout. I let out a high-pitched scream and dropped a bowl of wet onions and potatoes. The potatoes rolled on the dusty floor. I squinted up at the large man. Rays of sun shot into the room from behind him, revealing clouds of dust motes. In the blinding light, I couldn't see his face at first, but I smelled his sweat and felt heat coming from his body.

He stepped into the house and shut the door, not soon enough to prevent a large horsefly from entering and buzzing around my head. I'd just killed all the flies inside, and I was disappointed to see another one, especially one so large. Some people claimed flies had spread the disease that killed my parents, so I feared the loathsome insects.

Uncle Luther shook his head at the shattered clay bowl I'd dropped. He frowned at an escaped potato, which now resembled a ball of mud. He removed his black bowler hat and ran a rough but jeweled hand over his greasy, sweat-drenched salt and pepper hair. I'd never seen such jewels. He looked like a dirty aristocrat. His eyes were hooded by dark brows so bushy and scraggly I couldn't see the color of his irises. He bore no resemblance to Ma. The yellowed shirt under his brocaded vest showed signs of once being white. He pulled a red bandana from his neck and wiped the sweat from his face. His gun belts crossed in gunslinger style. Yet he was clearly no gunslinger. I tried to suppress a giggle because his potbelly made him look like he was with child.

He'd been surveying our small log home, but when he heard me giggle, he whipped his head toward me and narrowed his eyes suspiciously. He looked at Zeke, who was sitting at the table staring at him. Then he looked me up and down like you might a prize heifer.

"Well, if it ain't beauty and the bastard." He grimaced at his joke, which felt to me like a blow in the stomach. Zeke closed his eyes, shook his head, and held his tongue.

"See to my horse, boy."

Zeke gathered his fishing line and walked out the door. Heat and light from outside penetrated the room again. Uncle Luther thumped down onto the chair at the head of the table. "Get your uncle a drink, girl. It's been a long journey."

I took a Mason jar from the shelf, cleaned the dust out with a rag made from a torn gingham dress, and poured him a dipper of water from our drinking bucket. I put the water in front of him. He studied it as if it were a specimen of something he'd never seen. "I come two thousand miles and this is what you offer me?" He shook his head, gulped down the water, and slammed the jar on the table. He hollered, "Get me some whiskey, girl."

I spoke softly. "Sir, we're Saints. We frown upon liquor."

A dark look crossed his face. He slammed his hand on the table and laughed. "Lord knows I ain't a Saint. Must be something stashed around here somewhere." He sighed and narrowed his eyes, searching around for a place Pa might have been hiding spirits. He roamed our small house like it was the mercantile, picked up several things, and put them down. "You hide your valuables someplace safe I hope. Otherwise the Mormons will want a cut. That's what I hear."

"We raise what we need and give the rest to people in need. We're simple folk anyway, don't go for anything fancy." My eyes fell to his jeweled fingers.

"In most locales a bottle of whiskey is a necessity." He caught me looking at his rings. "You like these rings?" He twirled his hands in the air.

I looked over some jars on the shelf and ignored his question. "We have some Valley Tan. But it tastes worse than castor oil." Then I remembered, on cold winter nights, Ma and Pa would sit at the table and huddle around a bottle. "Wait a minute, we do have something else, sir. But I'm afraid it's also medicinal spirits—might not be fit for enjoyment either." I dug through the pots and pans—found both bottles and set them in front of him.

His spirits lifted. First, he opened the bottle of Valley Tan, smelled it, and took a big swig. He choked, spat, and wiped his mouth with the back of his sleeve. "That tastes like it's made of pig shit!" His eyes watered as he opened the second bottle and took a smaller sip.

"Medicinal spirits?" He chuckled. "Now that's whiskey if I ever tasted it." He snorted, picked up the bottle, and inspected it. "Mighty fine whiskey, too. Is there more of this somewhere? What else you have hiding around here?"

"That's the only bottle. But I can take you to the man who makes it. He lives in Rockville. They say he's not really right in the head, though he knows his medicinal tonics."

"I'll bet he does." He took another swig.

Uncle Luther's mood seemed to be lightening. My initial fears about him were starting to lift. I decided to be a good hostess and make him as comfortable as I could. He was probably just ornery from the trip.

"I'm sorry, sir—Uncle. Where are my manners? You might need some repose after your trip." In one corner of our small log home a curtain hung around Ma and Pa's old bed. A pot-bellied stove in the middle kept us warm on cold winter nights. Shelves lined the walls. Grain sacks hung from hooks affixed to the ceiling. One rodent had outsmarted us, and a tiny pile of flour had trickled to the floor. Attached to the house outside, a makeshift lean-to sheltered a cot, tools, and farm equipment.

I walked over to Ma and Pa's bed, which was hidden by a curtain. I'd been sleeping there since Pa passed, and Zeke had moved from his cot in the lean-to outside to my old bed. I picked up Dolly and placed her under my arm. I wondered if Uncle Luther knew about the ruby necklace. He seemed to be fishing around for something.

It was only right to give him the best bed, so I slid the curtain aside and revealed it. "Would you like to lie down, sir? I can shine up your boots and wash your clothes down in the river. If we're lucky, Zeke will soon be back with fresh chub. I'll cook it up nice. You'll feel good as new."

Uncle Luther looked at me and rolled a fat tongue over his dry, cracked lips. He smiled, but his smile was sly—not friendly. My optimism leaked out like water in a bucket full of bullet holes. He rose from the table, grabbed the bottle, sauntered over to the bed, and dropped himself down on it so hard I was surprised it didn't collapse. He was tall and his boots dangled off the end, which was a good thing because they were filthy, and I prided myself on keeping the linens clean. After Ma and Pa had died in that bed, we'd burned the linens and we only had one set left.

"Oh," he moaned, "take off these boots will you?"

I pulled off his boots. The smell almost knocked me to the ground. A big, hairy toe exposed itself from a hole in his left sock. What looked like decades of dirt was embedded in his cracked skin and toenails. He saw the look on my face and wiggled his toe obscenely. I tried to ignore that long toe waving its hairy face at me, but the image of it stayed with me. I averted my eyes and studied the hole in his sock. "I'll darn this for you, sir," I said and turned to go.

"Girl, I been wearing these clothes here for fifteen, sixteen days now with no wash. Help me get 'em off and be so kind as to draw me a bath."

I had helped Pa undress when he was sick, and I'd seen Zeke wearing nothing but his birthday suit. But I didn't want to get too close to Uncle Luther. I barely knew him, and so far what I knew of him gave me the willies. His eyes never stopped roaming my body. As I slid off his trousers and shirt, he touched my hair and rested his hand in the crook of my hip.

I carried bucket after bucket of water from the river up the hill until the washtub was full. After retrieving a fresh cake of soap and the scrub brush, I went back inside to fetch Luther. His right arm hung over the bed, his fingers curled just inches from the neck of the whiskey bottle. The rest of him was splayed out for the whole world to see. He had dark patches of hair and some faded ink drawings on his chest. His ridiculous belly rode high, but failed to conceal his manhood, which spilled over like the intestines of a gutted rabbit, and looked like something I could use to make stew.

After he'd finished his bath, I gave him some of Pa's old clothes to wear, while his dried. The pants only reached his shins and were so snug he couldn't button them. At dinner, Zeke sat across from him on a bench that he and Pa had made from an old oak tree that had been swept downriver. The river sometimes carried timber from the high country. Much of it was rotten, but we managed to salvage some. Uncle Luther finished his fish, pushed away his plate, and pulled out a deck of cards. Zeke was about to stand up and put the plates in the washing bucket when he saw those cards. His eyes lit up like Christmas and he slid back onto the bench and stared at them like a dog begging for a bone.

"Ain't you ever seen a deck of cards, boy?" asked Uncle Luther.

"It's been awhile," said Zeke.

"You know how to play?"

"A little."

"This here's my practice deck. I made a good living playing on the riverboats till the war broke out and then some fellas decided they wanted to kill me. That's one of the reasons I came to this Godforsaken place."

"Ma didn't tell us you were a riverboat gambler." My voice came out high and breathless. "What's it like? Being on one of them big boats?"

"Oh, your ma doesn't know a thing about me. I was surprised her letter even found me. Being on a boat is the same as being on land once you get used to it. Except for the people who can't swim. They always seem to be in a state of high anxiety. The river and the constant motion relaxed me. That's probably why I had such luck with the cards." Uncle Luther sized up Zeke. "How about a game, boy? What do you have that I can win? Is there anything of value in this warren?"

In my whole life, I'd never seen Zeke play a game of cards. The church forbade it. I was nervous. Uncle Luther had looked around at all our household items and livestock, and you could see him calculating what he might get for all of it. I could tell from his belly that Uncle Luther was no farmer. He was a man who ate, drank, and chased easy money. Zeke went outside and came back with a sack, which he pulled from our cold storage. Uncle Luther looked at the sack perplexed. Zeke set it on the table and said, "Let's start with this until I learn the game a little better."

Uncle Luther peered into the bag. "Walnuts?" He sighed and shook his head. "Well I guess it's not as bad as playing for peanuts."

"Sorry, sir, you asked if we had anything of value, and I neglected to tell you about our secret walnut stash," I said.

He narrowed his eyes and stared daggers at me. Again, I wondered if he knew about the ruby necklace.

Three

The next day Uncle Luther told Zeke they'd ride over past Rockville to old man Jack's Trading Post. Even though there was work to be done, Uncle Luther's main priority was whiskey. He hadn't realized that Grafton was a dry settlement. They were gone most of the day. I did my chores and most of Zeke's, and was outside cleaning potatoes for dinner when I heard their horses neighing and clomping up the path. Uncle Luther sat straight in the saddle, but Zeke was slumped over and nearly falling off his horse. I ran over thinking he was hurt.

When I tried to help him down, he practically fell on me. I smelled the sweet, fiery smell of spirits. My brother, always a bastion of strength and composure, collapsed on my shoulder and babbled, "Little O, it's my Little O." I couldn't stand it. After just one day of Uncle Luther, all my parents had believed in—hard work and temperance, humility and obedience to the Heavenly Father, all they had worked so hard to build—had started to crumble.

I guided Zeke to the lean-to and helped him into bed. He fell back on the cot and shut his eyes. I sat on the edge of the bed and assessed his small arsenal of weapons: the Henry Repeater, which he had inherited from Pa, several spears, bows and arrows, slingshots, and an old shotgun. I removed a six-shooter from under his pillow. I'd never taken care of someone who was all liquored up and I had no idea what to do, but I didn't want him to wake up and accidentally shoot someone. I removed a clump of loose earth from the wall. From a peephole, I could see the table. Uncle Luther was doing some fancy card tricks. They made a *phlltt, phlltt* noise. It sounded like the devil whispering.

In the short time he'd been here, Uncle Luther had not done one dang thing of use. I was exhausted. I felt a foul mood coming over me like a spell. I covered up the peephole, brushed Zeke's hair back, kissed his widow's peak, smoothed out my gingham dress, went back round the front, and resumed cleaning the potatoes. I tried to hide my sour disposition because a man's temper could be a dangerous thing. I didn't want to experience Uncle Luther's.

The two of us ate in silence. I was curious about his life as a card sharp on the riverboat, but I was too mad about him getting Zeke all liquored up to ask even one of the hundred questions I had. I put the dishes in a big metal bucket and carried them down to the river. By the time I walked back up the hill, the sky had turned pink and purple. I wanted to rest my head on the fluffy pink-edged clouds. Uncle Luther was watching the sun set. His figure and the cloud of tobacco smoke swirling around him seemed soft and harmless in the heavenly light.

He heard the clanging of my metal bucket against the wire brush, looked over his shoulder, and said, "Come here, girl."

I put the bucket down and stood next to him.

"Can't put a price on that, now can you?" He smiled a sideways smile like he was resigned to it all. "God's closing the curtain on another day."

He put his arm around my waist and pulled me to him. "It's almost as pretty as you. Can't put a price on you neither." His smile dropped and his face turned sour. "But I can put a price on the ruby necklace your ma stole. When were you going to tell me about it?"

"Sir, I don't know what necklace you're referring to, unless it's the one Ma sold to buy our tickets."

His eyes went mean and hard. "Tickets? What tickets?"

"Our tickets to paradise."

"You bought tickets to come out here? My sister traded a priceless ruby necklace so that she could join a wagon train and settle down in a fool's paradise? I don't believe it."

"This is Zion, sir. A lot of people will do anything to come here."

He looked around with skepticism. "I don't see anything here, unless there's gold or silver in the hills." His squinted, inquisitive eyes stared toward the horizon.

I inched away from him, but he pulled me back with a hard jerk. "You're a good girl. We'll get along if you do as you're told, but you disobey me and there'll be trouble. I want to know where the ruby necklace is." His hand clamped around the back of my neck. I cinched my shoulders and winced. He let go. I stumbled and rubbed my neck.

"You don't have any claim to our possessions or property anyway. Pa made a will and it all goes to me and Zeke." I realized too late that I'd wagged my tongue without thinking.

"I see you decided against my advice on being a good girl. Listen Miss Know-it-all, you're forgetting a couple things. First of all, you think anyone's going to believe that the half-breed Indian boy is your father's kin? From what I can gather so far, this here settlement is at war with the Indians, and they don't look too kindly on savages. You, missy, are just a girl and a minor. Far as I know, you don't even get to decide which side of the bed you get up on. Even if you did have any legal rights, this place here's a territory. All there is out here to protect you is Winchester litigation. Second, those jewels are rightfully mine. Did your mother think that I'd forget? That time heals all wounds? I'm not here to do charity for you and your bastard brother. I'm here to claim what's mine."

"I'm sorry you feel that way, sir. But that necklace was sold long ago." It was hard to believe Uncle Luther was Ma's brother. As far as I could tell, Zeke and I would have been better off if the devil himself had walked in the door. I had to swallow all the poisonous thoughts in my head before they spilled off my tongue. Uncle Luther would give me a hiding if I crossed him again.

"You are welcome to as many walnuts as you like," I said.

"Don't sass me, girl." He shook his head and clenched his jaw.

"I find it hard to believe you're Ma's brother."

He narrowed his eyes at me and said, "Hard to believe that Injun bastard is your brother." He swooped on me, grabbed my hair, and pulled my head back. In his nostrils, the hair was dark and as thick as a briar patch. Pieces of his dinner clung to his mustache. He looked at my lips, and for a second I was afraid he might kiss me.

"You got a mouth, girl! If those jewels are here, I'll get that sassy little mouth of yours to tell me where they are." He released his hold on my hair. "Go fetch a cake of soap and bring your behind back here, pronto."

I could run and hide somewhere till morning. There was whiskey on his breath and he might sleep off his cantankerous mood, but he wouldn't forget about the necklace. I was afraid. The Indians were known to attack at night. I figured nothing Uncle Luther could do to me could be worse than what they did to the Berry brothers. I fetched the soap, went back, and handed it to him. He stared down at it.

"This isn't for me, girl. This is for you. Now eat it." He handed it back to me.

I raised the soap to my mouth and hesitated.

"Go on," he yelled.

I put the soap in my mouth and felt the lye sting my lips. I wanted to spit it out so bad I could hardly stand it.

"You think about the sassy way you talked to me and you think real hard about where that necklace might be hiding."

The longer the soap sat in my mouth the more it burned. It mixed with my saliva and made me gag. I threw up and then wiped my mouth with my sleeve. "I told you. It was sold long ago."

"Go clean yourself," he said and walked away.

I hated him so much. I would never give the necklace to him. In all my life, I'd never felt this way about anyone. Maybe if he'd been nice, it would have been a different story. But he'd been tired and ornery from his journey and had let his true colors show. I had heard that hate was a powerful drink that could slowly poison you. I lay in bed that night trying to read *Hamlet*. Just as Hamlet wanted to kill his uncle, I wanted to kill mine. Poison was the most realistic of my sinister schemes.

I woke up that night to his hot breath in my ear. "Let's make up," he whispered. Dolly lay on the bed covers with the necklace hidden inside her. He tossed her onto the floor. Crushed beneath his weight, I could hardly breathe. I struggled to push his hands away as they tore at my night clothes.

A swift motion from behind him stirred the air. A loud clang filled the room. His inert body collapsed on top of me. I cringed and then opened my eyes. Zeke stood shirtless with the cast-iron skillet in his hand. The veins bulged from his muscled arm, which still held the heavy skillet. I saw then, he'd be an even match for Uncle Luther.

"I should have shot him," said Zeke. "But I was afraid the bullet would go into you. It's not too late—best to do it now when he's passed out."

I pushed the unconscious body to the side and freed myself from its smothering heaviness. It rolled onto the floor with a loud thud. "They'd hang you, Zeke. And besides, thou shalt not kill, remember?" I said that, although I had been scheming to poison Luther right before I fell asleep. A deep groan filled the room. I feared Luther'd come to.

"What should we do then?" Zeke asked and looked around the room.

"Let's drag him over near his bed. Maybe he'll figure he just rolled out of bed. I'll sleep out in the lean-to with you from now on."

"That's okay for now, but I'm going to set him straight in the morning."

"What are you going to do?"

"I'm going to tell him if he ever lays a hand on you again, I'll blow him to kingdom come."

We barricaded the door of the lean-to so we'd hear if anyone was trying to bust in. I felt safe with Zeke. But I didn't know how long he could protect me. Uncle Luther seemed like a man who didn't stop till he got what he wanted. He wanted the necklace, and if he couldn't have it, he'd have me. Zeke had no idea the ruby necklace existed. I didn't want him to get killed trying to protect me. But for some reason, I would not give Uncle Luther the ruby necklace. I don't know why. Maybe it was the same stubbornness that caused my mother to hold onto it for so long. Whatever that stubbornness was, my uncle knew it in my mother and so he had not bought my story about her selling it.

I started thinking about poison again, how I could kill Uncle Luther and make it look like an accident. I couldn't believe it had come to this—thinking of ways to kill Ma's brother. Obviously, there'd been some bad blood between them. Why did she write and tell him to come here? After just one day, he'd sure worn out his welcome. "Thou shall not kill" kept going through my head. I wracked my brain for other ways to get rid of him.

FOUR

If Uncle Luther had any memory of climbing into my bed and being knocked out by Zeke, he sure didn't act like it. For the next two days, he mostly sat at the table playing with his cards. Whenever we'd happen by, he'd try to get me or Zeke to sit down and play. Even though I didn't know the first thing about cards, he instructed me, "Just watch my hands. Watch them real close and tell me if you notice anything funny." It could have been raining pigs outside and he wouldn't have noticed because he was so focused on those cards. As long as he had food and some whiskey, he didn't seem to care about much else.

Zeke told me that Uncle Luther had asked him a few times about the ruby necklace. Zeke asked me if I knew anything about it. I told him yes, it was the one Ma had sold to buy our tickets to Zion. He looked at me as if I was crazy and said he'd never heard anything about it. I told him to tell the story to Uncle Luther if he happened to ask again.

He told me Uncle Luther had posted a notice at old man Jack's Trading Post about a high-stakes poker game at our place. Apparently, Uncle Luther had seen cattlemen, drovers, and prospectors pass through Rockville and he hoped to attract them to the cabin so he could swindle some money.

One day I was nooning from work in the garden, because it was getting too hot to be outside. Zeke sat at the table playing a practice game of poker with Uncle Luther. Zeke was getting good. He was learning Uncle Luther's tricks and could spot how he used sleight of hand to slip a stacked deck. It seemed like Uncle Luther was taking a liking to Zeke and was right impressed with his card skills. I don't know what provoked it, but from nowhere Zeke blurted out, "If you ever touch my sister, I will kill you."

I turned around. Zeke had his six-shooter pointed square at Uncle Luther's head. Uncle Luther put his right hand up, but I could see under the table that his left hand was on his gun. "Whoa, there's no harm in looking, boy. No harm in looking." He shook his head and focused on his cards. "Let's get back to the game."

That evening a strange thing occurred. Uncle Luther refrained from drinking whiskey. "Ophelia, is the council meeting tonight?" He came to me and asked.

I looked up from my book. "Yes."

"It's about time I met the Saints who make decisions for this piss-ant settlement. You come and make the introductions, then get right back home. I got some business to discuss, and it don't concern you."

He brushed his coat, greased down his hair, and was busy tying a yellow silk cravat around his neck. I was about to tell him that no one around here could be bothered putting on airs, but I decided to let him go on and make a fool of himself. I started toward the door. When we got outside, he turned to me, put his finger under my nose, and said, "They'll be no mention of my affinity for cards and whiskey. You hear?"

We stood in front of a big old army surplus tent set back between two cottonwood trees where the council held meetings. It was dark, but two torches illuminated the tent entrance where the elders stood. When I introduced Uncle Luther to Bishop Marley and Brother Thompson, he said, "Gentlemen, I'm pleased to make your acquaintance. Thank you for allowing me to visit your quaint hamlet. I can see why you call this land

Zion. It's like the hand of the Lord himself has blessed you."
His voice was conspiratorial, awe-stricken, as if he were trying
to conjure their own religious fervor and enrapture them with
it.

I could hardly believe my eyes and ears. Uncle Luther had
managed to transform himself from a lecherous swine into a
perfect gentleman. Gone was the Uncle Luther from the cabin.
He was an actor in a playhouse. His voice and his manner of
speaking, his posture, even the soft, watery look in his eyes, gave
the impression of a charming, but helpless, oversized dandy. In
front of the elders, before they disappeared into the tent, he
turned to me, patted my head as tender as a preacher, and said,
"Dearest Ophelia, go back home now and read the good book,
then work on your penmanship." As he was walking into the
tent, I heard him say to Bishop Marley, "She'll be a proper lady
soon. Then I might be able to take her back east and marry her
off to a wealthy gentleman."

I couldn't move. I stood there stunned by what I'd seen and
heard. Marry me off to a wealthy gentleman? Uncle Luther
would be more likely to sell me to a brothel. I doubted he even
knew any wealthy gentlemen he hadn't robbed. Instead of going
home, I went around to the back of the tent.

It was dark under the cottonwood trees. I crawled as far into
the tent as I could and sharpened my ears so I could hear.
Uncle Luther spoke so well he almost fooled me. The men
exchanged pleasantries, and talked about the soil and Luther's
long journey from Missouri. Uncle Luther brought up "the
problem of Ezekiel" and I strained to hear.

"I followed the boy," he said. "Followed him straight out of
town and watched him climb the high mesa. I kept a safe
distance, but I could see he was meeting with the Injuns. I
wouldn't be surprised if it were Black Hawk himself because I
could see even at night the shape of a large headdress."

I've eavesdropped on a lot of conversations in my life. Most of them weren't that interesting, but this was dire. I didn't have to hear any more. My heart thumped as I inched back, extricated myself from the canvas tent, and ran as fast as I could to our homestead.

I found Zeke at the table playing with the cards, transfixed. I still heard the devil whispering every time the cards made that *phlltt, phlltt* sound, but I had grown accustomed to it. "Zeke!" I screamed. He didn't even look at me, so intent was his concentration, and I feared he would become like Uncle Luther. But he wouldn't live long enough to become like Uncle Luther if he didn't get on his mare and hightail it out of town. I grabbed a gunnysack and stuffed food into it. "Get up! Get up!" I shouted. "Saddle up your horse. They're coming for you, Zeke. They're going to hang you if you don't get on your way."

Zeke stood up from the table. Puzzlement covered his face and he shook his head. "Calm down, O. What are you talking about?"

"Uncle Luther! He told the council you're a traitor. He said he saw you meeting with Black Hawk. You've got to get out of here."

Zeke ran out of the house and over to the lean-to, where he gathered his guns. After he saddled and mounted his horse, I handed him the gunnysack and tightened his saddlebags for him. He looked down at me.

"Don't tell me what direction you're going," I said. "They'll make me tell them. I'm not going to watch you go. I'm going to close my eyes so I can't even see which way you ride." My voice broke and the tears came. I bit my bottom lip to stop them.

"I'll be back for you, O. I promised Pa I would protect you."

"You can't protect me if you're dead. They'll be looking for you, and they'll hang you if they find you. Get as far away from here as you can. I love you, brother. We won't be apart for long."

"I can't leave you with Uncle Luther. What's going to happen to you?"

"Don't fret about me. I'm going to marry a gentleman." I kept my voice light, but hot tears ran down my face. "Now go!" I slapped his horse.

Hooves pounded the earth. My stomach felt hollow, as if someone had punched me real hard. I doubled over and tried to breathe. I couldn't think, I couldn't breathe. I paced in front of our place trying to gulp the night air, which buzzed and chirped and grunted—the sounds of insects coming out and the livestock settling in. I could hear horses coming up the rutted track. I ran inside and pretended to read my book. Blood pumped through my veins and a loud thumping resounded in my skull. My chest tightened around my heart.

Minutes later, the bishop and four men burst in and started searching the cabin. "Where's Ezekiel?" Bishop Marley shouted at me.

I looked up from my book. "Ezekiel," I said slowly as if I had never heard the name.

He ripped the book out of my hands, frowned at the title, and threw it on the floor. "Where is he?" he asked again through clenched teeth. Spittle landed on my face. I winced in disgust and turned my head away.

"Last time I saw him, he was right outside, sir." I was so scared I almost vomited.

Uncle Luther and toothless Brother Thompson stepped into the cabin. Uncle Luther was still playing the dandy. He put his hand on his jaw and struck a thoughtful gesture. "The Injun boy and his horse are both gone, and he has taken quite a number of his possessions with him. It looks as if he has absconded."

A gummy smile spread across Elder Thompson's face. "This girl's been known to eavesdrop. Bet she tipped him off."

Bishop Marley was furious. He grabbed me by the ear, dragging me out of the cabin and all the way back down to the council tent. I was in such pain I expected my ear would come off in his fingers. By the time we got there I was wailing and carrying on—begging and crying without shame. Bishop Marley pushed me into the tent. At first I was shocked because women and children weren't allowed in the tent. I looked around, disappointed at how plain and void of mystery it was. Chairs, some benches carved out of logs, a rickety looking table, and a pot-bellied stove piped through a hole in the ceiling—this was all I'd been missing.

I curled up on the ground. Bishop Marley stood over me. Other men were loading their rifles and running in and out of the tent. I could hear a posse gathering out front. "Give me a minute to work on the girl," the bishop called out to them.

He looked at me with fury. "I have a flock to protect. By not telling me where your bro—" He stopped himself and started again. "By protecting that savage, you are jeopardizing my flock. Do you understand that?"

I kept my head down and nodded. With my head still down, I raised my eyes. Uncle Luther was pacing the room, picking his teeth in deep thought.

"I think it's best if you leave us alone for a minute," said the bishop. "You just arrived and it would be unfair to ask you to assist in the harsh discipline this situation calls for."

Uncle Luther's voice was soft as a sparrow's. "I understand the girl needs to be punished." He leaned close and whispered to the bishop. "But do not disfigure or scar her. If that happens, custodianship will be a heavier burden than it already is." He slipped out the tent door.

I was alone with Bishop Marley. Someone entered the tent

and handed him a horsewhip. I made myself as small as I could and shielded my face with my hands, but the whip still cracked the air and stung my back.

"Tell me where he is!"

"I don't know," I screamed. "I swear I don't know."

A group of men entered the tent, their faces stern and their bodies alert and ready to move. "We should get going, or else we'll lose him."

My back stung and felt wet. I touched my shoulder and looked at my fingers—blood. Uncle Luther stood over me and looked down. "Pardon me, Bishop, but I said no damage to the flesh."

The bishop grabbed me, raised me to my feet, and pushed me into a chair. "Then how do you propose we get her talking?"

Uncle Luther struck that thoughtful gesture again, stroked his chin, and calmly said, "I propose we cover her with honey and let the fire ants do the work."

"There's no time. Besides honey is a valuable commodity."

"It will only take a minute to fetch a jar of molasses," said Uncle Luther.

The thought of fire ants crawling all over me was too much. "He went west." I screamed. "But he's not a traitor. Zeke doesn't know any Indians. I've spent every day of my life with him. There's no way he could visit the Indians, without me knowing."

"West! Start riding west!" the bishop commanded.

A group of men rushed out of the tent. After a minute, I heard their horses gallop away. I was pretty sure that Zeke would have ridden east. Uncle Luther, Brother Thompson, and the bishop remained in the tent.

The bishop looked from Uncle Luther to me. "Are you calling your uncle a liar?"

I started screaming hysterically. "In our whole lives, the only day Zeke and I have ever been apart was yesterday when that devil took him to Jack's Trading Post and brought him home dead drunk! There's no way Zeke is cooperating with the Indians. Don't you see, my uncle is just saying that so he can—" I stopped screaming and was silent. I looked at the blank, expectant faces of the men. What would they do if I spoke the truth?

"So he can—what, girl?" yelled the bishop. He furrowed his white brows and looked from me to Uncle Luther.

I could not form the words. I could not speak the truth. I looked over at Uncle Luther and Brother Thompson. They stood behind the bishop near the flap door. Brother Thompson had a glint in his eye and he ran his tongue over his lips. Uncle Luther lifted his chin in a dignified manner.

"So he can what, girl?" the bishop repeated.

I looked at the ground. "So he can run Zeke off the place," I mumbled.

"Now why would any man want to run off a strong boy who can help him work the land?" He wiped his hands together like he was sharpening knives and wiped them down the front of his coat as if to cleanse them. "I've had enough of this. I'm going to go calm the womenfolk and then I'm going to pray." He looked at Brother Thompson. "Tie her to that chair. She needs to stay here all night and contemplate the gravity of her actions."

Brother Thompson nodded and left the tent to fetch some rope. The bishop stopped and stared at Uncle Luther—stared long and hard enough that Uncle Luther flinched. In a great trembling, thunderous voice the bishop said, "Do not bring your wicked ways upon our people! We are the Saints, the Lord's chosen ones. Any offense to us and you will feel the wrath of God."

FIVE

I sat in the forbidden tent alone with my hands pulled behind me and tied together at the back of the chair. The spines of the old frayed rope pricked my wrists. Every muscle ached. My back and shoulders stung. My ear still hurt and my throat burned, but I was too thirsty to cry anymore. A crust of dried dirt and slobber caked my face. I licked my lips and tasted salt.

Hours passed, and although the settlement became silent of human activity, the crickets and grasshoppers tirelessly chirped. A lone coyote howled. Others joined in. The constant tinkling of river water reminded me that I was both thirsty and had to go to the privy—conflicting desires.

Anyone who was not hunting Zeke was probably fast asleep dreaming of the fresh apricots they'd eat for breakfast. In the orchard, fuzzy swollen orbs hung from the trees waiting to be picked. I was supposed to join the sisters in apricot picking the next day. I'd been looking forward to both feasting on the sweet fruit and some female companionship. I didn't know what would happen to me. I figured I'd be deemed a traitor and everyone would hate me.

I fussed and fidgeted, unable to ease the aching in my back. Zeke was gone and I was alone. I felt like I'd been split in two and my heart had been ripped out. I tipped myself over and landed with a painful thud on my shoulder. Like a helpless infant without even the comfort of a thumb, I lay there all night and let the grief and pity pour out of me—for Ma, Pa, and

Zeke, but mostly for myself.

I must have fallen asleep because the next thing I knew someone was fussing with my roped hands, trying to loosen the knot. Fingers brushed my wrist and clasped my lower arm, and I knew from the gentleness that it was a woman. May Belle Hopkins whispered assurances in an uncharacteristically soft, sweet voice. She released my hands and put her arm around me. Her kindness broke a wall within me. I cried again but this time from relief. She got me to my feet and led me out of the tent. It was before dawn and the stars were out. "I'll get you home and cleaned up," she said.

I stopped, looked at her, and begged, "Can we please go to your place instead, ma'am?"

She was taken aback for a minute till understanding washed over her. She nodded. "Why of course, child."

When we got to her place, May Belle sat me at the kitchen table and set down a jelly jar of water and a scone. I gulped down the water, but found my stomach too cramped to eat the delicious-looking scone. Between dawn and sunrise, May Belle went to the orchard to pick apricots. She allowed me to rest on a bed at her house. She had been the first wife of Abraham Hopkins, one of the settlement's most prominent members, until he passed away last summer. All of his younger wives had been married off to other husbands. May Belle was the only woman I knew who lived alone in comfort.

She came back just before noon, her face flushed with heat, her fingertips stained orange, and the sweet, almost bloody, smell of ripe apricot on her apron. She had been allowed two big baskets full of apricots for herself. The rest went to the common pantry or were put in the storehouse after being preserved. She'd have to go back later to dry the fruit, can it, and make preserves. Anything that wasn't used by the settlement would be sold, and the profits would be managed by the bishop. She sat in a chair and fanned her face with her hat. I brought her the water bucket.

She took two dippers full before she spoke. "I'd really fancy a tall glass of lemonade right now. You know lemons are plentiful in the California Territory. Someday we'll be able to go into Rockville and buy them. The wagon men and gypsies will come with carts full to sell or trade. Imagine being able to have a lemon whenever you want one!"

"I reckon that would be some life," I said and managed a smile even though dread had made me fidgety and sick to my stomach. I wondered if the other Saints knew that May Belle was harboring me. I wondered if the posse had found Zeke. He could be hanging from a tree right now. I wanted to ask her if she'd heard anything, but I didn't want to ruin our chat.

May Belle clasped her hands in prayer. "Lord, forgive my transgression. I lust for lemon when you have given me a bounty of apricots." In solemn repentance, she bowed her head and closed her eyes. She raised her head and said to me, "Every day we must thank the Lord for what he has given us and never ask for more. Even if we're thirsty, if all we have is air to breathe, we need to praise the Lord. Do you remember the crossing, child?"

I didn't want to talk about the crossing, and I was certainly in no mood to praise God. All I wanted to do was ask May Belle if she had any news of Zeke. But she was being kind to me. I didn't want to remind her of what I'd done. But then I remembered I hadn't done anything at all. Zeke was no traitor. They'd punished me so hard, I'd almost believed I'd done something evil when all I'd done was save my brother's life.

I looked at May Belle and then stared at a basket of apricots so fresh they still seemed alive. "I remember a lot of walking. I remember watching people die and being afraid. I remember how the look of the land kept changing. Most of all, I remember finally arriving and seeing the Great Salt Lake Valley stretched out below with shimmering water in the distance. I thought we were there. But we had to keep on walking for some time. Of the entire journey, those last few miles felt the longest. What stays with me the most is how every day we just kept moving— till finally I felt like a force—like I was a river or something, and I just moved on each day without thinking about it. Even now that movement lives within me. I've lived in Grafton since the crossing, but I still feel that movement pulling me toward somewhere else. Every day I have to fight it."

From May Belle's expression, I could tell I'd said too much. She looked at me like she was trying hard to understand what I was talking about.

"I don't mean to change the subject, but is there any news of Zeke?"

Her stern look returned. "I haven't heard, nor have I inquired."

"You know he's innocent, don't you? Zeke has never in his life talked to an Indian."

"That's up to the men to decide. You should not have interfered with men's business. It's no easy job to run a settlement and keep everyone safe in these hostile times. Child, do you realize we are at war with Black Hawk?"

I was going to tell her about the war I'd been fighting with Uncle Luther for the past two days. I was going to tell her what a bad man he was and how he'd tried to get in bed with me. That would let her see his true nature. The words were forming in my head and I was deciding how to tell her, when someone knocked on her door.

May Belle rose, smoothed her skirt, touched the back of her head, and patted the sweat off her face with a hanky. With a straight spine and even countenance, she opened the door. "Why, hello. You must be Ophelia's uncle—so sorry about your sister's passing. Do come in."

Uncle Luther stepped in. He wore the same getup he'd had on last night at the council meeting. He took her hand and pressed her fingers to his lips—still playing the dandy. I rolled my eyes and sighed. He said, "I was expecting a much older and much less vital woman."

May Belle giggled, blushed, pulled her hand away, and covered her mouth. "Oh, my! Well I'm no spring chicken, but I'm alive and well. My mind is sharp and I do my best to stay out of the sun."

May Belle usually spoke confidently, but now she seemed shy and fumbled for words. It was as if Uncle Luther had walked into the room and cast a spell on her. I eyed him. He wasn't a good-looking man, but with his yellow silk cravat and his gentlemanly ways, he had turned a hardened widow to jelly.

"Can I offer you something? I think I have a slice of pie left."

"I don't want to trouble you, ma'am. I just came to collect my niece."

"It's no trouble. I need to gather a few things for Ophelia before you take her away."

"Well, okay. I'd be honored to eat a slice of your pie—made by those most delicate nubbins." He picked up one of her hands and admired her fingers as if they were sparkling diamonds. "My, how do you keep these hands so dainty out here on the frontier?"

May Belle shook her head and pulled her hand away again. "Oh! You do go on." She blushed. "They're stained with apricot and covered with calluses. Save your charm for the young ladies," she chided. "I'm an old maid and I intend to stay that way." She cut a piece of pie, put it on a china plate, and placed it on the table with a fork and a red and white checked napkin. "Now, I regret that I have no cream for your pie."

"This is fine, ma'am. I do appreciate your hospitality."

I winced. When I had seen Uncle Luther, my stomach got all knotty and now it was beginning to hurt again. I followed May Belle into another room. She had one of the only brick houses in Grafton. From the kitchen, Uncle Luther groaned with pleasure and shouted his approval of the pie. I wished he'd shut his trap.

She led me to a coach trunk. It was worn and a little tattered from the journey to Zion, but it was made of expensive leather and brass buckles. She knelt in front of it, her smile an invitation. I knelt next to her. She peered and slowly opened it—never taking her eyes from my face.

With anticipation, I looked on. But the trunk was only full of quilts. Quilts? Did Sister May Belle think I'd be excited over quilts? She removed two quilts from the top of the trunk. Underneath, it was full of books. I gasped. She put her finger to her lips.

"This is our secret. I smuggled these books on the wagon. We were forbidden to take anything but necessities. Now that Abraham has passed, these books are my companions." She stared at me intently and whispered, "There are books the Prophet hasn't sanctioned."

Why was she sharing her secret with me? Maybe it was because I was a traitor and she knew I wouldn't tell on her. She picked up a plain, black book. On the cover embossed in gold was the word, *Hymns*. She handed it to me. A thin smile of false thanks crossed my lips. I couldn't imagine I'd ever want to sing again.

"Open it," she said with a sly smile.

I opened the book and began turning pages. Every page was blank. I didn't understand and looked up at May Belle.

"I don't know what the Lord has in store for you. But I don't think you're destined to remain here. Write down your thoughts and feelings. Record your first love and all of your adventures.

50

Write things in here you'd never say." She stared down at the book and a wistful shadow lingered on her face. "There are times in life, child, when the best thing you can say is nothing at all—when you have to hold your tongue even though the words are burning it. The hardest lesson I've learned over the years is when to hold my tongue. I see a lot of me in you, and I know you will face the same challenge. This book will help you. Everything you want to say but can't, you write down here. On the cover it says *Hymns* because if it said *Diary* that would invite snooping, now wouldn't it? Some diaries, they have bitty little locks outside—but that's just temptation for prying eyes."

I thanked May Belle and hugged her. Her kindness gave me strength.

"That book is to keep. Go on now and borrow a few more. You can exchange them for others when you're done. But be sure not to let anyone see them."

From the kitchen, Uncle Luther hollered. "I'm fuller than a hog at fair time. That was the most delicious pie I ever ate!"

I wanted to tell May Belle about Uncle Luther—tell her not to trust him, that his charm was a big act. But when she heard his voice her cheeks turned a pink color that made her look like a girl no older than me. It was too late. She'd fallen for his false charm.

On the way back to our place, Uncle Luther picked pie from his teeth with a reed he snapped from the river brush. I walked behind him. I cradled the books tight to my chest like a baby, so he wouldn't see the titles. Uncle Luther didn't seem to notice or care about those books. He probably didn't realize how valuable books were in Grafton. He was most likely preoccupied with the whereabouts of the ruby necklace, obtaining whiskey, and his impending high-stakes card game. "Did you learn your lesson, girl?" was all he said.

I made no reply.

Six

Darkness shadowed the lean-to until I couldn't read anymore. My feet ached to be free. I wanted so badly to take off my shoes. Every night I slept with them on in case Uncle Luther came for me. He'd call at all hours, "O-phe-ya!" and stumble out of the cabin, all liquored up and obsessing about me and the necklace. I'd run as fast as I could out of the lean-to, down the hill, into a ditch covered by willow grass. All the while Dolly lay on the cot stuffed with the treasure he was seeking. I could hear him from my hiding spot, but he couldn't see me.

He'd yell into the night, "O-phe-ya, come out now, or I'll give you a hiding you'll never forget!"

He didn't put much effort into looking for me. I'd outwait him and often fall asleep in the brush. By the next morning he'd forget his threats in favor of hot coffee and breakfast. With no one to help, I was now tending all the animals, fixing the meals, and doing all the chores myself. Every few days Uncle Luther would ride over to Jack's Trading Post for supplies. Besides that he practiced his card tricks and smoked tobacco.

With my head resting on an old feather pillow, I lay on the cot in the lean-to and stared at the ceiling. A final ray of sunset illuminated a spider web. I imagined a different life in a big town where I had money for fancy dresses and sweets. Dolly lay next to me. Her soulless black button eyes hid her secret. It was difficult to hide mine. If Uncle Luther saw hope in my eyes, he'd become suspicious about the necklace again. My pinky toe rubbed the side of my boot where the seam had started to come loose from the sole. When my shoes fell apart, I'd have to hoof it like a poor farm child.

I picked up Dolly and stared into her button eyes. Mother had made Dolly for me when I was just a little girl. I'd carried her on the emigration trail all the way to Zion. When my weary bleeding feet felt like they'd fall off, Dolly helped me carry on. I had not wanted to join the dead children who had been thrown into shallow graves along the route, so I'd hugged Dolly tight and pulled little pieces of cotton from inside her. I had let the cotton melt in my mouth and pretended it was crusty bread. Both Dolly and I lost weight on the trail. When we got settled, Mother stuffed her with scraps and me with food to make us both plump again.

Right before she died, we hid the necklace inside Dolly. Mother had called me to her bedside and sworn me to secrecy. Sparkling rubies had hung from her shriveled hand. They were her secret. Not even Pa knew she possessed them.

She had pulled me to her and with a quivering, weak voice whispered into my ear. "These rubies belonged to your great-grandmother. They are both sacred and cursed. For years, I've hidden them. If life ever became unbearable, if your Pa took to beating me, or my children were starving, I figured I'd sell them. I came close on the emigration trail, but I couldn't imagine what I could trade them for out there. Ophelia, go get me Dolly."

I fetched Dolly from my bed and handed her to my ma. She tried to undo Dolly's stitching, but her hands trembled too much, so I helped. We took out some of Dolly's stuffing, wrapped the rubies in the cotton, and stuffed them back inside. Then I stitched Dolly back up again. With a faint smile of re-assurance, Ma watched me from her bed. "Now you have something, Ophelia: insurance against desperate times. But I have to warn you, when my mother gave me these jewels she told me of an old family superstition that there is a curse attached to selling them." She swallowed, then licked her lips. So much talking had made her weak. There was so much I wanted to ask her, but she was too feeble to speak.

I put Dolly on the chair and brought a dipper of water from the bucket. Since my mother had been sick, Zeke and I separated her bucket and had been careful not to put anything to our mouths that she'd touched with hers. It was too late for Pa, as he was already showing signs of her disease.

Ma drank gratefully and rested her head back on the pillow. "The rubies may bring you good fortune for a few years, but I can't say what will happen later. This life has been a trial, but I was too stubborn and scared to sell them. Don't let your pa or Zeke know that I've been hiding these. Especially your pa. He'd be very angry."

I continued to stare at the spider web and imagined how life would be different if I were a wealthy lady. During the day I'd teach poor children to read. Then at night a gentleman suitor would take me to a ball. He'd be tall with blond hair, blue eyes, and straight teeth. I imagined my suitor might look like Joseph Smith because his picture was the only image of a handsome young man I'd ever seen.

The neighing and clomping of a horse coming up the path startled me out of my fantasy. I grabbed the Henry Repeater, which Zeke left behind, and peered out to see who it was. Bishop Marley saw me. He dismounted, hitched his horse, and strode over to me. I put the Henry down, folded my hands, and looked at the ground. I wanted to get on the good side of the bishop because he could easily decide my fate.

He looked into the lean-to and noticed my makeshift

quarters. "What on earth? Ophelia, why are you sleeping out here?"

I took a breath to answer, but he didn't give me time.

"The Brown homestead was just raided by Indians. Child, you need to go inside where it's safe. Right now! Where's your uncle?"

I pushed my hair from my face, tucked it behind my ears, and looked him square in the eyes. "What happened? Are they all right?"

"The women and children are unharmed. Brother Alonso drove them off. But they got away with three steers. Alonso is wounded."

"Will he live?"

"With the grace of the Almighty, he'll survive. Go inside now and pray."

Uncle Luther burst out of the cabin with a shotgun raised. When he saw the bishop and me, he lowered it. "Good evening, Bishop Marley! What brings you to our humble abode at this late hour?" The way he put on that dandy voice every time he talked to the bishop nauseated me. I sighed loudly. The bishop threw a quick vexed glance in my direction.

"Evening. I came to warn you that Black Hawk has made another raid on the settlement. People are gathering in the meeting hall and sticking close together in case he strikes again. You're welcome to join them. Grafton is not prepared for this right now. Most of our strong fighting men have gone to the high country to set up a sawmill. Black Hawk's timing is fortuitous. It's almost as though he knew we would be unprotected."

The bishop stared at me. A tremor ran through my body. He didn't trust me. He thought Zeke had something to do with this. I opened my mouth to protest, but Uncle Luther said, "We'll be just fine here." He held up the shotgun and shook it.

"I was in the front lines at the Battle of Bull Run. Men fell all around me, but I kept up the charge till those Union boys ran all the way back to Washington with their tails between their legs. I will not run from Injuns."

"Well, then, I had you all wrong. You're not a greenhorn after all. I expect a man with your battle experience can protect his kin. Make sure the girl is armed. I hear she's a good shot. You'll need all the help you can get if they attack again tonight."

I ran and grabbed the Henry. "Yes, sir," I said to the bishop as if he were my sergeant. "I'm ready to fight any enemy that comes my way." I looked square at Uncle Luther. His eyes shifted and rolled before a smirk crossed his face. "Go inside, Ophelia. I won't let any harm come your way, my dear sweet child." With the rifle tucked under my arm, I strode past Uncle Luther toward the cabin door. "Lord, help me," I heard Uncle Luther say to the bishop. "She's incorrigible."

The bishop shook his head and looked at the ground. "Each day, I thank the Heavenly Father for not bestowing the curse of a red-headed child upon me."

My ears and eyes burned with anger. I went into the cabin and slammed the door behind me.

Seven

With my rifle draped over my lap, I sat on my old bed and stared at the floor. Uncle Luther sauntered back into the cabin and placed the shotgun on the table. He settled on the bench, folded his jeweled hands under his chin, and studied me. I refused to look at him.

"What could be better than a quiet evening with your dearest uncle, holed up together against an impending Indian attack?" He cocked his head sideways and shook it in mock sympathy. "You won't be able to hide in the bushes tonight because the red savage might come scalp you." He made a dramatic gesture with his hands, banged them on the table, and laughed. Had he known where I was hiding all along? The threat of Indians seemed of such little consequence to him. An invasion of red ants was coming, for all he seemed to care.

"Were you really at the Battle of Bull Run?" I finally asked.

"Of course not!" He stood and removed a large burlap sack from a high shelf. With great ceremony he pulled items from it and laid them on the table. Even from across the room, I could smell chocolate, buttery biscuits, and cheese. He set down a green bottle with a long slender neck and uncorked it with a knife. He rose and fetched a cup from the kitchen. He wiped out the cup with a rag, placed it on the table next to the bottle, and settled back down onto the bench. I looked away as soon as he looked at me, but I could see his jeweled hand in the air. His index finger beckoned me to the table.

"Dearest Ophelia, if you must spend an evening with the devil, you might as well drink the nectar of the gods."

I glanced at the table. It was a mistake. I couldn't take my eyes off the feast he had laid out. The forbidden bottle had an elegant shape and exuded a wonderful grape aroma, which drew me forward. I stood clutching the rifle, three feet or so from the table, and looked at the sumptuous spread. If I had ever seen or tasted such delicacies, I had no memory of it. My tongue salivated from the rich smells.

"Sit," said my uncle. "We can at least make this pleasurable."

I sat on the bench across from him and rested the rifle across my lap. "Where did you get all this?" I asked.

"I have my ways." He smiled, poured some wine into the cup, and slid it toward me. "Let it linger in your mouth before you swallow it."

"Saints aren't supposed to drink spirits."

"It's only wine." He leaned forward and searched my eyes until I felt thoroughly exposed. "Besides, are you really a Saint? Or do you keep secrets from your elders? Do you tell lies and have impure thoughts?"

His questions penetrated and rattled the very core of my being. I'd always assumed I was worthy enough to call myself a Saint. I wasn't sure of anything anymore. I lifted the cup from the table and was about to drink.

He reached out and wrapped his long jeweled fingers around my wrist. "Let it linger on your lips," he said and steadied the cup. As my lips touched the wine, they tingled and seemed to grow. He took his hand away and nodded. I drank and lowered the cup.

"Now your lips are red, just like a painted lady." He smiled and reached for a deck of cards.

"*Phlltt . . . phlltt . . . phlltt,*" the devil whispered as he shuffled.

In the distance, coyotes yipped and howled. For as long as I could remember, all I'd had to drink was water from the Virgin. The wine made my mouth both come alive and melt in the most delicious contradictory sensation. "Aren't you afraid of the Indians?" I asked Uncle Luther.

A knowing sideways smile crossed his face. "Black Hawk won't come here," he said assuredly, as if he knew Black Hawk and his ways.

"How do you know?"

He snorted and slammed down the cards. "I know what I know, and you don't have to know it, or ask how I know it. I just do!" He blew air through his nose and gestured at the chocolate and cheese. "Go ahead. Help yourself. I know you want some. Don't be shy. If I didn't want to share, I wouldn't offer."

I placed the rifle on the floor next to the table, stood up, and chose a small piece of chocolate. I put it in my mouth. It tasted wonderful. I drank a little more wine and ate some cheese. It is hard to describe the rapture of eating those things to someone who has never been hungry or looked upon a simple slice of cheese as the grandest luxury. Partaking of those pleasures filled me with such warmth and good cheer, for a moment I forgot my uncle was a treacherous swine. As I ate, I stared at his fingers laden with heavy sparkling rings and marveled how nimble he was with the cards. I'd never seen such jewels on a man—or a woman, for that matter—and they mesmerized me.

He caught me staring at them. "Do you like jewels? Enough to lie and keep them hidden from a poor relation fallen on hard times who has come so far to see you? I earned these here"—he held up his ringed hands—"gambling on the riverboat, won them from the unlucky hands of babes, babes at the card table. The jewels your mother absconded with are my birthright and believe me, if they are here, I will get them back." He glared at me and then admired his rings. "I don't do physical labor anymore. I make it my business to know things. I acquired these rings through skillful application of knowledge." He spread out his hands and tapped his fingers on the table. "I wear a fortune on my hands because I play my hand with knowledge and skill." He tapped the deck of cards.

I wanted to know the story of my mother and the scandal that destroyed her family. But I didn't ask Uncle Luther, because I could see he was a liar and a cheat.

"You mean through trickery," I said.

"Through knowledge and skill," he scowled. "Now let's play a simple game called vingt-et-un. Do you remember what I taught you?"

EIGHT

After we played a few hands of cards, drank more wine, and ate our fill of the delicacies, Uncle Luther started to act funny. "Come on over here," he babbled. "Come on, sit next to me. Sit on my lap. Let me tell you a story."

I should have run away right then, but I was afraid of the Indians, and the wine seemed to make Uncle Luther silly, not mean and dangerous like the whiskey had.

The wine had loosened my tongue. "You're an old fool!" I said and got up from the table. "I'm too old to sit on men's knees and hear children's stories." I grabbed my rifle and sat on the bed in the corner. He glared at me with anger and injury.

I recognized at once that I'd been too bold. "I didn't mean old fool, sir. I meant to say, I'm too heavy for your lap. I'd break your knee." He rose from the table. I trained the Henry on him.

Shock and hurt crossed his face again. "Ophelia, is this how my sister raised you? No manners! Put that rifle down. You should be ashamed of yourself."

I put the rifle next to me on the bed and hung my head.

"Now come over and help me clean up. We can save all these delicacies for another day."

I got up, went to the table, and started cleaning up the leftovers from the feast. Uncle Luther walked to the bed and picked up the Henry. He hung it out of my reach across some high hooks near the ceiling.

61

After he put the rifle out of my reach, he turned to me. A dark shadow crossed his face. Within seconds his hand was at the back of my neck. He grabbed my jaw and yelled in my face. "If you ever, ever, point a gun at me again, I will beat you so hard you'll wish you were dead. Do you hear me?"

I nodded. He turned me around, pressed my body down onto the table, pulled my bloomers down, and lifted my skirt. "If that ruby necklace is here somewhere you better tell me!" He beat my bare bottom. I cried for mercy. But I did not tell him about the necklace. He finally stopped beating me. Yet he held me there with my skirt still lifted.

"Stop crying and listen good," he whispered into my ear. "The hiding is over. But if you don't tell me where the rubies are right now, I'm going to make you my jewel. Do you understand?"

I struggled to free myself. I kicked him and tried to bite his wrist. He overpowered me and pressed my face against the table. My family had prayed, shared meals, and laughed at that table. Deep shame and mourning came over me. Still, I couldn't bring myself to give up the rubies. I'd spend the rest of my life trying to figure out why I didn't save myself and give them to him.

He followed through with his threat. When he entered me, I felt a pinch and then burning. It didn't hurt as much as the hiding, but the pain was deep in places I didn't even know could hurt. I felt as low and dirty as a barnyard animal. Where was the Heavenly Father? Where were my mother and father? Could they see this? Why did my mother write to this horrible man? Why did she let him know we existed? As he pounded himself into me, I felt ashamed. Why hadn't I just given him the necklace?

When he finished, I pulled up my bloomers. He grabbed my chin and stared into my eyes. "I'm sorry I had to do that. Now

I know you're telling the truth. Only a whore would trade her virginity for a ruby necklace." He released me. I ran out the door.

The Virgin pulled me to her. I had never felt her call so strong. Transfixed, I stumbled down the hill as if pulled by a magnetic force beyond my control. I picked up a giant rock and entered her waters fully clothed. I intended to follow Shakespeare's Ophelia and drown myself. The cold water numbed and cleansed my body. I held the rock and lay down, letting her water engulf me and cover my head.

Uncle Luther's hands grabbed me, pried the rock from my grasp, and dragged me out of the Virgin River. As he carried me up the hill, I heard the sickening sloshing of his wet shoes and clothes. My body shook uncontrollably. Water dripped from his brow onto me like a steady agonizing rain. My head fell back and I could see the glorious celestial light coming from the heavens that I would never be part of. I was damned.

After that horrible night, Uncle Luther scarcely looked at me. He acted as if I were invisible. He was no more interested in me than in a blade of grass. Somehow this was worse than all his lecherous advances. I couldn't help but think that he had discovered some vile thing inside me. I hated him for what he'd done to me, and I hated myself too.

I made this entry in my journal soon after it happened.

Dear Heavenly Father,

Why did you take my mother, father, and brother away? Please forgive me. I was greedy and stupid. I should have given him the jewels and saved myself. Now I'm his slave in this place, which was once a home—filled with laughter and the kind voices of my family—my family of Saints. We believed in you. With minor exceptions we followed the church law. We prayed to you daily. Yet you struck us down. You took my parents so slowly, so painfully. I had to watch them waste away and become skeletons. Why have you forsaken us? What has become of Zeke—only you know. Please keep him among the living. Please let me see him again someday. I pray Mother and Father are in a place of divine glory and peace, their suffering in the earthly realm now over.

What of me, Lord? Do you plan to keep me here with Uncle Luther? In the presence of the Saints, he pretends to be a gentleman and a believer. But here with me, he is a demon. I gave my virginity to the devil himself in order to save a ruby necklace. Am I damned? Will he try to take me as a wife? I would rather die. Please forgive me. Please, please, send a sign of your mercy. Your humble servant,

Ophelia Oatman

NINE

The day of the big card game, Uncle Luther woke early and shook my bed while cursing a flock of noisy ravens. "Goddamn squawking bluegums! Ophelia, wake up! Get me some coffee."

I boiled water and set to making his coffee while he maimed the cantankerous ravens with a slingshot. All my life I'd awakened with a sense of purpose, whether it was walking with the wagons to Zion, stitching quilts, planting, harvesting, or tending the crops. Whatever the chore, I had always been eager. They might have said I was prideful and had a loose tongue, but no one had ever accused me of being lazy.

During that terrible time, I had to drag myself out of bed each morning. I dreaded each day. My only pleasures were reading Sister May Belle's books and tending the garden. I was ashamed of making myself a whore and that I'd tried to drown myself, the same as Mr. Shakespeare's Ophelia. She was a silly, weak girl, who had gone mad, and I didn't understand why Ma had named me after her. Each day I dreamt and prayed that a young man would ride into town and save me from my hopeless existence.

On the day of the card game, he did. When I first laid eyes on him, I thought the Heavenly Father had answered my prayers and sent me an angel. I had been toiling in the garden all morning until the sun grew too hot. I squatted by the river and was contemplating wading in for a dip. The clomping of hooves alerted me of someone's approach. I stood and squinted down the path. I didn't know who he was, or what he wanted, but when I saw him, I thanked the Lord.

From a spotted white pony, he looked down at me with pale blue eyes that matched the hot August sky. I wasn't frightened of him. His face was hairless, and his cheeks had a rosy hue. From under his brown buckskin hat, hair flowed like strands of fresh-spun gold. His constant smile showed teeth as white as the sun-blanched bones that I had collected from the sandy washes and rocky hillsides. I had always admired the whiteness and purity of those bones, especially considering they came from death.

He stared down at me from his pony and said, "Well, looky here!" His smile was sewn on like a badge. "Ain't you a sight for sore eyes?"

I could neither speak nor breathe. I felt like a lady in a tight corset. I'd never worn a corset, or been to a ball, but I'd read about them, and that was how I imagined it. For a moment I thought Joseph Smith himself had risen from the dead. With the boy's golden hair, they were so similar. My angel looked around in confusion and spoke again.

"Is there supposed to be a card game around her somewheres?"

"Yes, sir, my Uncle Luther is hosting it, at our homestead up on the hill there." I pointed toward our place. "You're a little early. It doesn't start till sundown."

He looked up the hillside and then at me. Then he dismounted and said, "Where are my manners? I'm Samuel. Samuel Cox. But you can call me Sam or anything you want. You're just so purdy I forgot myself. And what might your name be, fair lady?"

I'd never had a young man fuss over me like that. My whole body tingled and my stomach fluttered. "I'm Ophelia. Ophelia Oatman. My brother used to call me O for short." I smiled and then felt sad. In my mind, I could hear Zeke's voice calling me Little O. It seemed so long ago that he had called me that.

He slapped his knee. "O! Ophea? Why, I like that. It's got a nice ring to it. Never did meet an Ophea before. May I?" He reached for my hand. I nodded. He lifted my fingers to his lips. I was glad I'd just rinsed them in the river. If he'd caught me a moment sooner, they'd have been covered with dirt.

From the moment I laid eyes on Samuel Cox, I was in love. Falling in love was just like I'd read about in books. I'd never thought something out of a novel would happen to me. He was perfect in every way. The only peculiar thing about him was that the smile never seemed to leave his face.

"Well, I got some time to kill. Say, this looks like a nice shady spot to rest my head. Do you mind my company?"

"No, not at all. Why, it was getting so hot, I took a break from working. Good thing you didn't come around a minute later. I was just about to strip down and go for a dip."

His smile grew even wider and his eyes danced. He took off his hat, raised his brows, and searched the ground for something to say. "Shucks. That would have been an awkward first meeting, Miss Ophea."

I didn't mind that he mispronounced my name. He could have called me just about anything. I had an overwhelming urge to hug him. Sam Cox hitched his pony and unrolled a blanket on the gama grass in the shade of a cottonwood. He tossed a burlap sack down onto the blanket.

"We can have ourselves a nice picnic. I got enough chow for the two of us." I sat on the blanket. He sat down, took off his hat, and then reclined on his side facing me. "I like to wait a few minutes and settle my stomach from the ride before I eat. This here's some rocky, uneven country."

I sat straight with my legs out and smoothed my skirt. "Yes. My stomach is a little jumpy too. You gave me a start. Most days I'm alone and don't see a soul."

He shook his head and clucked his tongue. "That's too bad, a pretty girl like you, alone every day."

I tried to smile. After what happened with Uncle Luther, I never thought I'd want anything to do with a man again. But Samuel Cox was different. I wanted to be with him so badly it hurt. I wanted to feed him, bathe him, shave his tiny whiskers and lay myself open for him. But how could it be? I had traded my chastity to keep possession of the cursed ruby necklace. I was ruined. They said a man could tell if you weren't a virgin. I wondered how old Samuel was, but I didn't want to ask him because I didn't want him to ask me.

"This is about the extent of my life—tending this here struggling garden, some livestock, and the ramshackle house over yonder," I said.

I eyed his hat on the blanket. It was the sort the cowhands and vaqueros wore. He sat up and started pulling off his boots. They had rusty spurs on the heels. Heat and a cloud of fine dust rose from his foot.

"Do you mind if I take these boots off and let my feet breathe a little?"

"Why, no—not at all. Your feet must be hot and tired."

He pulled off his sock. I braced myself for a ghastly sight, but his feet, even though they were dirty, were the most beautiful I'd ever seen—besides a baby's, of course. They were perfectly formed, strong yet hairless. So far everything about Samuel Cox was beautiful.

He sighed and looked down at the river. "That water looks mighty inviting."

I looked at the river and smiled. His pony neighed as if in agreement. "That's a beautiful pony you've got there, sir. Are you a cowboy?"

"Call me Samuel or Sam. I'm only nineteen, can't be much

older than you. No reason to call me sir. And I'll call you Ophea."

I couldn't bring myself to correct him.

"I came out here to do some cattle herding and trading. Earned some capital, and then I discovered my true calling." The smile, which never left his face, grew wider and I got another glimpse of his white, polished-bone teeth. I wanted to touch them.

"What's that?" I asked.

"You see, I have a gift for the cards. In one night—in one night—I doubled the cattle-driving money it took me six months to earn." He fingered a jewel-studded cross around his neck while he shook his head. I could tell he was reliving that glorious card-playing night.

From everything my parents had told me and from Uncle Luther, I knew cards brought nothing but trouble. The *phlltt-phlltt* of the deck still sounded like the devil whispering. "I hope you didn't come all the way out here so you could make money at cards. Listen—" I looked up the hill just to make sure Uncle Luther wasn't suddenly within earshot. I spoke low. "You watch out for my Uncle Luther and the cards. He was a riverboat card sharp. Sitting down to play with him is like taking tea with a wolf. Unless you want to lose everything, it's a very bad idea."

Samuel Cox squinted and studied the sole of his boot. His grin had changed from one of pleasure to a challenge. "We'll see about that. I got something that can never be learned or practiced." He leaned back on his elbow again, relaxed.

"What's that?" I asked.

"Luck."

"Luck? How do you mean?" I tilted my head and waited for his explanation.

As he pulled Johnny cakes and jerky from his sack and spread a picnic lunch out on the blanket, he proceeded to rattle off all the various ways he'd narrowly averted disaster, starting from the time he was a young-un up until his recent escapades driving cattle from Texas to the Missouri. He'd had close scrapes with Indians and bears, angry cattle ranchers, outlaws, road agents disguised as Indians, even a three-hundred-pound woman named Little Molly. In his nineteen years, he'd already had enough adventures to fill a lifetime.

I thought about telling him a story or two about myself, but they seemed boring compared to his. He should have been dead ten times over. He was right—his luck was amazing. He stopped talking and started devouring the Johnny cakes. He kept offering me food till finally I managed a few nibbles even though my stomach was knotted from the excitement of being so close to him. He hadn't asked anything about me, which was just fine. I figured the less he knew, the better.

I was too excited to eat much. I reclined on my back and felt the earth beneath my body, the places where it touched me and where it didn't. In the presence of Sam Cox, my body felt alive, like something almost separate from me—something I could barely control. A slight breeze tickled the hair on my arms. My belly sank and my rib cage expanded. Even though it was hot, my nipples were hard. I had a strange sensation, which I later recognized was the ache of desire. I tried to ignore the feeling, but I was giddy and my head was light and full of air.

Tiny white tufts of cotton floated around us. With squinted eyes, I'd try to follow the path of one before it was lifted out of sight into heaven. I wanted to be that light. I wanted to float.

"We're surrounded by angels," I said.

Samuel Cox laughed, stopped eating for a minute, and looked down at me. "I think that's from the cottonwood trees. Ophea, may I ask you something?"

I turned from my back onto my elbow. He was serious but the smile was still there. His eyes ran the length of my body. My desire intensified under his gaze. I nodded.

"Are you one of them Saints?"

I flipped onto my back again to study the floating cotton, which looked so much like tree-born angels in the hot wavering air. "I was," I told him. "But I'm becoming less and less a Saint each day."

I believed my own earthly angel was right next to me, and I never wanted to leave his side. I'd been afraid we'd have nothing to talk about. As it turned out, Samuel Cox was quite a storyteller. I decided to give myself to him. I would do whatever he asked. I hoped he would not see how defiled I was from Uncle Luther, because then he would surely forsake me.

After eating, we lay on the blanket, faces turned up to the hot shimmering sky. Monarch butterflies flew by and landed in puddles of horse urine. High above us, white, puffy clouds spun into shapes before they unraveled and floated away. All manner of insects, some you could barely see, floated in that July sky. The air contained a web of life I had never noticed.

The sun dropped to the west and took some of our shade with it. Beads of sweat formed on my brow. I was about to get up and move with the shade.

Samuel Cox sighed. "That river is calling my name." He sat up and looked at me. "Would it be too bold or improper to ask you to join me for a swim? I promise I'll keep my eyes averted."

I sat up and looked toward the Virgin. "There's nothing I'd like more than to go for a dip. But what will you think of me? Stripping down in front of a man I just met?"

His ever-present smile grew wider and I glimpsed those whiter-than-polished-bone teeth again.

"I'd say you're my kind of girl."

I left my bloomers and chemise on, even though I knew full well that as soon as they got wet they'd be see-through. It was brazen to take off my clothes and swim with a man I'd just met.

But part of me figured I had nothing left to lose. I was already ruined.

"Can you swim?" I asked. "Her current is stronger than it looks."

He stood in his underclothes and looked at the Virgin. "I've taken herds of Texas Longhorns across rivers that make this here one look like a puddle."

"Okay then. I usually take the next eddy out to the bank. By the time I walk upriver, I'm dry. Ready?"

The sun glinted off his teeth. "Ophea, I'm ready whenever you are!"

We walked into the river. The shock of cold water tensed my body and my hands went up under my arms like chicken wings. "Whooh, that's refreshing." The bottom gave way and the Virgin's current carried me downriver. I put my head back into the water and lifted my feet. Liquid cold swirled around me. I pointed my feet downriver and raised my head. Samuel Cox was beside me. He bobbed above the surface, his smile wider than ever. He yelped with pleasure. I saw the eddy coming up and swam toward it. Sam started swimming too. I got to the bank and grabbed a low-hanging branch. I held tight to it with one hand and reached out with my other. He grabbed my arm. I pulled him out of the current into the eddy and toward me. We made our way to the river's edge and scrambled onto the bank, dripping wet and laughing. The heat of the day had drained us, but the Virgin had renewed us.

Sam laughed and grabbed my arm. "This little arm saved me from a long walk upriver." He kissed the inside of my forearm and then the crook of my arm. I smiled and laughed. He pulled me toward him. Even though his body was wet and cool, I could feel his heat. He leaned down and looked into my eyes. I tilted my head toward him and looked into his eyes. Our lips touched and I tasted the river. I wasn't a virgin, but that was my first kiss.

TEN

The deafening crack of gunfire interrupted us. Sam pushed me to the ground. He looked around, reaching instinctively for his six-shooter. He must have forgotten that he had no pants on and no gun to draw. Uncle Luther walked down the hill scowling with a rifle trained on us—as if we were dangerous—half-naked and shivering like lambs.

"Girl, come to me!" he yelled.

I looked at Sam. Strangely enough he still smiled, but now his smile was doing a twitchy dance of regret and apology, both toward me and Uncle Luther. He put his hands up and took a step away from me. I crossed my arms over my chest to hide my breasts. I hung my head and walked toward Uncle Luther. As soon as I was within reach, he struck me hard across the face. The force of his blow knocked me onto the sand. Blood dripped from my mouth. Sam took a step toward us, but Uncle Luther raised his gun. Sam took a step back and put his hands up higher.

"What in damnation is going on here? Who the hell are you?"

"I'm Samuel Cox, sir. I saw a notice at the trading post about a poker game around here this evening."

"Looks like you're playing the wrong kind of poker. You're going to pay for this." Uncle Luther spat tobacco juice onto the ground next to me.

"Uncle Luther," I shouted, "don't hurt him. It's my fault. It was all my doing, I swear."

Uncle Luther squinted and studied me hard. Samuel lowered his hands a little. Uncle Luther swung the rifle back in his direction. Samuel raised his hands again. Uncle Luther studied him, sizing him up. A sly smile broke out on his face. "My, my, he is a pretty boy. Turned you into a right river-nymph, now didn't he?" He turned his head from Sam and looked down at me. "Didn't know you had it in you. With your nymph ways and red hair, I ought to sell you to a brothel."

He spoke to Sam. "You're not the first to fall under the spell of this little strumpet, and I suspect you won't be the last. I'll let you in the poker game, but I'm going to have to fine you for the use of my girl."

Sam protested, "Sir, we didn't . . . It was just a swim and one little kiss . . . There was no . . ."

Uncle Luther raised his gun again and aimed it at Sam. "I ain't going to argue the details. You pay a fine or I shoot you. That's all there is to it."

"Okay. I'll pay the fine, sir."

"Good. Now start walking and git your clothes back on before anyone else comes along and you ruin the reputation of my family."

Samuel started walking upriver toward his pony and our clothes. Uncle Luther fell in step behind him with the rifle. I started to rise from the ground to follow them. Uncle Luther turned toward me and shot me a sinister look. "Be wise to stay out of my sight for a while till I figure out what I'm going to do with you."

I sat back on the sand and watched Uncle Luther follow Samuel down the path and away from me. If I'd had a gun I would have shot Uncle Luther there and then for telling my angel that I was a strumpet.

★　★　★　★　★

Later, I crept back to the house. Uncle Luther would be expecting dinner. He and Samuel were sitting outside. Uncle Luther was in the rocker taking one of his afternoon naps, his feet up and his hat down almost covering his face. Samuel sat on a tree stump strumming Zeke's old guitar three feet from Uncle Luther. He smiled at me and I smiled back even though my lip hurt from where Uncle Luther had struck me.

Sam stopped strumming and was about to say something. But as soon as the music stopped, Uncle Luther's head rolled and he started mumbling. Sam strummed again. Uncle Luther's head dropped and he snored. We looked from Uncle Luther to each other with perplexed smiles. Samuel stopped playing two more times with the same effect. We nodded to each other, silently agreeing that it was best for him to keep playing so that Uncle Luther would keep sleeping.

While preparing the evening meal I tiptoed so that I wouldn't wake the sleeping demon. I tried to imagine that Uncle Luther didn't exist, and that I cooked dinner only for Samuel. I wanted to hear more of his stories and finish our interrupted kiss. By the time Uncle Luther awakened, the stew was done. I scooped some from the Dutch oven and handed him a bowl. As I handed Samuel his bowl, our fingers grazed and I felt a tingle. I wanted to touch his hands more or at least just sit and watch him eat. But I needed to disappear before Uncle Luther could finish eating and berate me again. I took my dinner bowl and went to sit on a stump around back of the house.

A man was riding up the hill toward our place. In the twilight, I could just make out the dark shape of a second man. It looked like Uncle Luther would have his card game after all. I figured if I was lucky, one of the fellows would catch him cheating and shoot him dead. It seemed like a distinct possibility. As that fantasy started to take shape in my mind, my spirits rose. If it happened, I could run away with Samuel Cox.

Each year the house had become smaller and smaller. Once it was filled with happy memories, but the echoes of sickness, of my parents' grunts and tortured moans, lingered. Even the beautiful patchwork quilt I had once associated with comfort reminded me of sickness. Uncle Luther had destroyed any lingering fond feelings I had for our log home to the point it felt like a suffocating prison. I often hoped he would get the fever and die on my parents' featherbed with the patchwork quilt twisted around him. He deserved it. But I couldn't wait to see if sickness would take him. Disease chose its victims with a strange sort of whimsy that I couldn't understand, and it made me question the nature of the Lord.

After darkness fell, I went into the lean-to. I'd rather live with spiders and scorpions and the threat of an Indian attack than with Uncle Luther. Pickaxes, shovels, and all manner of other tools hung from the walls and were piled up in the corner. Before Father died everything in the lean-to had been in its place. Zeke had kept things up all right. But now, when Uncle Luther needed something, he'd storm in like a tornado, and I refused to clean up after him.

I liked the lean-to because it made me feel closer to Zeke. His getaway was so fast that he didn't have time to go through his belongings, and he'd left behind many of his personal treasures. Besides the cherished Henry, which he inherited when Pa died, he had a collection of minerals, arrowheads, knives, and some wood figures that he'd carved in the scarce moments when his hands were free from toil.

Through the peephole in the lean-to I could see the men sitting around the table. One man looked like a Spaniard. He had short black hair and a very thin mustache. His mouth never moved, but his eyes studied everything and he watched the others. The other gambler had a beard so long and bushy I could hardly see his face. He kept his slouch hat on. I imagined his head was bald. A lantern hung from a hook above the ceiling casting an eerie light around the room. Uncle Luther faced me. I could only see the back of Samuel's head. He was by far the youngest of them all.

The pile of money in the middle of the table kept getting swept away and built back up. What would happen after the poker game? Would Samuel Cox ride away into the night without me? Or would he ask me to go with him? Uncle Luther would never let me go. That much I knew. My heart felt like it was way up in my throat and my stomach fluttered. I had to escape with Samuel. If I stayed, I'd either drown myself in the river like Ophelia, or go absolutely mad lamenting Samuel Cox.

The Henry was tucked under the cot mattress. I had retrieved it from the high hooks when Uncle Luther was out getting whiskey. As a joke, I put the barrel into the peephole and squatted down. Every time Samuel moved his head and I had a clear line of sight on Uncle Luther, I pretended to pull the trigger. "Bang," I whispered to myself. I was just fooling, though I couldn't help but wonder what would happen if I really shot him. "Thou shalt not kill" kept going through my head. Would my soul be damned? Pa had always said, "God helps those who help themselves." And the Prophet Brigham Young also said sometimes it is righteous to shed blood. He even employed Porter Rockwell as his own avenging angel.

I dug at the peephole until it became bigger and my line of sight into the room was clearer. I squeezed one eye shut and trained the gun at Uncle Luther's heart. But Samuel kept swinging his head and there was no way I could shoot Uncle Luther without risking Samuel's life. I sighed, leaned the gun against the wall, and began throwing things into a grain sack. One way or another I was going to leave with Samuel.

I looked at Dolly on the cot. Knowing what was inside her

gave me courage, but scared me too. What if the curse was real? Not yet sure of my plan, I stuffed her into a saddlebag. I didn't know exactly how I was going to do it, but I was determined that when Samuel Cox left our homestead, I would leave with him. I pulled my dress over my head and stuffed it into the sack. Zeke's old clothes were worn and dusty, shredded and patched, but at least they were sturdier than my gingham dress. I'd need outdoor clothes and a good blanket because I'd be sleeping on the ground.

The gamblers' voices startled me as curses exploded from inside the house. I looked through the peephole. Uncle Luther was sweeping all the money and gold from the middle of the table. Samuel rose from his chair. I couldn't see his face, but from the heaviness of his shoulders I could tell he was burdened. "You're going to give me another chance to win something back, aren't you?" he asked Uncle Luther.

"What do you have left to lose? Your pony? I hope you got good boots. This is no country for walking."

"I got to go to the privy. I might have something you don't know of, so don't think you've cleaned me out yet," said Samuel.

My heart thumped and my body throbbed with urgency. Would Samuel lose even his pony to Uncle Luther? Then what would we do? Uncle Luther would shoot us both before he let us leave. I grabbed the rifle and stuck the barrel through the peephole. With Samuel gone, I had a good enough line of sight. I trained the rifle on Uncle Luther. As he threw down a shot of whiskey, I squeezed the trigger. A roar filled my ears. Uncle Luther fell back in his chair. Gun smoke filled the house. The sound of the shot echoed in my ears and the smoke burned my eyes and nose. Inside the cabin, two more shots were fired in quick succession. The room filled with more smoke. I peered through the hole. The other two men had fired on each other and all three lay on the ground writhing and moaning. I hadn't even thought about them. That's how detailed my plan was.

I ran out of the lean-to and stepped cautiously into the house through the front door. Blood flooded around the men's bodies and dripped through gaps in the floorboards. Three men lay dead because of me. I didn't check to see if they were dead. I just assumed it because blood seeped from their still bodies and pooled like a community well. Samuel Cox ran into the cabin with his six-shooter drawn. He looked from me to the bloody bodies on the floor. "What in the name—"

"Samuel, grab all that money and let's get out of here. If anyone from the settlement heard those gunshots, they'll come up to investigate and we'll be hanged."

At the mention of hanging, he sprang into action and followed my orders. I had saddlebags packed and ready. I just had to strap them onto one of the horses. "Samuel, which horse should I take? Which one do you reckon is strong but even-tempered?"

He grabbed my saddlebags, and started strapping them onto a pinto. The horse was nervous under my unfamiliar touch, but I fed him some hay, patted his nose, and sweet-talked him while Samuel fastened the bags. He hoisted me up onto the horse's back. "What happened in there?"

"I'll tell you about it as soon as we put some miles between us and Grafton."

Over the years, I had come to love my home in Grafton. I was even fond of the cantankerous Virgin, which periodically threatened to wipe us all out. I believed in the Heavenly Father. I believed in the Prophet Joseph Smith. But most of all, I believed in my family. Unlike most other Mormon men, my father had only taken one wife. You can get away with a lot when you're willing to live so far from the luxuries of civilization. My mother and father had been the lords of my world. Ezekiel was the mysterious half-breed angel. I didn't know how he came to be born from my mother and not of my father's seed, but it didn't matter. I loved him all the same.

I felt guilty about the men I'd left bleeding to death in Pa's house. I could have been an obedient girl. I could have given the ruby necklace to my uncle. He probably would have absconded and then I would have become the third or fourth sister-wife of some toothless man twice my age, most likely Brother Thompson. But Pa's words kept coming back to me, "God helps those who help themselves." Even as his hands were busy helping others, Pa had always tried to teach people to do things for themselves. Yet he had never taught me to shoot. It was up to Zeke to do that. And I couldn't stop wondering why Ma had called on Uncle Luther for help when he was such a devil.

After Sam and I crossed the wooden bridge over the Virgin, the dirt road came to a T. I wanted to ride east. But he wanted to ride west. Although the rugged cathedrals of rock to the east beckoned me, they put Sam on edge. They reminded me of happy days with Zeke, exploring the winding canyons, discovering waterfalls and swimming holes. But Samuel saw it as a land of rock mazes, places where we could be cornered by Indians or trapped by a posse of Saints, who would soon enough come looking for us. In some part of my heart slept a glimmer of hope that if we went east we might find Zeke. We had always taken refuge in the east, and I knew Zeke had ridden that way on that horrible night when Uncle Luther condemned him to live as an exile. I also knew Zeke could have hidden in those canyons long enough to outfox the Grafton Saints.

Being a man, and a cowboy, and now an outlaw, meant that Samuel Cox was not forthright with his fear. Our horses pranced and neighed, their haunches still full of our frantic getaway gallop. "Let's go this way," I said leading the pinto toward the east.

"That's Indian country," he said.

"It's all Indian country," I replied. "If we go west, there's nowhere to hide. People will see us coming from miles away. That might be all right for you alone, cowboy, but with me and this orange hair, we'll stick out like a sore thumb. And they'll be looking for me. We can take the winding paths east and north. It's the road less traveled."

"I want to go west," said Sam, "to California."

I convinced him to go east, at least for a little while. They'd only bother looking for us for a few days, a week at most. Then we could double back or find another way around Grafton and go west toward California. I told him I knew of a trail that cut through the rock canyons and led out to the main road, but that was only half-true. I'd heard of one, but I'd never been that far myself. As we got deeper into canyon country, Samuel looked spooked.

Eleven

When the stars shone brightest and deep night fell, we found a flat spot and spread Samuel's bedroll on the sand next to some sage and rocks. We lay next to each other. Our bodies were as taut as the strings of a finely tuned guitar. The excitement and the furious pace in which we had ridden out of Grafton kept us both awake, even though it was late and we were tired. I didn't know what would happen to us, or where we would end up, but because I was with Samuel it didn't matter.

He turned toward me and stroked my hair. His strong hands cupped my face. We finished our interrupted kiss. The still night air carried no chill and he unbuttoned his shirt. I slid my hand over his muscled chest, down over his ribs to the cavity of hardened flesh around his naval. The strength and power of his body excited me in a way I had never known. If the devil was responsible for the feelings, then I could see why he was in competition with God. I had asked God for help, for a sign, and he had sent Samuel.

With difficulty, I coaxed Samuel to remove his holster. He placed his six-shooter on the blanket next to us. Even as his hands caressed my body, his focus continually returned to the gun. After all, she was a lover whose power could save us. We began to consummate our relations. I wanted him to focus completely on me and the magic our bodies exchanged. But he couldn't help looking over his shoulder every once in a while. He seemed to expect a hatchet in his skull, or to find a Mormon posse with their rifles trained on our naked bodies.

When he entered me, he forgot himself and our danger. Finally he seemed lost in our union. A brief memory of the night with Uncle Luther came to me, but Samuel's tender kisses and loving embraces brought me back to his arms. From the pleasure I felt and the great expanse of stars overhead, I knew this act was divine and celestial. For the stars seemed born of the same expanding and contracting that connected our loins. I understood then that this deed was only evil when the male forced himself upon the female—then man truly became a beast.

Samuel Cox shuddered. His moan echoed off the canyon walls so loudly you never would have thought he was a man in hiding. He sighed, rolled over, collapsed on his back, and looked up at the stars. I laughed so hard my belly hurt.

"What?" he asked. By the starlight, I could see that he still smiled, but concern had crept into his voice. "Makes a man feel a little insecure when a woman he's just known laughs."

"I'm laughing at the way you yowled. They probably heard you all the way in Grafton."

He snorted. "Hmm, was it that loud? I lost my abandon."

I got up and gathered my clothes.

"Where are you going?" he asked.

"Over to the creek to wash myself."

"Alone?" He started to get up.

"Just relax a spell. I'll be all right." I grabbed the Henry rifle I'd used to shoot Uncle Luther and headed for the creek.

When I got back from the creek Samuel had dressed and was preparing the horses. "We ought to keep riding," he said. "Be easier on the horses, if we rode at night and rested during the heat of the day."

We followed the faint trail, never losing sight of the creek for too long. Unaccustomed to long journeys on horseback, I became saddle sore, but I didn't complain. Samuel looked like he was born in the saddle and could ride for days without rest. When dawn broke, the sun illuminated the pink and orange rock. The sage seemed to open and wave while birds chattered and sang. I had fought off fatigue a few hours before, when the air had finally cooled and my shivering body ached for sleep and warmth. The beginning of a new day renewed my spirit, and I felt I could keep riding till noon.

Samuel tore a piece of jerky from his mouth and offered it to me. I rode up alongside him, took it, and chewed off a piece. I had to rip it with my teeth and shake my head as an animal would. He squinted and surveyed the land. "You know where we're headed, Ophea? You ever come this far before?"

"Oh, sure," I lied. "This'll take us where we need to go. Don't you worry."

At noon when the sun reached its zenith and the air shimmered with heat, we bedded down in the shade of a rock overhang. It was about seven feet deep, four feet high, and twenty feet wide. Black bat feces hung petrified in the far corners, but a nice layer of sand covered the rock. Samuel spread out a bedroll. His sideways gait showed weariness and fatigue. Without hesitation he removed his holster and placed one of his six-shooters on the corner of the blanket. He stripped off his shirt, stretched out on the makeshift bed, and used the shirt for a pillow. I took off Zeke's old heavy clothes, spread my bedroll out, and lay next to him in my bloomers. Within minutes I heard his snoring, and I soon joined him in the land of nod.

TWELVE

Cool air chilled me awake. The sun had dropped out of sight and a strong wind created a constant high-pitched whistle. Under the rock ledge we were mostly protected, but when I stepped away from it, sand whipped up and scratched at my eyes.

Samuel must have felt the disturbance too, for he was awake and buttoning his shirt before I could turn around. We ate some hard tack and dried apricots while we packed our things. We unhitched the horses from a log near the river where we had left them to rest and drink. With the speed and efficiency of seasoned gypsies, we left our temporary encampment and continued riding down the trail.

We rode until we reached a place where the rock walls met and created a small slot. Only a thin slice of sunlight remained on the western horizon. The slot was too narrow for our horses. Without the horse, I could just barely squeeze through the rocks straight on, and Samuel had to position himself sideways. We puzzled over why the trail went straight through this small rock slot. He looked at me, the horses, and the slot with a perplexed smile. "Who would travel this country without horses?" he pondered aloud.

"Paiute?" I answered, worried now that I had truly lost the way.

"Ophea, you been living on that homestead too long. These

days even the Paiute have horses. Don't you know anything, girl?"

The way he said "girl" was like a slap, or a blow to the stomach, because he sounded like Uncle Luther, and for the first time I doubted my actions. I doubted Samuel, and myself, and everything I'd done. I'd put my life and soul in jeopardy. I'd gone against everything I'd believed in and everything my parents had believed in, but it was too late for second thoughts.

It was a dead end. We had to turn around. We rode back in the direction we had come, back past the place where we'd slept, and followed the trail by thin starlight. At least we wouldn't starve. We could always eat cottontails. As we rode along, they scurried in and out of sagebrush and formed a startled procession. The horse's rhythmic movement mesmerized me. I stopped thinking about my sore backside.

I focused on the trail and occasionally looked up at the stars, or the rock walls surrounding us. Fatigue and hunger muddled my mind. Dawn broke and we decided to rest. We dismounted and walked to a rock overhang like the one we had slept under the previous day. We looked closer. Hoofprints and footprints covered the ground. The sand was matted down as if someone had slept there. The last stars were fading. Dawn was breaking as it had the day before.

How many days had we been riding? I could have sworn it was only one. Someone had been in this very same spot not long ago. As the sun came up, we realized it was us. We stood and looked down at the spot where we had slept the day before. Or was it the day before that? All the events blurred together, and I couldn't separate day from night. It seemed like an eternity ago that we had tried to squeeze through the slot.

As he gazed in utter disbelief at the place where we had slept, the smile disappeared from Samuel's face. For the first time he seemed angry. When he turned toward me, I saw in his eyes fear and revulsion mixed with wonderment. He looked at me the way you might a witch or a leper. A raven announced its arrival, its caws echoing in the otherwise silent morning. The raven landed on the bed of sand where we had slept, and looked from Samuel to me as if he were a judge who had arrived to settle our dispute. Yet the raven's arrival seemed to confirm some suspicion inside Samuel—some suspicion about me.

"You brought me bad luck, girl."

He had called me girl again. Fear turned my stomach into one hard knot. Girl—girl—I was nothing but a girl to him—a girl who had brought bad luck.

"I never lost at cards before. They even called me Lucky Sam. But I see you there by the river with your red hair glowing in the sunlight. You entice me into the water. Then we're kissing and next thing you know, I got some old fart pointing a gun at me. After that, I lose at cards. And you kill three men! Now, I'm an outlaw, a desperado—lost in the desert, surrounded by rock walls in a place that can only be the devil's playground because it's so hot my flesh could just about melt off my bones." He took his hat off and wiped the sweat from his brow, then looked at me hard and sad before he looked to the horizon and shook his head. "You're a beautiful girl, Ophea. My eyes—upon seeing you—were revived from a long, dreamless sleep. But you brought me bad luck, and I have a terrible suspicion that you are cursed." He stared absently at the raven who sat on the rock with his head cocked as if he were listening. The raven cawed, squawked, and flew to the safety of a tree. Yet he was still there, looking down on us.

Sam's accusation scared me. Both of my parents dead, my brother gone, I'd traded my chastity for the cursed ruby necklace. I had been taught to believe in the will of God. But Samuel didn't speak of God. He spoke of luck and curses. Had I enticed him into the river? Had I been too forward? Three men were dead because of me, and only one of them had deserved it. Had I incurred the wrath of God? I didn't believe the Heavenly Father wanted me to end up in the hands of a devil like Uncle Luther. Yet he had given man dominion over all things, over the land, and the beasts—even woman.

I spoke in a hushed mother's tone, "Samuel, we were tired and we took a wrong turn somewhere. We probably got mixed up when we stopped at the creek and let the horses drink." He was silent and his mouth formed a hard thin line. I tried to alleviate his foul mood with a chipper response. "Think about it this way, if anyone is trying to track us they'll be as vexed as we are." He stared at me, squinted, and waited.

I dismounted from my horse and pointed at a big rock mesa. "Look, I will just scurry up on top of that rock there and see where we lost our way. Don't fret. We'll be back on the main trail in no time."

He looked at the rock mesa with skepticism. "That's a fine idea, but how do you propose to get up there, Ophea?"

"Easy, I'll climb."

"Climb?"

I pointed to the rock mesa, which rose up next to another rock formation. "See how those two rocks form a chimney? I can climb up there and squeeze myself in till I get higher. Then the angle eases off, and I can just creep catlike to the top. From there I'll get a bird's-eye view of this rock maze."

Samuel shook his head and looked at the tall rocks. He'd been shifting his body in the saddle but now he was dead still. "I don't like it," he said. "What if you fall? What then?"

I laughed. "My brother, Zeke, and I have been climbing rocks like these for years. I'm sure-footed as a mountain goat. Don't worry. I won't fall."

At first, I'd felt confident. But the mention of falling made me tremble with dread and panic. I'd never been afraid of heights before. Zeke and I had often climbed rocks just like that. Once we'd even stolen eggs from a redtail's nest and had to get back to solid ground while trying to avoid her angry attacks.

I rolled up my tattered pant legs and tightened the laces of my boots. I noticed again that my right boot was coming apart at the seams. Before I started climbing, I removed my bonnet and placed it on a rock. I rubbed my hands together and wiped them on my trousers for good luck. I smiled at Sam, and wished he'd show a little encouragement, maybe just a nod to condone my actions. I longed to see the white of his polished-bone teeth. But he just stared at me—his smile gone.

Fear cast a nervous shadow on each little movement and my palms sweated, making it difficult to grip the rock. As I climbed higher, my heart thumped louder. Finally, I reached the top just in time to see a beautiful sunrise. From there, Samuel looked small. The air moved and I felt free. Giant rock walls formed mazes and spread as far as I could see. I could not figure how to navigate us out of the rock labyrinth and back to a beaten trail. I wanted to stay on top of the rock, where I felt above all my trouble. Samuel looked up at me and I waved to him. "I can see!" I called. "To the northeast the trail opens up, it's not far!"

"Ophea," he called back, "git down from there before you fall!"

I wished he'd quit saying the word *fall*. Sometimes just talking about something too much could make it so. With all his superstition, he should know that. But I had made it to the top when he was too scared even to dismount from his horse. I had probably made him feel like a coward. My actions were unladylike. I did not seem to have the sort of disposition that a man admired. I'd been told more than once that I was too headstrong to make a good wife, and that my red hair would lead to nothing but trouble.

I started lowering myself back down the rock chimney, careful where I put each foot and hand. I tapped and shook every bit of rock to make sure it was attached. One section had been a little tricky to ascend. I'd had to hoist myself up and match one of my feet to where my hand was in order to make progress.

I didn't anticipate how hard it would be to come back down. I lowered myself from the ledge and scrambled my feet around for something to step on. But my feet didn't find the rock, and because the rock protruded at my chest I couldn't even see them. As the strength drained from my arms, panic filled every muscle and nerve. I wondered how much longer I could hold on. My forearms and chin were flush with the ledge, while my feet flailed beneath me. I looked to my side but it was no use. I couldn't see what was below. In a moment of faith and desperation, I extended my arms and held the ledge with my hands. Luckily my foot found the rock, and I lowered myself down to the next ledge. In that moment of relief, my other foot slipped on some sand.

I plummeted down the rock chimney. The most overwhelming terror and pain overcame me as I heard my body smack onto each rock ledge. Unable to grasp anything to stop myself, I kept tumbling. More than death and injury, I feared Samuel and how angry he'd be with me because I'd fallen.

Thirteen

I lay at the base of the cliff. So many parts of my body screamed in pain that I could not tell exactly where I was most broken. My right cheek pressed against the sand. As everything else throbbed, I tried to take comfort in that one soft spot under my right cheek. Unable to keep my eyes open against the agony, I squeezed them shut. A scream exploded in my mind, but I did not have the breath or courage to make it heard. The pain turned into a thousand points of flashing light. Something inside my head leaked as if a cool trickle of water ran through it. That trickle released me from my agony.

I opened my eyes. Samuel's serious unsmiling countenance hovered over me. Each whisker and speck of dirt on his face looked enormous. His eyes flicked and roamed the length of my body, finally resting in horror and disgust on my lower half. I tried to catch his eye. I tried to speak. But the pain swallowed me into darkness again.

The next time I opened my eyes again, I saw the ceiling of the rock overhang. I turned my head and found Dolly's black button eyes staring at me. Memories of the exodus out of Winter Quarters and the long trek to Zion flooded my mind. Dolly no longer provided comfort. I couldn't hug her for reassurance. I had the ruby necklace sewn inside her, and yet in the desert wilderness, it didn't do me a lick of good.

I don't know how long I was unconscious. I squinted toward the creek and saw Samuel with his horse. Sunlight reflected off the water and cast points of flashing light so bright I could barely focus on him. I struggled to keep my eyes open. The midday air shimmered and buzzed with insects. Samuel's horse lapped water from the stream. From the way his horse was saddled, I could tell he was about to leave.

I tried to scream to him, "Wait! Don't leave me here!" He didn't even turn his head in my direction. My throat was so dry and hoarse from my effort to yell that I wasn't sure if any sound had escaped me. I tried to scream his name over and over until my throat burned. He mounted his horse and began to ride away. I was finally able to produce sound. His name echoed off the canyon walls. He stopped. He turned a quick, sad glance over his shoulder then began to ride again. With tremendous effort I pushed myself up on one arm. I tried to crawl after him, but the pain was too great and I collapsed.

When he was gone from sight, my body convulsed with sobs, fear, and terror so intense I felt like I would split open. All my dreams of romance, of chivalry, and knights in shining armor, died that day as I watched Samuel ride off and realized no one was going to save me.

FOURTEEN

Maybe he'd gone for help, I thought. After all, he'd placed me on a bedroll, put Dolly beside me, and pulled a blanket over me. A canteen of water lay beside my head and Pa's Henry lay to the right. The sight of Pa's Henry filled my heart with hope. Maybe I wouldn't die after all. Bedding, a canteen full of water, and a gun—what else did I need to survive? My horse was tied to a branch near the creek. I wondered if I could get on him and ride after Samuel. My leg had no sensation. I had to gather my courage and assess my injuries. My head throbbed when I sat up. I slowly removed the blanket. "Mother of God!" I screamed and re-covered the horrific sight of my mangled and twisted leg.

Where could Samuel go for help? Even in Grafton, there was no doctor. My hopes for survival were ruined by the misshapen mess under the blanket that had once been my leg.

I'd complained to God about so much, the death of my parents, my brother's exile, Uncle Luther—but I'd never once thanked him for working legs, my health, food, and water. I'd never once thanked him for my life; for the absence of bodily pain; for the sweet breath that I drew from the sacred air in each and every moment. I had never thanked him for any of these things. I'd had so much and never realized it. Now I'd lost everything, even the things I'd taken for granted.

Worse than broken, I was alone. The loss of Samuel stung more than the pain in my leg, which had subsided and remained tolerable as long as I was absolutely still. I'd believed Samuel to be an angel of light and earthly perfection. Never had I seen such physical beauty in a man, and I thought he was as handsome as the Prophet Joseph Smith must have been before they lynched him. I believed that my feelings for Samuel were sanctioned by the Heavenly Father. I had sealed myself to him in the union of our flesh, and that union had transported me to a higher celestial body. It had meant everything to me.

Yet our union had meant nothing to Samuel, and, therefore, it was born of our lust. In truth, I was no better than a woman of convenience, a soiled dove, a harlot, a painted lady—a strumpet. I was a whore who had traded her virginity for jewels, and the Lord had struck me down.

The next morning I opened my eyes and saw the soft pink morning light. I lay and watched the color change as the sun rose. Turkey vultures circled high in the sky like dark angels descending to earth. They flew lower and lower in a beautiful spiral. Rays of light illuminated their wings, and I marveled at their magnificence.

Soon, realization that these dark angels could eat me replaced my wonder and filled me with dread. If I died, they would nibble on my corpse for months—call their brethren and have a feast with me as the main course.

I decided to live, that I'd do everything I could to survive. I wanted to taste peach pie again, and try an ice-cream cone. I wanted to sing and dance, and one day swim in the ocean. But most of all, I didn't want a flock of turkey vultures feasting on my flesh. I'd transgressed against the Lord, and my chances of salvation were gone. I wanted to live before I died and was cast into eternal darkness.

I survived for two days on hard tack and jerky. Dolly's stuffing couldn't sustain me as it had on the Pioneer Trail. I had to figure out how to kill an animal with the Henry, or a way to set traps. As soon as the last drops of water slid out of the canteen and down my throat, I knew I was in trouble. My throat burned as I peered into the empty canteen. I could survive for a while without food but not water.

My horse stood by the creek. At least he had water, but how long would he last without food? He'd eaten all the greenery from the bushes and was sniffing around for more. If I could make it to the creek, I could get water and untie him. The creek wasn't far from my spot under the big rock overhang. I put the canteen strap around my neck and used my hands to scoot myself toward it. As soon as my leg moved, pain shot through my body. I held still and scrunched my eyes as the horrid sensation exploded in my brain.

It had seemed so simple—just scoot down to the creek. But with the promise of agony every time I moved an inch, the journey to the creek felt impossible. I thirstily licked the salty tears that ran down my cheeks. My sole desire, my single point of focus, was the creek. The water called me.

The sight of my mangled leg made me gasp and pant. I took a deep breath. Cuts and scrapes had caused some bleeding, but luckily there was no deep wound. Although my lower leg was twisted and my foot faced the wrong direction, at least the bone was not protruding. I lay flat on the rock and reached for the saddlebag. From inside, I pulled my clasp knife. I carefully squirmed out of Zeke's old clothes and cut them into long strips. When finished, I straightened my leg and foot the best I could and wound the strips tightly to stabilize the bone. The pressure made my leg feel more secure.

This time my leg didn't flop when I moved, so the pain wasn't as bad. I lowered my upper half from the rock onto the sand below and then reached up to lower my leg with my hands. Once down, I scooted on my belly, careful to avoid cactus and spiky plants, through sand and over rock until I finally reached the creek. From all the effort, my thirst had grown even stronger. I lapped water like a parched animal.

I could have followed the creek downstream to a place where the water ran faster and clearer, but my thirst was too great and the distance too far. I drank as much as I could, filled my canteen, and started crawling back to my spot under the rock. The homing instinct drew me to my bedroll and my meager belongings spread out around it. I lay down and propped my head with the saddlebag. At least I had accomplished a few things. I had set my leg straight and bandaged it. I had water. If I could figure a way to eat, I might survive.

I fell asleep and awakened under starlight. My stomach cramped and ached so badly, I wished for death. I rolled onto my side and vomited into the sand. After throwing up the small amount of apricot in my stomach, I heaved and threw up bile. My body shook and convulsed. The pain and misery was so great, I prayed for the Lord to take me. The stomach malady seemed a fate worse than death, and I wanted an end to my suffering. If I'd had the strength, I would have taken the Henry and shot myself. But I couldn't even raise my head. I squirmed, moaned, and pleaded to the stars. I cursed, prayed, cried, and whimpered.

Sleep was my only comfort. I went in and out of it with no will of my own. A thin thread held me to the world. I closed my eyes and conjured the emerald pools I had swum in with Zeke. It wasn't long ago, but it seemed an eternity. I opened my eyes. A hairy tarantula crept across the sand close to my face. I looked briefly into his black beady eyes before the weight of my own eyelids became overwhelming. I slipped back into sleep. In my dreams, Pa pushed me on the swing he'd just built, the wind blew my hair back, and sunlight warmed my face.

I opened my eyes to a chilly, starry night. A coyote sat on a rock across from me, watching, wondering, and panting. I closed my eyes and dreamt of the crossing. Snow melted and dripped into my worn shoe. My mother pulled a shawl around me. I kept walking, pulling stuffing out of Dolly and eating it. My dry mouth was full of cotton.

I opened my eyes to circling coyotes. They sniffed the saddlebag and taunted the horse, who neighed and stomped. I didn't have the strength to lift the rifle or shoo them away. Cotton filled my mouth. I looked at the canteen, but I couldn't drink the water. Not that water, which had made me sick.

During the heat of the day, my skin burned. Flies swarmed a pile of my vomit. The odor made me wretch again, but there was nothing left inside me. A slice of sun penetrated my rock shelter. Red ants marched over me like an angry army. I spent my last bit of strength swatting them off. I poured the useless water over my body and drowned them. I fell back into a black hole of sleep and woke up in the middle of the night trembling with cold. I wrapped the blanket around myself and curled up like a scared baby. As I listened to the night life, demons of terror descended upon me.

By sunrise when clouds stretched like pink blankets over a soft blue sky and the tall red rocks glowed as if they were on fire, I finally felt at peace. I waited for the Lord to cut the thin thread holding me to life. My throat was dry and parched. I was close to death. Yet somewhere I found the strength and voice to sing. In hardship and trouble, Saints had always sung.

I remembered reading of Frederick Douglass and slave songs born from the deepest misery and suffering. Maybe I'd gone mad, but the impulse to sing filled me even though my life had not been noble. Instead of a fallen woman dying alone in the desert, I imagined myself a dying soldier who had fallen fighting for justice and freedom. I didn't witness The Civil War, but I'd heard plenty of stories. Deep inside, I feared that I would soon be damned to eternal darkness.

Even as my emaciated body approached death, I sang the words to "The Battle Hymn of the Republic" loud, soul-stirring, and strong as if I could perhaps sing my way out of sin and into heaven. The echo of my voice in the rocky canyon startled me. Like Shakespeare's poor Ophelia I too became mad with babble and visions. I whispered strange lyrics in tune with The Battle Hymn . . .

> *I have seen the fury of the coming of the Lord*
> *He frees the horses and they gallop across a ford*
> *The devil presses on me, until my legs must yield*
> *The Lord strikes him down and I run across a field*
> *Glory, glory, hallelujah*

Somewhere in the canyon, boulders broke loose and exploded like gunfire. The sound was worse than a waiting demon gnashing his teeth. To keep the fear at bay I kept babbling my song.

> *The crack of gunfire breaks sunrise's quiet mood*
> *Mourning doves are deafened by the musket's ball*
>   *and groove*
> *Ricocheting lead leaves mothers with no brood*

I imagined soldiers on the battlefield, writhing in pain, begging for mercy. I wanted to kiss their pain away. I wanted someone to kiss my pain away.

> *Beside each fallen soldier a Valkyrie will kneel*
> *She will kiss the righteous and to their fate will seal*
> *Glory, glory, hallelujah*
> *I see my mother writhing and my father in a box*
> *In the desert lays a piano beside a fallen ox*
> *His bones are blanched and polished; her keys are*
>   *marred with pox*

Ophelia's War

I was poisoned by the river and broke my leg on rocks
My hour is coming soon

FIFTEEN

Smoke tickled my nostrils. It felt as if someone was moving my leg. The sweet, pungent smell of burning sage awakened me. I opened my eyes and tried to raise myself. A hand—fingers spread across my forehead—gently pressed my head back down. Bracelets dangled in my face. Some were made with tiny colorful beads. One bracelet was braided with fiber that resembled my hair.

As my focus became clearer, I realized the bracelet *was* made from my hair. The wrinkled person stood, and I realized she was a woman. Her naked breasts sagged unashamedly. A necklace of smooth pearls hung around her leathery neck and a bandolier of bullets crossed under her naked breasts. She wore a tattered top hat with three feathers sticking out of a maroon band. A hip holster with one rusty six-shooter held up her buckskin skirt, which came to just below her knees. Worn moccasins that came up to her ankles looked like a second pair of feet.

I could not stop staring at the pearls. Who was this savage woman, and how had she come by such an extravagant strand of pearls? If not for the jewelry, her bare breasts, and the skirt, I would not have known she was a woman. Her face was deeply etched with wrinkles and fell somewhere between masculine and feminine. For in her countenance, I could see both, depending on the angle of her head. She looked about as old as the towering rock walls surrounding us.

She walked down to the creek and washed some clothes. Her breasts swayed as she swished and wrung the fabric. She seemed neither aware nor ashamed of her nakedness. She moved as if completely clothed, her posture upright and yet natural. I longed to be in her skin, to have the movement of my leg again and not feel ashamed of my body. I sat up. My head felt light, but the nausea was gone. A splint had been created with sticks and some unrecognizable woven material, which immobilized my leg.

A mule, laden with strange objects, stood near the creek and swatted flies with its tail. The woman spread the clean clothes out over his back, took the bit, and led him toward me. She looked like a jack-ass miner going to stake a claim. But instead of pickaxes and miner's equipment hanging from her mule, there was a cast-iron pan, a stringless violin, a Confederate saber, a blanket, and a human head.

The head swung casually as if it were any ordinary thing. I locked gazes with the head's brown eyes. They stared back out of a man's thickly bearded face frozen in terror, as if he had gazed upon Medusa. The horrific sight sapped my strength, and I fell into darkness again.

When I opened my eyes, the woman was squatting at a small fire with a dagger in one hand and a squirrel in the other. She disemboweled the squirrel, and tore off the last pieces of skin with her teeth. She skewered it and placed it over the fire next to another one that was already crackling. She fetched a woven Indian style jug, came over to me, and pressed it to my lips. I looked toward the creek, put my hand on my stomach, pressed my lips tight, and shook my head.

She shook her head and pointed at the creek. "No," she said. "Is good." These were the first words she had spoken to me. I hoped she spoke more English.

The water tasted bitter. But my thirst was so great I gulped it anyway. The muddy water of the Virgin River had never made me sick. I'd been drinking it most of my life. I usually drew our drinking water from where it flowed fast. But I hadn't had that luxury when I drank from the creek. Whatever festered in the stagnant water would have killed me, if the strange old Indian woman hadn't come along and nursed me. Yet who was she? She seemed part medicine woman and part nomadic scavenger roaming the desert for abandoned treasure.

I wondered about the pearls and the violin. Wagon trains often fell on hard luck—a wheel damaged beyond repair, or a broken axle, meant precious family heirlooms had to be abandoned. Volumes of rare books, china and silverware, fine dresses, even the odd piano were often left lying in the sand and sage, surrounded by cacti. Perhaps the Indian woman had found the pearls and brooch lying next to a pile of sun-blanched ox bones.

But what could explain the head? Was it the head of a man who had wronged her? Maybe it was the head of an outlaw, and she would turn it in for the bounty. I tried to convince myself that she had no evil intentions for me. She had, after all, nursed me from the brink of death and done a fine job with the splint.

I took the squirrel meat reluctantly. When I put it in my mouth, I ate ravenously and my body felt grateful for the food. I gained instant strength from the flesh of the squirrel. I could feel its life enter my bloodstream.

After we ate, my head cleared and I found the courage to ask her a question. "Where are your people?"

She stared at me, her face blank of emotion or recognition. "Where are your people?" she echoed and looked off into the distance.

Was she just repeating what I'd said, or was she asking me the same thing? Either way, it was a good question.

I spoke slowly. "Who are your tribe?"

She spoke slowly back. "Who are your tribe?"

I stared off into the distance, still unsure whether she was asking or simply repeating. My people were dead and I had no tribe. Maybe it was the same for her. She too looked off into the distance, and although it appeared that she looked at nothing, I could tell she saw something—something greater than the sand and rock cliffs all around us. She turned to me and said, "Sing."

"Sing?" I kept my focus on her and tried to make eye contact, but she looked away.

"Sing," she said and stared at the unseen point.

She must have heard my death song. My voice had echoed off the canyon walls and led her to me. She wanted me to sing again. But I couldn't sing as I had when I lay dying. A voice had come out of me that was not my own, and it had both calmed and unsettled me.

I smiled and shook my head. "I can't—I can't sing very well, except when I'm dying."

She stared at me. "You sing," she commanded and kept her eyes fixed on me.

I couldn't look directly into her eyes. I smiled, shook my head again, and accidentally caught the eye of the severed head. Would she cut my head off if I didn't sing, or worse, sang out of tune? I pointed at myself. "No good."

She narrowed her eyes and nodded. "Sing."

I cleared my throat and began to sing "The Battle Hymn of the Republic" again. The words sounded weak and pathetic, squeaky and too high.

Her face looked as if she had just tasted something rotten. She shook her head and looked off into the distance again. "No good."

She closed her eyes. We were silent. I was sorry to disappoint her, but grateful she didn't behead me for my poor performance. Singing had always been that way with me. I could only sing when the spirit moved me. When I tried to perform or impress others, it came out all wrong.

Her hat sat on the rock next to her like a small quiet companion. Wind stirred a strand of her silver hair. Otherwise, she was still enough to be just another rock in God's desert garden. What a strange savior he had sent me. His ways were indeed mysterious. Fatigue filled my weakened body. I was about to shut my eyes and lie back down when the woman began to shake. She opened her mouth and sounds came out. She didn't seem to be making the sounds. It seemed as if they were pouring out of her like water. If they were words, I didn't know them, but they didn't sound like words.

The sounds reverberated and seemed to express some kind of truth that predated spoken language itself. My body responded to those sounds in the most powerful way. Overwhelmed by emotion, I choked, unable to breathe as if I were frozen. Those sounds expressed both the origins of life and the inevitability of death. Those sounds could create and destroy worlds.

In the past, my spirit had been moved by hymns, but the sounds she emitted transcended any hymn I'd ever heard. I began to question my whole conception of the world, the Heavenly Father, and everything I been taught about the spirit. For this woman, this nomadic savage, was a Godless heathen in the eyes of society. Yet I witnessed in her presence, in her song, a miraculous manifestation of spirit. Tears poured down my face, for I had been transformed—transformed and saved by a head-toting, nomadic heathen scavenger, who wore a strand of pearls and a bandolier of bullets.

Sixteen

The next morning she rummaged through my belongings. She turned the pages of my diary, put it down, picked up my mother's steel pen, and studied the tip. I wanted to show her how it worked, but in the chaos of fleeing Grafton, I'd thrown the diary into my saddlebag and forgotten a bottle of ink. "It's a pen," I said and mimed writing. "But I have no ink." I shook my head. "No ink."

She put the pen down and picked up the Henry. I prayed she didn't want the Henry. Not only did I need it, but it was the only thing I had that reminded me of Pa and Zeke. She held it up, aimed at something in the distance, and put it down without firing.

"No bullets," I said. "Only five or so left." I held up my hand to indicate five. She held up her hand back to me. Her mule stood in the sand near the rock overhang. All of the things attached to his back had been unfastened and were spread out under the rock overhang, not far from my belongings. Flies swarmed the decaying head, which at least faced away from me. The old woman untied my horse and brought him over to stand by the mule. She fed him some grain from a sack. I could tell by the way she handled him that she hadn't lived with horses her whole life, and so I figured she must be Paiute.

She emptied my saddlebag and began to pack my horse. Terror and fear spread through my body. Was she going to take my horse and belongings and leave me here alone? Maybe she planned to leave me with the head—maybe she considered it a fair trade. She seemed to sense my panic. As she continued to pack the horse she said to me, "Come back. Two suns. He need food." She pointed to the horse.

Before she left, she placed a woven jug of water beside me and a sack filled with pinon pine nuts. I spent the next two days crushing the tiny brown nuts with the handle of my knife and sipping the water. Their hard shells released a pleasant pine odor and the pure white nuts soothed me for a while. By the time she returned, I had tired of them and wanted something else to eat.

In the evenings, frenzied cricket chirping gradually slowed, and the nights came fast and cold. Aspen and oak leaves turned gold. At night I shivered, and each morning I had to rub the tip of my nose and my fingers to keep them from going numb. The old woman went on a few journeys, but she always returned after two or three days. I figured we were within a few days of some kind of settlement, or at least a trading post, because she seemed to be bartering items. I hoped the settlement wasn't Grafton. I was relieved she had gotten rid of the head. I wondered what she had traded for it and with whom. On her final journey she brought me a crutch and a woolen shawl.

With the crutch and her assistance, I limped along with the slow, pained gait of a cripple. But at least I was up on my feet. On the day she began packing our makeshift home for good, I felt sad. For all the anguish and suffering I'd endured in that spot, you'd think I couldn't wait to leave it. But I was afraid of what would come next, where I would go, how I would survive, and most of all—of being alone.

I rode my horse, and the old feather-light Indian woman trailed behind on her mule. She navigated us out of the rock labyrinth to a main trail, which headed north toward Provo. Where the trails converged, she halted. It was as if she were unable to go any farther. I stopped and looked at her. Her eyes had that faraway look I'd grown accustomed to.

"Go, where the iron horses join. Your fortune, my death." She nodded and watched me.

I got off my horse, took the Henry from my saddle holster, and held it out to her. "A gift," I said.

She nodded, took the rusty six-shooter from her holster, and held it out to me in exchange.

SEVENTEEN

I could have stopped at a Mormon farmhouse and asked for food and shelter. If I were still a Saint, the Mormons would have fed me and turned my idle hands toward industry, even though I couldn't work in the fields on account of my leg. But Saints don't trade their virginity for rubies and go around shooting their elders. For all I knew, Brigham Young had already dispatched one of his avenging angels to destroy me.

I could have given up the jewels. But I didn't. I kept them. And for what good? Even though I had the jewels, I was still hungry. I couldn't eat them. The image of the two dead gamblers and my uncle haunted me. They had lain on the cabin floor like butchered animals with that big pool of blood dripping through the wide-gapped floorboards. Those horrible memories turned all my dreams into nightmares.

Word among Mormons traveled fast, and I was afraid that news of the triple murder and my disappearance had already made its way across the territory. But from what I understood, Gentiles were accustomed to murders, rapes, robberies, and debauchery. They wouldn't give a hoot about a missing Mormon girl, unless there was a reward, and the settlers of Grafton were too poor to post one. I steered clear of Mormon communities and only stopped in Gentile mining and railroad towns. I wasn't ready to be found. I didn't know if I'd ever be ready.

My guilt was so heavy I felt others could see it like an albatross around my neck. I avoided the main trail, favoring the trails through high country to get to the Salt Lake Valley. One night, before I could find shelter, a storm hit, the temperature suddenly plummeted, and it began to snow. No bed of boughs and pine needles could possibly shelter me against the storm's fury. After a while, my body ached from cold. I could barely keep hold of the reins. All my instincts screamed for warmth. The wind whipped my face and cut through me. I rode on with my head down, barely able to see a foot in front of me. Finally, the faint smell of smoke filled my nostrils. I followed its scent like a hungry wolf until I arrived at a small cabin. I didn't care what kind of trouble might be waiting inside as long as I could escape the biting cold.

The trapper had already heard me coming and greeted me with his rifle. But when he opened the door and saw me, he put it down and whisked me inside. My body shook. My fingers and toes had lost all color and feeling. He wrapped me in furs, stoked the fire, and gave me hot broth. Musk and smoke emanated from his beard and large body. At first it was difficult for him to speak. He was advanced in years, at least half a century old, a mountain man who rarely saw, let alone spoke to, another person.

He was obviously a skilled trapper, as his cabin was filled with skins and furs. Beaver pelts hung from every inch of the walls and ceiling. It felt like we were in the pouch of some giant furry animal. After he found his tongue, a torrent of words poured forth. He spoke of the decline in the beaver trade; how pelts had once fetched a fortune.

"The snooty womenfolk moved on to some other damn hat— with feathers," he said. Then he looked shy and excused himself for cussing. He bore a strange resemblance to a beaver: deep-set brown eyes, a chocolate brown beard, and hair poking out from his shirtsleeves that was identical to the beaver pelts. I wondered if he'd always looked this way, or if he had grown to resemble the animals he'd tracked for so long.

I was too cold to be afraid of his loneliness and desire. If I had to run back out into the cold night, I would surely freeze to death. He asked me how I came to be out there in the high country all alone. I told him my parents had died, and I was on my way to the valley to live with distant relatives. He said there was a more direct route.

I tried to make up a plausible explanation. I told him I was drawn to the beauty of the mountains and hadn't thought a snowstorm would come in September. He lectured me on mountain weather, freak snowstorms, bears, wolves, and mountain lions. He told me stories of strong men he had known who'd lost their lives to the elements or Indians. I listened, nodded, and pulled the fur around me.

"Don't suppose you'd like to stay here with me? Become my wife and start a family? I'm not as old as I look. I have a good life. Gets cold here in winter and the food supply thins, but I plan for it and never go hungry."

I told him that I'd be honored, but I was already betrothed to a distant cousin, who was expecting me to arrive in the valley. He asked me what kind of man would force me to travel all alone. Said if it was him, he'd escort me. Said if it was him, I'd never go hungry or cold. Said if it was him, I'd never have to knock on a stranger's door for help. He riled himself up against my imaginary fiancé whom I struggled to defend until the trapper grew suspicious.

"There's no cousin, is there? You concocted that story so you wouldn't hurt my feelings, didn't you?"

"There's a cousin, but I don't know anything about him, don't even know his name. They just sent word I should come."

"I see," he said and nodded. The night grew darker and fatigue seemed to settle into him from so much talking. He sat next to me on the bench in front of the fire. I stared vacantly at the dying flames. He slid his hand inside the fur shawl and under my clothes. His hand was as warm as a baked potato and despite what it might lead to, it felt good and warm.

"Your flesh is as cold as ice, missy. Come, let me warm you." He guided me to a bed piled high with furs in the corner of the cabin. I melted into the soft fur. He squeezed in next to me and pulled fur blankets over us. Heat radiated from his body as if his insides were on fire. Against him, I finally felt the chill melt.

Yet his hands reached for my female parts, followed the curves of my body, and pulled me so close I felt his hard member pressing into my buttocks. Tears came and my chills were replaced by sobs.

He removed his hands from under me, smoothed my skirt down, and stroked my hair. "It's okay now. I just got carried away." He rose from the bed, wrapped a fur around his shoulders, and with his back to me, stood wide legged in front of the fire. He became a large dark silhouette in a fur cape. "I'm not a bad man," he said. "I'm just a man."

I heard flesh smacking and then a groan. The fire crackled with his ejaculation. He sighed and returned to bed with no anger, only tenderness and soft apologies, which he cooed into my ear like a lullaby.

The next morning he fed me breakfast, wrapped me in a small buckskin coat, and waved goodbye.

By the time I made it to the Salt Lake Valley, my horse was sickly. I couldn't afford to keep him, so I sold him for three dollars. I found work doing laundry for a Gentile-owned hotel on Whiskey Street and settled down for nearly seven months. I didn't know how or why my destiny was tied to the completion of the railroad, but the Indian woman's words stuck with me.

"Where the iron horses join, your fortune—my death."

I was so exhausted from working long hours in the laundry I

never wrote in my diary. Even though I doubted the Lord would answer the prayers of a fallen woman, every night I prayed for Ezekiel's safety. I imagined scenes of a happy reunion with my dear brother until I fell asleep.

One day in early May, I read this article in a discarded Deseret newspaper. I cut it out and tucked it in my diary:

PROCEEDINGS SCHEDULED AT PROMONTORY SUMMARY

"The last tie will be laid; the last rail placed in position, and the last spike driven, which will bind the Atlantic and Pacific oceans with an iron band. An electric flash will bear the tidings to the world!"

I decided I'd had enough of the Great Salt Lake Valley. I packed my meager belongings and planned to travel north so I could be closer to my destiny. The night before my journey I washed my only dress, careful not to scrub too hard as it was threadbare. Early on the morning of my departure, May 7, 1869, I bathed in the creek so I would be fresh for the long journey ahead.

I set out on foot with my belongings stuffed into a grain sack and a bedroll tucked under my arm. I didn't have much, but I still had my knife and the rusty six-shooter, a bedroll and blanket, my diary and my mother's steel-tipped pen, as well as the buckskin coat the trapper had given me. Most important, I still had Dolly with the ruby necklace stuffed inside her. I was not ready to sell the necklace. Every day I tried to forget about it and resist the temptation to sell it because I was afraid of the curse. The necklace was all I had left of Momma.

For provisions on the journey to Ogden, I packed a stash of saltwater taffy, six strips of dried elk, and a box of hard tack. For a couple of years after the Civil War ended, you couldn't give away a box of hard tack. But times were tough and it was hard to come by anything.

★　★　★　★　★

People from every walk of life—from the lower classes to ladies and gentlemen sporting finery—crowded the road north toward Ogden. There were horse-drawn carriages, mule and ox teams pulling wagons and carts, single riders; a few brave souls had even ventured forth on bicycles. I saw Chinese donning their traditional lampshade hats, miners, bullwhackers, mule skinners, gamblers, pimps, clergy, soldiers, simple farm people, and whores.

The Mormon Church was in favor of economic progress, yet they feared that the influx of despots and nonbelievers would taint the purity of Zion. The Saints had been warned not to socialize with Gentiles and only to deal with them for purposes of commerce. Yet Mormon families had still set out in hopes of seeing the famous locomotive and witnessing the final laying and driving of the famed golden spike, which would join the union and its territories from East to West by rail. It was a momentous event, and I felt like I was witnessing history.

I walked beside the rutted wagon trail in the willow grass alongside others who were trying to hitch a ride. It was difficult for me. The gentry held their heads high, and turned from me as if I were nothing but a foul stench. The hard-up miners and dirty railway laborers, themselves sorely in need of a bath, preferred the painted ladies to a scrawny lice-ridden girl. Whores piled on to stopping wagons. Their bulging bosoms bounced as they swigged whiskey and let men feel them for a penny. I had not stooped that low yet.

But the words of Doc Perkins haunted me. When I had first arrived in the Great Salt Lake Territory, I went to see a Gentile doctor on Whiskey Street about my injured leg. After he looked at my leg, he examined my head and warned me that my skull had the same characteristics as a prostitute. He gave me a lesson in what he called birth control, genital hygiene, and disease prevention. I had never known that birth could be controlled. I assumed, depending on your circumstances, that it was either a gift or a punishment from God. He told me stories and showed me drawings of people stricken by cupid's curses. The images were so gruesome I thought I'd be cured of sexual feelings forever.

Doc Perkins took a liking to me and said he'd give me money for a room and a weekly bath, if I'd come to see him every Friday. I took the money and absconded to the north end of the valley where, after several weeks of begging and sleeping in the bushes, I found a bed at a charity station in the basement of Saint Mark's. The nuns helped me find employment as a laundress. They never even asked if I was Catholic.

Each day I feared I'd be arrested for my crime in Grafton. I kept to myself and didn't speak to anyone, just nodded or shook my head pretending to be mute. Christmas day passed without my family or a special meal to mark the day. Work in the laundry hardly paid anything. I'd inhaled so much lye it hurt just to breathe. Momma and I had always done our laundry outside where the fumes weren't so bad. Although I had a bed, it was infested with bugs and after waking up with bites I finally gave up and slept on the floor. I was so sad and miserable I often wondered if I should have taken Doc Perkins' offer.

Although I'd been raised in a desolate place, I'd never felt as lonely as I did in the Great Salt Lake Valley surrounded by people. All I had to show for months of honest labor was a torn threadbare dress. I did enjoy regular nourishment. And thanks to that I'd gained weight and my menstrual cycle had returned. Still, I had worked twelve to sixteen hours a day, six days a week and couldn't even afford to replace my worn shoes.

On that May morning, I'd started my journey to the driving of the golden spike ceremony with high hopes, considering I didn't know what I was going to do, or where I would end up. The weather was fine, not too hot or cold, perfect for traveling. After two hours of walking, my feet hurt. I fought the desire to take off my shoes and go barefoot, since wearing shoes, even ill-fitted shoes with holes, gave a better impression than hoofing it like a child.

The early morning rush of wagons and carriages slowed. All my hopes were dashed after three hours passed and I still hadn't managed to hitch a ride. I doubted I'd make my destination in time for the Saturday ceremony. I gave up on my goal of Promontory Point, figuring Ogden was close enough and that I'd be lucky just to make it there. The sky blackened, the temperature suddenly dipped to about forty degrees, and the wind came to life. I cinched my bonnet tight so it wouldn't blow off. Foreboding storm clouds brewed and swelled with darkness. They swept across the sky faster than any clouds I'd ever seen.

At first, rain spat down in cool gentle drops, but then the sky opened and water came down in buckets. Until that day, the spring had been mild. The valley had greened and the orchards filled with delicate pink and white blossoms. The hummingbirds had returned. Their high-pitched trill and sudden frantic appearance always filled my heart with joy. I had not prepared for the return of freezing rain and snow, but I knew it often happened. Even down south in Grafton, a fine spring or summer day could fill with fury and spew angry hail or snow upon seedlings just starting to grow.

Several carriages passed without even slowing. The rutted trail had turned to mud and the wagon wheels splashed muck onto my face and dress. Despair and fear overtook me. No shelter could be found on the open road, not even a cottonwood that might break the heavy violent rate with which the rain soaked my dress. I put on my buckskin coat, but it didn't help much. I was on the verge of throwing myself under the hooves of the next passing team, when a mule-drawn, covered wagon pulled up and stopped.

A man and his wife sat in front. Rain dripped from the brim of the man's wide hat. White-blond hair poked out from under a wool blanket, which the wife pulled over her head. The man smiled in a friendly manner, but the woman looked skeptical and concerned. I knew right off they were Mormons, and I was scared they'd ask me where I was from. But the man spoke to me in broken, heavily accented English, the awkward singsong of a Swede. "Swere roo hoin lahs?" Before I could answer he said, "Huhee rop on!"

I scurried to the back of the covered wagon and hoisted myself up and inside. Six small faces framed by the same color of white-blond hair as the mother's stared at me. The children barely had room to move. One sister picked up a small girl to clear a spot. I sat cross-legged, and the sister placed the little one on my lap.

All six children were barefoot. The bottoms of their feet were hardened and brown like leather. Their huddled bodies provided warmth. We bounced along the trail. The children shifted to avoid getting dripped on by leaks in the wagon cover. They stared at me as if I was from the moon. The little girl on my lap fingered the buttons of my dress and sucked the water from my rain-drenched hair. I felt a pang of love for her, the other children, and their parents. The closeness of that family facing life's trials together made me ache for my own lost family.

They had so little, yet they had stopped to help me. I wanted to give them something in return. I pulled out my precious cache of saltwater taffy and handed each child a piece. Their faces went from blank inquisition to excited happiness. They unwrapped their taffy and gazed upon me with gratitude. I reluctantly took Dolly from the grain sack and handed her to the girl on my lap, hoping she would understand the doll wasn't to keep.

The children chewed the taffy like cows. Smacking and sucking sounds filled the wagon. The little girl on my lap, whose teeth were not yet formed, seemed to enjoy the taffy. But she kept removing it from her mouth and handing it to me.

I had guessed the family wasn't on a leisure trip to see the driving of the golden spike, and I was right. At the fork of the Weber and Ogden rivers, the wagon stopped. The father came around, pointed eastward, and chortled something I couldn't understand. But I knew what he meant. I pointed north and removed the girl from my lap. As I feared, she was reluctant to relinquish Dolly and gave a scream of protest when I reached for her. Her older sister lightly slapped the tiny girl's arm. I quickly took Dolly and shoved her into my sack. I jumped down from the wagon. The ground was wet and muddy, but at least the rain had stopped. I waved to the children and went to thank the mother for her kindness.

"Thank you," I said and smiled.

She nodded, her eyes betraying fear and concern for me. I sensed her relief at my departure.

EIGHTEEN

I had saved enough money for one or two days' lodging, but as it turned out there was a shortage of beds in Ogden. The only beds left were being sold at triple the regular rate, and I couldn't afford one. The proprietors of the rooming houses told me even the bathtubs were sold out. I wondered if they refused me because of my disheveled state. But surely men from the mines and railways were filthier than I. Yet the innkeepers preferred them to me, as dirty men from the mines could have pockets lined with silver and gold. As one place after another turned me away, I thought of Dolly and my secret riches and held my head high despite my dejection.

Compared to Great Salt Lake City, Ogden was not much of a place. Compared to Grafton, it was thriving. The railway track had been laid on the western edge of town. The station consisted of a few clapboard shacks and some canvas tents. A rickety looking grandstand stood uneasily, anticipating the upcoming ceremony. A quarter mile of narrow boardwalk extended over swampy land to connect railway travelers to merchants and businesses, which crowded together in a one-mile radius around the railroad tracks. I walked from the railway stop where the first transcontinental train would soon pass all the way to Fifth Street where the merchants and saloons were clustered.

Buildings were in various stages of construction. Fancy shop fronts attached to tiny clapboard buildings gave the illusion of prominence. Most of the people in Ogden that day appeared to be Gentiles. They stumbled in the streets with whiskey bottles, laughing and jostling and sometimes brawling. The town was crowded, and I was often forced off the boardwalk into the muddy road.

Ladies strolled along accompanied by gentlemen. You could tell the Mormon women because they wore sturdy homespun dresses and always had children clutching their hands and skirts. The wives of important railway and business men wore tailored dresses the likes of which I'd never seen. To the shock and disgust of both the Gentile ladies and the Mormons, scantily clad whores paraded around like they owned the town.

I took refuge from the crowd on a bench beside the bakery and wondered why I had come to such a place. I had no idea where I was going to sleep and although the rain had stopped, the sky still threatened rain or worse—snow. I took off my bonnet and wiped my face with it. At that moment, Pearl Kelly and Johnny Dobbs came around the corner.

Whore or not, Pearl Kelly was hands down the most beautiful woman I had ever seen. Amid velvet ribbons, her blond hair came down in perfect shiny curls from under her black riding hat. Although her face was painted, she didn't look like a clown. Cheek rouge accentuated her high cheekbones, and lip rouge brought out a healthy rosy hue on her sensuous mouth. Her eyes were deep blue, the color I imagined the ocean to be. In some strange way Pearl looked like a grown-up version of a beautiful doll.

She rushed over to the bench where I sat. She was the first person in town to notice me. Before her attention, I'd felt invisible and alone. She knelt down in front of the bench. "Sister, sister, we're reunited at last," she cried and hugged my head to her bosom.

Johnny Dobbs stood with his arms crossed. He wore a black bowler hat and a brocade vest. The tortoiseshell handles of expensive six-shooters poked out from holsters at his sides. A knife sheath was strapped around one of his pinstriped trouser legs, which was tucked into a fine leather boot. A cigar perched comfortably at the side of his mouth as if it were a second home. They'd both been drinking, but not as much as some of the other staggering Gentiles.

"Now Pearl, you know she ain't your sister, unless it's her ghost."

Pearl Kelly pushed my head from her bosom, cupped my chin in her hand, turned my face from side to side, searched my eyes, and looked at my hair. "She looks just like my sister, Annie, God rest her soul, the orange hair, the blue eyes, and those little freckles on her nose. Oh, poor Annie, God have mercy." Pearl wept.

Johnny Dobbs pulled a hankie from his pocket and handed it to her. "Pearl, this here's a celebration. Don't ruin it by mourning the dead." He shook his head. A man passing by stopped and gawked at us. "Women, they cry like dogs piss," Johnny explained. The man nodded in commiseration and moved on. Johnny addressed Pearl with urgency and impatience. "There's money to be made. Let's get back and see to business."

She dabbed her eyes, careful not to smear her makeup. "Girl, what's your name? You look so much like my beloved sister, Annie."

I hesitated and sputtered. For the past year, I'd been Elizabeth Jones, but I didn't want to be Elizabeth Jones anymore. I wanted to be someone like Pearl Kelly. Pretty and elegant, loved and protected by a frightening man like Johnny Dobbs.

"My name is Ruby. Ruby Doll House," I said. "It's very nice to meet you. I'm sorry I brought you grief by reminding you of your poor sister."

Pearl stood, twirled her skirt, and clapped her hands. "Ruby Doll House! Now that's a name! I don't believe it's your Christian name, but I like it! I'll just call you Sister. Don't you have any folks? How did you come to be such a wretch?"

I choked and tears welled in my eyes. No one had been kind to me in so long.

Pearl smiled and nodded in understanding. "Never mind about that. You come with us and I'll get you a bath, some new clothes, and some nice warm food. Would you like that, Sister?"

"Pearl!" Johnny Dobbs exploded, and I could see that he was like a walking stick of dynamite—explosive when lit. "No one's going to want that lousy girl. She's a flying mess, as poor as Job's turkey."

Pearl diffused his temper. She sauntered over, gazed up into his eyes, slipped her arms around the back of him, and said, "We can kill the lice and fatten her up. We've done it before. Look at that red hair—lot of men pay extra for that. Betcha five dollars I can turn this ugly duck into a swan!"

Johnny Dobbs melted as fast as a candlestick thrown into a forge. His eyes softened. He smiled admiringly at her. What power she had over him. He turned a doubtful, scrutinizing look at me.

"I'll work real hard, sir."

Johnny Dobbs and Pearl Kelly looked at each other. They smiled, and their eyes filled with amusement.

"Come on then," he said and strode away.

Pearl grabbed my hand and pulled me off the bench. I grabbed my sack and walked next to her, doing my best to hide my limp. Johnny Dobbs strode ahead and rudely bumped people out of his way. Pearl didn't have to bump anyone. When they saw her coming, they stepped out of the way and let us pass. It seemed she could part the Red Sea. She didn't look at anyone, but everyone looked at her with varying sentiments: awe, desire, scorn, condemnation. Whatever they felt, they could not help but gaze upon her. Some men tipped or even removed their hats, and said, "Good day, Miss Pearl."

"Good day Charles, Thomas, Willard, Benjamin . . ." She didn't even need to look at their faces to recall their names. She just knew them, and she somehow commanded their respect as sternly as a schoolmarm. But she was a whore. I knew it. Yet I couldn't bring myself to see her that way.

Excitement and the promise of prosperity hung in the air. It was rumored that Ogden would replace Corinne as the official Junction City. Anyone who took the train across the country would have to stop in Ogden whether they wanted to or not. The streets swelled with railroad transients finally ready to put down roots. While some men were busy hammering, sawing, and painting storefronts, others didn't even bother with permanent structures. They raised canvas tents—the same ones they'd inhabited as they had followed the railway all the way out from the Missouri. Those men had set up gambling dens, tobacco shops, and distilleries, and had followed the progress of the railroad, vying for the workers' pay all the way to the end of the line.

The Saints were horrified. Before the railroad, the Mormon settlers only had to contend with mountain men, Indians, and trappers. To them, the influx of Gentiles meant the influx of sin. The great curse they had cast upon the nonbelievers had arrived at their doorstep.

We arrived at Johnny's saloon, a two-story brick building situated next to the bathhouse. We entered through the back door. Johnny's saloon occupied most of the first floor, and Pearl's girls were on the second. At the time it was just called Saloon. But over the years it would go under different names: The White Elephant, The Brass Monkey, Buffalo Jill's.

Pearl opened the first door on the left and with great pride revealed an indoor bathtub. "No plumbing yet, but someday." She pointed under the tub. A hole in the floor lined up with the drain. "Water drains right outside. No need to carry it outside when you're done."

She told a plump, dark-haired girl to draw me a bath—a warm bath. Johnny Dobbs scowled. "You're gonna waste warm water on her! I'll never understand you, Pearl. You treat a street urchin like royalty." He stormed off toward the saloon.

"Five dollars!" Pearl called after him. "You're going to owe me five dollars! You'll see."

The plump, dark-haired girl who had been ordered to draw my bath grumbled. With a tin bucket in hand, she went in and out the back door, drew water from the pump, heated it on the pot-bellied stove, and poured it into the tub. "Looks like Queen Elizabeth has come back from the dead to grace us with her presence. I've never in my life had a clean warm bath." She wiped sweat off her brow.

Pearl Kelly crossed her arms and narrowed her eyes at the girl. "If you stop your whining, Nellie, you can go second. Otherwise you'll be at the end of the line. Go tell all the girls to be ready for a bath. Tonight's going to be busy. Lot of rich bigwigs in town, and some of them are sure to drop in. I don't want any dirty Sallies giving my place a bad reputation."

Nellie didn't look at Pearl, but she looked at me and her nose twitched. "Yes, ma'am," she said.

Pearl put her hands on her hips. "Wash her hair real good. Use some lye and whiskey. Try and get all the nits out, then send her up to my room." She hitched her skirt and climbed the stairs.

I took off my clothes and explained to Nellie. "Only my clothes are dirty. I bathed in the creek this morning. I won't sully the water."

She nodded, pinched my clothes between her thumb and forefinger so she wouldn't have to touch them, and threw them onto the windowsill.

"I've never had a clean warm bath in my life either," I said. "This is my first one."

"Congratulations! Looks like it's your lucky day," she answered with mock enthusiasm.

I put a foot in the steaming tub and immediately took it out. "Hot!"

"Go on. We don't have all day," she hollered.

I balanced my weight on the sides of the tub with my hands and eased myself into the water. Even though I was afraid of where I was and what would become of me, I closed my eyes and enjoyed the warmth. Luckily, Nellie's hands didn't match her sour attitude and she didn't scrub me too hard, or pull my hair. She had no shame in bathing a complete stranger. Her hands betrayed tenderness despite her hard exterior.

She took my dirty clothes away. They'd probably be washed and torn for menstrual rags because they weren't even fit for a whore. After my bath, wrapped only in a towel, filled with fear and trepidation, I climbed the stairs to Pearl's room, past girls sitting on the stairs waiting for their baths. A few jeered and tugged at my towel, but I yanked it back and ran out of their clutches.

Just as I reached the top of the stairs, Pearl burst out of her bedroom door. The girls quieted and looked up at her. She put her hands on her hips. "This is Ruby." She put her arm around me. "Anyone who is uncivil to her will spend a night in the tank. Remember those first days and nights in Corinne, when we had nothing but a canvas tent and a dirt floor. Now, look around. See where I have taken you. We have rules. You follow the rules, or you'll be spreading your legs out in the cold dirty alley." She let a moment of silence pass so her message would sink in.

Right next to Pearl's private bedroom, a man looking freshly bathed and awkward clutched a small bouquet of flowers and sat on a divan. Pearl smiled at him. "Won't be long, George." Pearl put a hand on his shoulder and whispered into his ear. "She's making herself pretty just for you." George smiled and squirmed a little. Pearl ushered me into her room and shut the door.

"Touches my heart when they clean themselves up and bring flowers," she said and smiled.

Over by the window, a writing desk sat strewn with papers, books, and an open ink bottle. A drop of ink hung from a steel-tipped pen. She walked to her desk and screwed the lid onto the ink bottle. A thick maroon and purple quilt covered her bed, which had a beautiful cherry headboard ornately carved with nymphs, sirens, and mermaids. I found out later that it had been made for her by a Prussian count. On top of the quilt, a dress and corset waited to bind my naked body.

I had never owned or worn a corset. All of my mother's dresses and undergarments were burned after she died—caution against the spread of disease. Pearl dressed me and gussied me up until I felt like someone else. My skin was raw from the bath and the corset squeezed me so tight, I could hardly breathe. When she powdered and painted my face, she looked at me as if she were seeing the dead. "Sister, sister, sister . . ." she whispered, "how I've missed you." She brushed, wound, and pinned my hair on top of my head. The height and weight of it pulled my neck and I realized why ladies with elaborate hairstyles held their heads so tense and high.

Pearl stepped back, assessed me, and smiled. "Now I don't know how long your hair will stay that way, but I'm going to get my five bucks!" She led me to the mirror.

I stood before it, transfixed, barely able to recognize myself. My breath caught, both because of the tight corset and my disbelief in what I saw. Just hours ago, I'd felt old beyond my seventeen years, wretched, scrawny, dirty, and sickly. Freshly bathed and dressed in all this finery, I looked, well—beautiful.

Pearl sat me on the bed and held out some stockings. She showed me how to put them on and pin them to the garter belt. "Now, when the time comes, take these off yourself—very carefully. Do not let a man take them off. His rough hands will tear them, and I can't afford to keep replacing them. You'll get another dress, a plain one, for daytime and chores. Come winter, you'll get one pair of wool stockings. If you need anything else, you'll have to pay from your earnings." She clapped her hands under her chin and sized me up again. "Ready?"

Besides Pearl's private room and the sitting area in front of it, upstairs consisted of one big long room that had been partitioned off into smaller rooms with heavy curtains. Those small makeshift rooms were only big enough for a bed, a washstand, and a chamber pot.

She led me down the stairs past the very last girl waiting for the bath. What was the point in bathing, when eight soiled doves had already cleansed their fannies in the water before you? When we walked into the saloon, I felt eyes, not just upon Pearl, but upon me—upon me, when just an hour before I'd been an ugly duckling not worth a second glance. A general din was building in the saloon, but even some rowdy men quieted and turned to look at us.

Johnny Dobbs stared in disbelief. He shook his head and placed a fin in Pearl Kelly's outstretched and waiting hand. Pearl picked up a fork and banged it against a glass until the din quieted. "I'd like to introduce our newest girl, Ruby Doll House." Catcalls, whistles, and cheers went up. Glasses were raised and libations downed to celebrate.

Johnny leaned against the bar and looked at Pearl. "Well, I got to hand it to you, Pearl; you found a ruby in the rough. I certainly never would have picked this one." He shook his head and wiped the bar with a rag he kept slung over his shoulder.

Pearl smiled. "It's a smart man who knows to give credit where credit is due. Thank you, Johnny." She turned toward me, tucked a piece of my hair behind my ear, and adjusted my dress. "Now, listen," she said to Johnny. "I'm going to get her some supper. She'll barmaid tonight. No whoring, unless I can find the right prospect. I need to get her trained and educated."

Johnny stopped wiping the bar and aimed an explosive look at Pearl. I felt like running out of the room, but Pearl stood her ground. "Are you out of your goddamn mind? Look how busy this place is already. We're going to need all the girls we have on their backs upstairs. I've got plenty of men to help me down here."

Pearl put her hands on her hips, tilted her head, and spoke as if she was trying to teach him something. "Johnny Dobbs, remember that you said the brothel is mine, to run how I see fit? I don't want to turn her out just yet. She needs training."

He put his hands on the bar, leaned over toward her, and yelled into her face. "What training? You open your legs, lie back, think of England, and let the man do his business!"

Pearl shook her head and looked exasperated. "I didn't build what I've built, the kind of reputation I have, on that kind of simple thinking."

"It's fucking, Pearl! Can't get much simpler than that!" A loud crashing sound caught his attention. He hopped over the bar and crossed the room to break up a brawl.

Pearl ushered me out of the saloon and into the adjoining kitchen where five or six men and one woman crowded at a big pine table and spooned stew into their mouths. A large pox-scarred old woman stirred a giant pot. Pearl nodded to her. Malice shone in the woman's one good eye. Her other eye was dazed, unfocused, and drained of color. She ladled stew into a bowl, and handed it over to me.

When we were out of earshot, Pearl said, "That's Old Nell, half blind and dumb as a bat. Don't let her scare you. She sleeps out in the shed."

Nineteen

In San Francisco, New York, Washington, London, and Paris, telegraph operators waited for the word "DONE" to come across the wire indicating that the golden spike had been driven. In Ogden, a steady rain fell, and Johnny Dobbs's saloon swelled with a wet, rowdy crowd. On the precipice of a great moment, celebrations waited to begin. But the word "DONE" never came across the telegraph wires. Instead the word "DELAYED" appeared. Politicians who had planned grand festivities in their districts didn't know what to say to the masses already gathered and waiting. In San Francisco the celebrations proceeded as if the spike had been driven. But in Ogden, the rickety grandstand shook in the wind and was battened with rain as disappointed spectators headed home or crowded into saloons.

I carried drinks to men at Johnny Dobbs's place and stuffed coins into a leather purse tied around my waist. Stories and rumors about the delay filled the crowded saloon until one emerged triumphant. A man stood on the bar. He clanged a knife against a tin mug. The room started to quiet. From behind the bar, Johnny Dobbs cupped his hands around his mouth and yelled, "Give this man your attention for one minute! He's got important news."

"Thanks, Johnny." The man nodded at Johnny, then addressed the crowd. "Many of you are wondering why Thomas Durant, the U.P. vice-president, never showed up for the ceremony today. Why the delay, you ask? Can't the railroad run on time? I look around tonight and see familiar faces, men who broke their backs and left their families to try and make a living by working for Union Pacific. Let me tell you, while the company men slept in warm luxurious railway cars, we slept in cold tents with only flea-infested blankets covering us. Countless men died in accidents or of disease and exposure. Some of you probably think we got rich. Sorry to say, you are wrong. The truth is, sometimes we didn't even get paid at all until we got our guns and demanded payment." He paused for effect. Grumbles and murmurs filled the room. "That's right! We had to demand payment at gunpoint for money that was rightfully ours. Then they called us criminals!" Heads shook and disapproval mounted. "We gathered here today to celebrate the driving of the last spike, a golden spike, to join the railroads. But Durant and his cronies are missing! They are missing because hungry men, who never got paid, had to take justice into their own hands. Don't worry, they'll show up, and the golden spike will be driven, but not until every man who broke his back to build the railroad gets what he's owed. The railroad companies would lay track with men's bodies if it would make them richer. But the cheated men finally came together. They said, 'Slavery's been abolished. We're not going to work for free.' They got organized, derailed the Sixty-Six, and are forcing Durant to pay! You know what they're going to do with the money? Maybe you think they are going to build houses for their families? No, they're going to eat, because while the railroad presidents enjoy four- and five-course meals, these men are starving!"

The man stopped his speech and looked around the room suspiciously. "Now I don't want anyone sneaking out to get the sheriff, because I don't have any more details. All I know is that the golden spike will be driven, but not until the workers get their pay. Let's drink to them!" He raised his glass. A cheer went up, everyone toasted. Then the din and chaos returned.

After the speech I served more drinks, and bustled around the room ducking elbows and bottles. Many men propositioned me. With one simple word whispered into their ears, I thwarted their advances. At one point, when I went back to the bar for more drinks and to empty the coin purse, I looked down and realized it was gone. Out of nowhere, Johnny Dobbs appeared. He gripped my arm and pulled me toward the back of the saloon. A man leaned against the door to the bathroom. When he saw us coming he stepped aside. Johnny opened the door and threw me in.

A candle lantern flickered on the windowsill. Slumped underneath it on the floor a girl sat with her knees drawn up. I recognized her as the girl who was last in line for the tub. The filthy tub water looked like a scummy pond and filled the room with a foul stench. "Is that the water from earlier?"

"Only the best," the girl said and scrutinized me. "You went from first in line for a bath to the tank? That's a long way to fall in a couple of hours. You must have made Pearl real mad. What'd you do?" She scratched her head and then leaned it against the wall as if the weight of it were too heavy for her neck.

"Not Pearl. Johnny Dobbs. Lost a coin purse, but I don't think it's just that. I don't think he likes me."

She smiled and let out a little laugh. "Only one person J.D. likes. Only person he's ever liked in his whole miserable life is Pearl. That woman's got a hold on him."

I stepped as far away from the tub as I could. I didn't want to sit on the floor and dirty my dress. "Looks like she's got a hold on half the town."

The girl nodded. "Yeah. She's got something. Wish I had it. What is it about Pearl?"

"She's beautiful."

The girl shook her head. "It's more than that. I've seen many beautiful women end up in ruins. Take Old Nell."

"The cook!"

"They called her Belle! She was the Queen of Hearts—was more beautiful than Pearl once."

"What happened?"

"Told you, it's more than beauty. You got to be savvy too. Pearl's savvy."

"What's savvy?" I asked.

She sighed and explained. "Comes from *savoir*—French word for knowledge."

"What about you?" I asked. "You seem savvy. How'd you end up here in the tank?"

She scratched her arm. "I've been chasing the dragon. If I was anyone else, they'd of turned me out by now. But I got so much dirt on J.D. they'd have to kill me."

"Chasing the what?"

She let out another exasperated sigh. "You really just fell off the turnip cart, didn't you?"

The door burst open. Two drunken men stumbled in. They smelled like pigs bathed in whiskey. I covered my nose with a handkerchief and turned away. One man grabbed me by the wrist and pulled me toward him. His hands pawed at my dress. He tried to suck at my neck like a vampire. His beard smelled like animal fat. I gulped air as my stomach turned and bile rose in my throat. I couldn't do it. I'd been better off on the street. This was horrible. How many more would there be? His hand lifted my dress and ran down my stocking. He pushed me to the floor. One hand was on me, and the other searched for his member. I pushed him back and tried to roll out from underneath him.

The chasing-dragon girl snuck up behind him. She looked at me, and put a finger to her lips. Her other hand clutched a hankie. A strong odor of ether nearly knocked me out. She reached around and pressed the hankie over the man's nose until he collapsed and rolled onto the floor.

"That's how you turn a trick," she said and smiled. She reached into the man's pocket and removed a few coins. The other man was also lying on his back and appeared to be out cold. "Don't be greedy and empty their pockets or they'll get suspicious and come back for you." She hopped up and banged on the door. The door man opened it and dragged the first man out by his feet. He came back a minute later for the other one.

"That was amazing. Thank you. My name is O—Ruby. What's yours?"

"I'm Sarah. O—Ruby? What are you Irish? Yes, I'm amazing, but it won't be long before word gets around, and one of them comes for me."

"What will they do?"

"Slit my throat."

I held my hand up to my throat. "Won't any of the men here protect you?"

She looked ahead as if she could see the day her death was coming, as if it were fated and there was nothing she could do. "No, Pearl's got a—"

Pearl appeared in the doorway. "Talking about me, Sarah? You're never going to get out of the tank. Are you?"

Pearl looked at me and softened. She came over and searched me for signs of damage. "Poor sister, are you all right?" she whispered and stroked my face.

Sarah screwed up her face in confusion. I nodded and looked down, smoothing my dress over my torn stockings.

Pearl turned on Sarah. "Why is she in here?"

Sarah shrugged. Pearl looked back at me.

"How did you get in here anyway? I told Johnny—Oh, that man! Did he put you in here?"

I swallowed and didn't say anything.

"Oh, I'll kill him!" She stood, put her hands on her hips, and fumed. She removed a key from around her neck. "Take this key. Go up to my room and rest. I'll be there when I can." She stormed out and screamed for Johnny.

I didn't know what time it was, but I climbed the stairs, curled up on a divan in Pearl's room, and fell asleep. The next morning someone kept knocking on the door, until Pearl half awoke and grumbled, "What is it?"

The door opened and a stick with a white rag attached to it appeared in the room waving back and forth. Pearl smiled despite herself. "Come in."

Johnny came in and shut the door behind him. He smiled at Pearl but frowned when he noticed me on the divan. He held up a giant sack. It was bulging with coins. They jingled as he put the sack down. He reached inside and came up with a fist full of bills. "We did very well last night—better than ever!"

He had bloody scratch marks on his face. Pearl sat up and pushed the blankets down. She had bruises on her arms. "Why'd you have to ruin it and throw Ruby in the tank over a couple of lost coins?" She cocked her head and waited for an answer.

He dropped the money sack, crossed his arms, and looked at me. "I tried to tell you last night, that's not why I did it!"

"Why then? Trying to break her in? Didn't she look broken enough already?"

"No. I did it because she told every man in the whole damned saloon that she has syphilis! It's all over town. It will probably spread round the whole territory by noon. That the kind of reputation you want? A brothel where the whores have the French pox? Your red-haired beauty is no damned good to us now. She needs to get the hell out of here."

Pearl's mouth hung open. I stared at the ground. She got out of bed and stood over me. "You did what? Tell me this isn't true."

The word I'd whispered into all those men's ears was—syphilis.

TWENTY

Pearl Kelly stood at the window in her nightclothes and surveyed the street below. Her bruised arms showed signs of a struggle, but the angry red scratches on Johnny's face revealed that she had been the aggressor. With one blow he could have crushed her. His restraint demonstrated his devotion.

We waited. The stifling air was stagnant, laden with odors from the previous night's revelry and debauchery. Scents of perfume, whiskey, cigarette smoke, and urine from the chamber pot mingled with our palpable anticipation. Bacon smoke, and what I now recognize as the fishy aroma of copulation, wafted in from under the closed door.

Pearl took a deep breath and opened the window. Sounds from outside became clearer. Hammering, sawing, horses clomping and neighing, the high-pitched whistle of a steam train, and the murmur of men's voices rose above the faint chatter of displaced birds. Chickadees and sparrows landed on the sill and flitted about the window twittering to each other as if commenting on the recent activity that had taken over the thoroughfare.

A cool breeze stirred the air and seemed to dissipate Pearl's fury. Johnny's menacing smile divulged his pleasure that her anger was now directed at me instead of him. Her eyes moved as she assessed the street scene. "Building Babylon," she said in a low whisper, which could have been an answer to the birds.

She turned to me. "Do you really have syphilis?" The hot

anger of her initial reaction had cooled, but her voice shook with challenge and a buried threat.

I hung my head and mumbled, "No."

"I didn't think so. Besides them freckles, there's not one pox on your entire body. Your skin is as pure as angel's milk." She stared at me with tight pursed lips already coiled with rebuke. "Have you ever had a loved one stricken with the pox?"

I hadn't felt the weight of disapproval that heavy since Mother had been alive. I braced myself for Pearl Kelly's wrath, averted my eyes, and shook my head.

"Well, if you had, you'd know it's nothing to joke about." Her eyes clouded over with memory and her voice trembled with loss. "Sores fester on the skin. The flesh begins to eat itself and then the disease spreads to the brain, causing madness. Victims have flashes of pain mixed with bizarre delusions. They can't walk, or talk, or see straight." She paused and shook her head. "And on top of all their suffering, the world looks upon them as monsters, to be hidden away, not treated in infirmaries, but cast out to die alone. People think the Lord concocted this disease to punish harlots and sinners, yet it even strikes infants. Poor helpless babies come into this world shriveled and wizened like old men ready for the grave."

Even though she was a whore, I'd managed to offend her morality. I had known her less than twenty-four hours, but the complexity of her moral code had already begun to emerge. Her anger turned to reproach and disappointment. I prayed to God she'd just hit me or have Johnny hit me, so we could get past this. I wanted to be in her good graces again. I wanted to be her phantom sister. Was that how her poor sister had died? Of syphilis? I could only guess at Pearl's past, the horrors and misfortunes that had led her to this life.

Silence filled the room. The noise from outside grew louder. She stood, hands on hips, waiting for me to respond.

I looked up at her. "I've seen sickness, miss. Both my parents died of fever. They twisted and writhed from the pain. They burned and broke out with sores and then drowned in perspiration. There was no doctor, no medicine. I didn't know how to comfort them. All I could do was witness them suffer and die."

Her eyes softened and flickered with interest. "Were your parents sinners?"

"No, they were Saints." As soon as I said it, I realized I'd just revealed more about my past than I'd meant to.

"There's no justice in this life that I can see," she said. Then she closed up—it was like watching a trap spring shut. "I've heard every sob story ever told—some unfold like the great Greek tragedies, others like penny dreadfuls, but they all end the same. We must do whatever we can to make our own fate. But I'm afraid your little prank has sealed yours." She wagged her finger at me, then turned back to the window. "Take off the dress."

I glanced at Johnny Dobbs. He smirked, reached inside his coat, and pulled out a cigarette case. Pearl sensed his movement and turned toward him. Her eyes snapped on the tin box. "Put that away! No smoking before noon," she said.

His face froze. He slid the tin back into his pocket. Then he sighed loudly, folded his arms, and turned his attention toward me as if waiting for a peep show to begin.

I assumed Pearl meant to throw me out. My mind raced with the prospect. The moment I'd walked into Pearl and Johnny's place, I'd tried to reconcile myself to life there. As depraved and wicked as it was, there was also camaraderie in it, a sense of belonging, as if they were a big heathen family. In my heart I knew I was damned, a whore and a killer condemned to dwell in eternal darkness. Even If I could live amongst the Saints again, in my heart I would always know that I didn't belong. It made sense that I could only find a home in a house of ill repute where my sins would bind me to my brethren in damnation.

"Can I have my dress and belongings back?" I dared to ask Pearl. The petticoat and dress that Pearl had gussied me up in restricted my movements and squeezed my rib cage, yet I'd felt some sort of security while wearing them. I had put on the dress and become Ruby Doll House for a day—a painted lady in a town full of desperate men willing to pay dearly for female favors. Why did I have to ruin it by telling all the men that I have syphilis? I'd never seen it in real life, but Doc Perkins had scared the daylights out of me with illustrations.

Yet Pearl was right. My parents had been righteous, and they were still stricken with disease. According to the doctrine and covenants, they'd be in the celestial kingdom, while I would dwell in outer darkness for eternity. The only thing Father didn't do, which the church asked him to, was to take multiple wives, and I prayed that the Heavenly Father didn't hold that against him.

Pearl strode to the chamber door, opened it, and called for Nellie, the girl who had bathed me. "See if you can find the rag she came in with!" she hollered. Pearl shut the chamber door and opened the door to a great oak wardrobe. She reached in and pulled out my burlap sack and my hole-ridden shoes.

With his large arms crossed over his chest, Johnny shifted about impatiently. Pearl inspected the old six-shooter and said, "Haven't seen one of these in a while." She held up my fringed buckskin coat and laughed. "You gonna wear this to trap beaver?" Then she picked up Dolly and stared at her for what seemed like eternity. Her brows furrowed as she weighed the doll in her hands. "This doll's heavy. There something in here?"

My heart raced. My skin turned hot, and I tried to steady my breath. If Pearl found the jewels inside Dolly, she'd take them because of the torn stockings, or the damage to her reputation I'd caused, or maybe for nothing at all. She didn't need a reason.

She had Johnny and any number of men downstairs who'd slit my throat at the snap of her fingers.

I smiled and answered quickly. "Just a heart of fool's gold, miss. I put it in there when I was a young'un. I've had that doll ever since I can remember. She's all I have left to remind me of my family."

Pearl's face softened again. Her eyes became moist and clouded over. She tossed the doll on the bed. "Yes, family, poor sister. Oh, Annie." Pearl looked at me and then walked back to the window. "You do so much remind me of her, Ruby. It's hard for me to be cruel to you even though you deserve it."

My heart filled with hope. Maybe Pearl would spare me. Maybe she'd even let me stay. I didn't know why, but for some reason I desperately wanted to be around her, even if it was just as a lowly servant.

Johnny Dobbs exploded. "Pearl, she ain't your sister. She's done nothing for us but damage our good reputation." He turned to me. "Now, missy, I believe she said to take off that damn dress. It don't belong to you." He turned to Pearl. "You got a soft spot for this one. You're not thinking clear. You best let me deal with her." He unbuckled his belt, whipped it out from around his waist, and looked at me like he couldn't wait.

My eyes fell to the giant brass buckle in his hand and I prayed his disposition wasn't such that he'd get carried away and beat me with that end. Some men dish out lashings with dutiful compassion. Yet I'd seen others become demons and with each lash, strike harder and more brutally until they worked themselves up into a frenzy that caused a bloodbath of their anger. How would I deal with the pain? Would I break through the agony and soar above, high in the sky where even birds can't reach me? Or would I be dragged down by the hot, burning agony? Would it be everlasting? Or would I be released into the good graces and compassionate arms of Pearl again?

She looked at the belt in Johnny's hand with distaste. "Put that down for a minute."

"Ruby, do what I said and take off the dress." They both watched me. I struggled with the eye hooks and laces until they became impatient. "Johnny, help her," Pearl commanded.

Johnny Dobbs rushed over to me and with his big clumsy hands began to pull and twist at the dress until it actually felt tighter. "Johnny, the dress didn't do us any harm. Use a gentle hand and don't tear it," she said.

He slowed down and panted from the effort to control himself. I felt his hot wet breath on the back of my neck as he fumbled. He finally loosened the petticoats and slid the dress to the floor. A cool draft from the open window stirred the fine hair on my body and hardened my nipples. Johnny stared. I crossed my arms over my breasts to cover them. His gaze went to my bottom half and I crossed my legs.

"You can't be coy in this business, love," said Pearl. "Don't you know anything about the art of seduction?"

"No, miss," I answered and looked at the floor again, genuinely ashamed of my nakedness.

"That pathetic posture makes me want to beat you, and it will certainly do the same to a man. Isn't that right, Johnny?"

"Yeah, that's right," said Johnny with relish.

"Now, put your hands down. Stand tall and proud, look him in the eye. You are Aphrodite, and you have nothing to fear."

I looked at her, confused.

"The Greek goddess of love," she said.

I put my hands to my side, straightened my spine, took a deep breath, and looked Johnny square in the eyes. Our gazes locked for a few seconds until his fell to my body and remained there as if nailed. I looked over at Pearl. She gave a slight nod, and I felt a small triumph.

"Johnny, do you still feel the overwhelming desire to beat

her?" she asked. He looked at Pearl, and then at me, and then back at Pearl, confused and hesitant with his words.

"No, but I still think—"

"You think, yes, I know what you think. But how do you feel?"

He scratched the back of his head, looked at the floorboards, and then back up at Pearl. "Something different."

Pearl smiled at him. "It's okay. I know she's beautiful. Come here, love." He walked to Pearl. They embraced and joined lips. I'd never seen a man and a woman display this type of affection toward one another, and I was embarrassed to witness it. I quietly gathered my things and inched toward the door. Pearl noticed and turned from Johnny. "I'm not done with you." She turned back to Johnny. "I need a few minutes alone with her. Find someone to tend the bar and come back a little later." He smiled and nodded at Pearl, but scowled at me as he was leaving.

Pearl turned to me and crossed her arms. "You're beautiful, but a man could poke his eye out on one of your ribs." When she spoke, I could sometimes hear a lilt break through, a brogue, which she tried to hide. She glanced at my belongings on the bed, then went over to the window and shut it. But she continued to look out as she spoke to me. "I do have a soft spot for you. I'm not going to force you to stay here. If you think there's something else you can do, some other way you can live, by all means go find it. I've got enough girls here, and more will arrive every day, now that the railroad is complete. They all want to work for me because I'm the best." She looked around the room, at the ceiling, and the walls. "We'll soon grow out of this building and buy or build another one."

She looked out to the street. "I see about a hundred men out there and maybe two or three women. Out at the farmhouses, each Mormon man has himself four, five, six, maybe even ten sister wives. I hear the rich can have up to twenty. They increase my business by keeping all the women to themselves. Most Gentile men in town won't be able to find wives. Even some of those righteous Mormon men who have harems will still come here. They'll come in the back door with their hats pulled down low and take the underground tunnels if they have to, but they'll be here."

She sighed and pressed a hand to the pane. "Maybe you'll find a good husband who doesn't beat you. But you'll never have your own money, or be able to own property like me. I didn't choose this life, Ruby. I was put out when I was very young. I was too poor to know God or religion. All I knew was survival, trying to eat and keep warm. Where I grew up, you couldn't even pull fish or pick oysters from the river because it was so full of excrement they'd make you sick. The smoke from the factories choked you, and it was all you could do to keep the soot off your face and try and look pretty for your next trick. I met Johnny. We hatched a confidence scheme, made some money, and got the hell out of there before the law caught up with us. This place is different. There are two rivers full of fish and clean sparkling water. You could fish or hunt. But I'm a city girl, and I never learned these skills."

Her gaze rose from the street to a towering snow-capped mountain north of town. "Just looking at that mountain raises me up. The air is so pure here I can fill my lungs without coughing. There is even a beautiful valley to the east called Eden. Despite the fact the Mormons hate me and would hang me if they had half the chance, this is my home now. Johnny and I are going to build something great here, and I invite you to be part of it. But I know it isn't an easy life for a girl like you to choose. I never had a choice; I was born into it. I don't sell myself anymore. I'm a madam and a business owner. You can learn a lot from me, Ruby, if you're willing. But if you are going to hate yourself for it, or spend the rest of your life cowering under the weight of your sins and fearing God's wrath, then I suggest you leave and never come back."

Someone knocked on the door. "Come in," Pearl called. Nellie opened the door, held my dress at an arm's length out between two fingers, and scrunched her face in disgust. "Is this what you're looking for?"

Pearl took the dress and shooed Nellie away. She shut the door and tossed it to me. "Get dressed. Take your things and go. See what you find, mull things over, and search your soul for an answer—search down deep in your real soul, the personal one, not the one some preacher has made you think you should have. If you decide to come back, there will be a punishment, and Johnny will administer it. It will be horrible and you'll want to die, but then you'll be forgiven."

I couldn't tell whether she wanted me to stay or go. Shouts from the street turned Pearl's attention back to the window. I swallowed a hard knot of saliva and forced myself to breathe as I gathered my sack. I would not have thought it possible, but my dress was in even worse condition than it had been when I arrived. It must have been used as a rag because it smelled like stale ale and sawdust. I pulled the dress over my head. The sawdust made my skin itch. I longed to take the dress off and throw it away forever.

I didn't want to sully Pearl's fine bed with my dirty dress, so I sat on the floor and squeezed my feet into my worn boots. I had to scrunch my toes together so the big toe would not protrude. From the neck down I was Ophelia again—a lost wretch, a fallen Saint, and an outlaw. Yet my hair still held some of the coiffure, and I could feel the rouge on my lips and cheek. From the neck up I was Ruby Doll House.

I was torn between staying and going. I wanted to stay with Pearl, but I couldn't submit myself willingly to Johnny's wrath.

The look in his eyes when he reached for his belt had been one of pure malice. Even Uncle Luther's evilest glare had always been laced with mischief. Satan did not cut his helpers from the same cloth. Johnny Dobbs was different from any man I'd ever known and he frightened me.

I needed fresh air. Pearl's door would be open. She had said I could come back. I decided to go.

"Thank you, Miss Pearl," I said. My hand rested on the glass doorknob and I waited for her response. Her brows raised a little as if she was surprised by my decision. She sighed and gave a slight nod without looking at me. I went through the door and closed it carefully, wishing to make a quiet getaway. For some odd reason, I felt like a traitor. I had known Pearl for less than a day, yet some incomprehensible seed of loyalty had been planted in my heart.

Morning light stirred the painted ladies and their customers awake. They clamored for clothes and negotiated trade, still clumsy from the rowdy night. I nearly tripped over a tuba case carelessly left next to the steep narrow stairs. Sarah, the chasing-dragon girl from the tank, was on her way up with an empty chamber pot in each hand. She shot me a confused look and seemed about to ask me something before she decided it was too much bother and continued on her way.

I passed the kitchen, which was bustling with activity. Bacon smoke carrying scents of fried egg streamed out the open back door. A man carrying a crate came barreling in straight toward me. I positioned myself sideways so he could pass.

"Thanks, doll," he said and winked. His smile revealed deep dimples nestled under high cheekbones set above a strong clean-shaven jaw. He was young like me.

The heat rose in my cheeks and my body tingled. I smiled back and watched him. Not all men were bad. If you could find a man of integrity like Father or Zeke, with the looks of Samuel

Cox, you'd be a lucky girl.

Johnny Dobbs stood in the hallway with his hands on his hips, directing the dimpled crate-carrier where to set it down. I turned and hurried on my way, feeling a pang of loss over a home I never had and jealousy for people who had somewhere to go, someplace to be, and people, however depraved, who at least knew them and called them by name.

A man emerged from the outhouse, and since there was no one else waiting, I seized the opportunity. I wasn't in there but two minutes when I heard someone stomping like a mare in heat. I missed the days when I'd lived outside of a busy town and could see to my bodily functions in peace.

As the morning sun mounted, steam rose from the muddy roads. I stuck to the boardwalk and avoided the deep muck caused by Saturday's heavy rain. My leg ached from walking so much. The smell of fresh bread led me back to the bakery at the edge of town. Hunger pains began to jab at my empty stomach. If I didn't get something to eat soon, my belly would turn into a hard knot, and I'd be unable to eat when I had the chance. That's how I ended up being so skinny.

The woman behind the bakery counter was plump with rosy, flour-smudged cheeks and tired eyes. She formed a weak, impatient grimace as I tried to decide what to purchase. I wanted to be careful with my savings. A finely dressed couple entered the store laughing, and the woman behind the counter turned her attention toward them. I stepped aside and pondered the baked goods and confections. She called the couple Mr. and Mrs. something or other and spoke deferentially to them. The lady clutched the man's elbow and cast a quick pitiful look at me before she scrunched her nose and turned her head.

The baker woman hollered to someone in the back of the store. "He'll be right out with your order," she told them and turned her attention back to me as if imploring me to be on my way before I offended the gentry.

I had been enticed by the confections, but ordered half a dozen rolls instead because they would last longer and provide more nourishment. I reached into my sack to retrieve some coins from my purse. To my horror, the purse was empty, totally and completely empty.

The baker woman saw my empty purse and lost her temper. "On your way! How dare you come in here painted up smelling like week-old fish and a casket of ale! You don't even have a coin to your name! What business have you got! Out—now!" She hollered.

The lady customer raised a gloved hand to her mouth, and her male companion shielded her as if the ugly scene might cause her bodily harm. I turned to go.

"Roger, for heaven's sake, pay for the poor girl's bread!" she gasped.

"Of course, darling." He patted her hand to calm her.

He looked at the baker woman and said in a loud condescending voice. "The Lord commands us to have mercy on the poor. Give the girl a dozen rolls. Just add it to our account."

"Sir, she'll—"

"That's enough. Do as I requested without another word."

I hung my head in shame as the woman stuffed twelve rolls into a sack. She came around the counter and thrust it at me as she opened the door. "Don't come back," she grumbled under her breath.

Fear and embarrassment had caused the hunger in my stomach to turn into a hard knot. I had planned to sit on a bench and bask in the morning sun while enjoying a fresh roll. The scene in the bakery and the realization that my money had been stolen took my appetite away. I walked around a surrey, which I figured belonged to the wealthy couple from the bakery.

Planks had been laid across the road. I hopped to each one trying to cross the wide road without sinking into the mud.

I did not want to believe that Pearl had stolen my money and
sent me back out into the world without a penny to my name.
That was the money I'd saved, slaved for in the laundry, scrimp-
ing and wearing rags for almost a year. Yet it probably wasn't
even as much as Samuel Cox had made away with from the
poker game the night we'd absconded from Grafton. I didn't
want to put Pearl in the same category as Samuel Cox, a cheat,
a coward, a fickle chicken who would leave you to die at the
first sign of trouble.

I tromped down the boardwalk and with each step, my fear
and shame turned to anger toward the people who had wronged
me. When I had lain dying in the desert, I tried to let go of my
hatred toward Uncle Luther and Samuel Cox. I knew in order
to die in peace, I had to let go of hate. But the anger returned
and filled me with fierceness—a fierceness that my survival
depended upon.

The image of the lady in the bakery flooded my mind. The
man had patted her hand and treated her as if she were some
delicate species of plant that wouldn't survive unless placed
under a glass globe. Yet in her helplessness, she held power. It
was different from Pearl's power, but it was there all the same.
She did not seem like a sister-wife fighting for her place in a po-
lygamist marriage. The man had spoken of the Lord, but both
he and she wore fine tailored clothes and didn't look like any
Mormons I'd ever known.

I never had the luxury of being a lady. My first memories
were of trudging across the frontier, following the wagons
through the mud and eating Dolly's cotton stuffing so my
stomach wouldn't feed on itself. Dolly! My heart leapt and a
sudden urgency filled me. I had trained myself to forget about
the cursed ruby necklace inside Dolly. It wasn't just the curse

that made me want to keep it. As long as I had the necklace, I still had a piece of Mother.

Pearl, or whoever stole my money, had not realized that my real wealth was hidden inside a dirty old ragdoll. Desperation had taken me perilously close to a life of shame. Mother wouldn't have wanted that for me. Damn the curse, I decided. If a worse fate could befall me for selling a family heirloom, I was prepared to face it.

Twenty-One

I stopped in front of a dry goods store, retrieved a roll from the sack, and held it between my teeth while I put on my buckskin coat. With the roll still hanging from my teeth, I hoisted the sack over my shoulder. Horses neighed from a livery set back a little distance from the narrow makeshift boardwalk. The sound of their whinnies and snorts filled me with longing. After I sold the necklace, I'd buy a horse, a rifle, and a new dress. I'd go to the bathhouse, get cleaned up, and find a place to live. Maybe the necklace would fetch so much money that I could get a place of my own. I imagined chickens and a garden but no husband. With the prospect of money, the world seemed full of possibilities. I ate my roll and marched with confidence down the boardwalk, keeping my eye out for a jewelry merchant.

The words, *Buy, Sell, Trade* were stenciled on the dusty glass window of a timber-frame building. It looked sturdier than most of the makeshift tents on the street. In front, a man sat in a bulging shaker chair, which looked like it was about to break under his weight. The man focused on his boots with what appeared intense admiration, the kind of doting look most people only bestowed on loved ones. The boots, full Wellingtons of fine black leather with shiny drover's spurs, appeared brand-new. His legs were outstretched and the boots were crossed and propped on a railing. Unlike his boots, his trousers were worn mounted-gray-wool and looked like they had once been part of a confederate uniform. They squeezed his short stout legs, which blocked my passage.

"Good morning, sir," I chirped. "Excuse me."

When he turned to me, the sight of his face nearly made me gasp. He had probably lost his right eye on a battlefield somewhere. It had no pupil, just a sky blue iris that seemed to bleed into the whites of his eye like runny yoke. On his left cheek was a raised angry scar. A lump of tobacco protruded from his lower lip. He spat a wad onto the boardwalk. His one good eye stared at me with penetrating hatred. I could tell he'd lost more than an eye in the war. He scowled.

Because I was full of courage and on the brink of becoming rich, I repeated myself like a schoolmarm waiting for an answer. "I said, good morning."

This time I got a small nod before his gaze fell, and he assessed my ragged dress with a mixture of both puzzlement and disdain. Even men who looked like they had just crawled out of roadside ditches had the nerve to judge a girl by her attire. Besides his boots and a black bowler hat, he wasn't dressed much better than me.

I sighed and looked around. When the hammering, sawing, and bustle of the street noise subsided, bird songs filled the air. Spring bloomed all around, and I felt the sun's warmth on my face. "Well, sir, I'm just happy to be alive on this fine morning. Excuse me. I have some business to attend to in this shop here." He briefly touched the brim of his hat and removed his legs from blocking my passage, a small victory for me.

I entered the shop. The very act of opening and closing the front door stirred up a storm of dust that rose and settled like a startled flock of finches. A disarray of items cluttered the walls and shelves. The discordant ticking of at least twenty-five assorted clocks created a tense, hurried atmosphere in the small cluttered place. I looked for the proprietor. He rose from behind a counter stacked with buffalo skins. "What can I do for you, miss?"

I walked over to him and set my sack on the counter. Lanterns, rifles, pots, pans, pickaxes, bridles, and ropes hung from the walls and ceiling. If you could imagine it, you could probably find it somewhere at the trading post. The cacophony of all those ticking clocks made my head pound. "How can you stand it?" I asked and put my hands to my ears.

"What's that?"

"The ticking."

"Can't hear them anymore. I wind them up every morning and none of them keeps the same time. Worthless junk! With the railroad, very important to have a clock that keeps time." He scratched his head and looked at me. "You here to buy, sell, or trade?" His voice was a tired singsong with an occasional high note of irritation.

I absentmindedly stroked a wooly buffalo hide. I wanted to rest my head on it, but I resisted. Frozen black buffalo eyes stared down at me from an enormous head mounted on the ceiling. I removed my hand from the hide and put it over my sack.

"Do you have the means to assess and purchase jewels, sir? You see, these jewels may be extremely valuable. Maybe worth more than everything here combined."

He seemed calm, but I could hear his breath quicken and whistle. He was thin and bald with spectacles perched on the end of his nose. "Of course I have the means. But I'm no fool. I don't keep large sums of money here. Truth be told, most of the jewels that people try to hock are fakes."

"Fakes?"

"Nothing but colored glass. Let's see what you got."

I reached inside my sack and pulled out Dolly and my Buck knife.

"That's a nice knife. Can't give you anything for the doll though."

"Wait a minute," I said. I turned Dolly over and began to slice her open. I just couldn't do it to her face. We'd been together too long. As I pulled out some stuffing and then the jewels from inside her, the man's breath grew louder than the tick-tock of the clocks. His hands fumbled and he licked his lips as he picked up the rubies. He took out an eyepiece and stood by the window. Dust motes danced around him as he studied the rubies for what seemed like eternity.

The stern glare of the buffalo head seemed to convey a warning. I tried to shake off the image of my head mounted next to his. Finally, the man came back from the window and placed the necklaces on the counter. "Sorry," he said and shook his head. "Glass, just as I expected."

I stared at him. He looked into my eyes for a few seconds, then dropped his gaze to the jewels and fingered them gently. "Good imitations—but imitations."

All my hopes and dreams rose into my chest where my heart clenched around them. I was afraid they'd fly out and leave me forever if I dared to speak. "Are you certain?" I squeaked.

"I've been doing this for thirty years and I'm sorry, miss, but those jewels are not real."

"Are they worth anything?"

"Only if you try to pass them off as real. But I can't help you with that. I'm out of that game. Too risky, especially around here. Town's too small. Maybe in Gotham, Boston, one of those big eastern towns, you might have some luck passing them off, but it's a dangerous game. You got to know what you're doing."

I tried to think of what to do. I had let Uncle Luther take my maidenhood for a pile of glass. I couldn't believe Mother had been carrying around fake jewels her whole life thinking they were real. Her ancestors must have been fooled too. Why would anyone bother to curse imitation jewels?

"This necklace has been passed down in my mother's family for generations. I just can't fathom that they are fake rubies. Why, there's even a curse attached to selling it!" I studied his face.

"Who is your mother?" he asked.

"What do you mean? My mother passed two years ago."

His breath whistled through his nose again. "Who was she before she passed? What was her maiden name? Who were her people? Did she come from a prominent family? Only a very wealthy and prominent lady would possess a necklace like this—if it was real, that is." He added the last part so quickly it raised my suspicion.

It occurred to me that I didn't know my mother's background. The only thing I knew about her family was that they had disowned her and she didn't ever want to talk about them. And she and my father had both loved Joseph Smith, perhaps more than each other. "My mother was a Saint."

"Uh-huh. Whole Utah Territory is full of Saints, except us Gentiles of course. We're the sinners."

My parents had followed Brigham Young's orders and gone to the farthest, driest corner of Zion to grow cotton. He had told them it was their calling. I wondered if they would have lived if they disobeyed, if they'd gone somewhere sensible to live that wasn't hot as hell and full of droughts, flash floods, and disease.

"Tell you what. I'll take these fakes off your hands and you can pick out anything here you want—got some real nice dresses and ladies boots in a trunk out back."

The hair on my neck stood up, and a warning bell rang in the back of my brain. I looked to the buffalo for guidance. "Sir, do I look like I just fell off the turnip cart?"

He studied me. "Well, not *just,* but maybe a few days or a

week ago." He stared at my dirty dress.

"Unless the jewels are real and you're trying to cheat me."

"Missy, I'd like to spank your skinny behind for the way you just insulted me."

"I bet you would. But that'd cost a pretty penny. Or maybe you'd just trade me for a dress?"

His demeanor changed and his mouth hung open as he tried to size me up under the buckskin coat and threadbare dress. "So, you're a whore. Had a notion that might be the case. Must not be a very good one if you can't make enough to feed and clothe yourself with all the desperate and lonely men around here."

I shoved the jewels and stuffing back inside Dolly and placed her in my sack. "I think I'll get a second opinion. Maybe I'll take them to someone who can see." I smiled and nodded in reference to the thick spectacles hanging off the end of his nose. "Good day, sir." I slammed the door behind me.

Outside, the one-eyed troll turned to look at me from his roost in the shaker chair. He had stopped admiring his boots and sucked on a pipe. The smoke hung in the air, smelling of licorice and bringing back some vague memory I couldn't place. I wanted to linger in the odor, but my anger set me in motion.

"Which way to the river?" I asked.

He pointed northwest. I nodded thanks. I needed to go to the river and clear my mind. Ever since I could remember, I'd been drawn to rivers. Although fording rivers on the long march to Zion had proved dangerous and slowed progress, the rivers had been our life blood. We'd travel miles from one to the next, always stopping to rest and revive. Even the cantankerous Virgin had seen me through many troubled times as I'd sat on her banks and watched the sunlight dancing on the water. If the river could keep flowing, then so could I.

As I walked, questions about my mother, Uncle Luther, and

Zeke plagued me. I didn't know much about my parents' histories. They were gone, and it was too late to ask. I wondered about Zeke. I prayed he was still alive and that I might find him one day. I wanted to believe Pearl loved me like her lost sister, and that she had set me loose without money only as a way to bring me back. Since I had no family, I could be her lost sister. I'd do anything or be anyone so I wouldn't have to be alone anymore.

I reached the river and stumbled upon what looked like a duck hunter's blind. Sticks and thatch covered a dugout. Vestiges of human activity lay scattered on the ground—a tinderbox, straw matting, a huge pile of feathers, a fire ring. None of it looked too fresh, so I figured whoever had been there had hunted the place out and moved on. I threw my sack into the dugout and walked down to the river. The area seemed safely abandoned, so I sat on a rock and took off my shoes. Then I stood up and stripped off my dress.

The cold water was dank and dark with mossy stones, much different from the Virgin's sand and silt. I tried to clean my dress as best I could before my feet and legs went numb. I stood barefoot on a rock, wrung out the dress and my bloomers, and then hung them on some branches to dry. Although the sun felt good on my skin, I crawled into the dugout just in case someone came along and spied me naked.

I emptied the contents of my sack and sat on it so I wouldn't get dirt on my bottom. The dugout provided adequate shelter. I thought maybe I could live there for a while until I figured out what to do. My stomach growled and I reached for a roll. My mouth watered as I held the bread to it. I took a bite, closed my eyes, and savored the buttery taste.

While eating that delicious roll, I smelled licorice. Panic-stricken, I dropped the roll and scrambled for my gun. As I gripped the six-shooter on my lap, I stared at the abandoned bread covered with dirt. I placed my buckskin coat on my lap to hide both the gun and my nakedness. Then I listened for the troll with his licorice-smelling tobacco. But the rushing river drowned out most other sound. The smell passed and I began to wonder if I'd imagined it.

Out of nowhere, the spurs of his black Wellingtons appeared right at nose level in the opening of the dugout. I cocked my gun and looked at Dolly. She lay beside me face down. Stuffing sprang from the gash on her back.

The Wellingtons turned in a slow circle until the pointy toes were aimed right at me. I could not control my breath or the loud pounding of my heart. As he crouched, I heard his knees crack and his new leather boots squeak. His face appeared. He stared at me with his one good eye. This time he did not hold my gaze. He looked from me to Dolly and back. "I won't hurt you. Just hand me that doll," he said and reached for her.

I raised the six-shooter from under the buckskin coat and pointed it at him. Dolly was all I had left. "Put your hands up and get out of here, or I'll shoot you right in the face," I said.

Crouched on his haunches, he put his hands up. A look of shock, confusion, and mild amusement crossed his face. I wish he'd been afraid. But he wasn't. It was too bad.

"Now, there's no need for that. Put the gun down before you get hurt."

I shook my head. He lunged at me and I did the only thing I could. I fired.

TWENTY-TWO

Blood and solid matter splattered onto my face and body. I suppressed the urge to scream. My ears rang from the gunshot. The close-range bullet had knocked the man backward onto the ground. He squirmed but did not make any noise.

When his writhing stopped, I assumed he was dead. I put my buckskin coat on, stuffed Dolly in the crook of my armpit, and crawled out of the dugout.

He lay curled with his scarred blind side pressed against the ground. The bullet had opened his old wound, and that side of his face, so full of anger and tension, had exploded. Blood oozed out, mixed with the earth, and pooled around his head, forming a ruddy brown halo. His quick, fast breathing was in step with the frantic roaming of his intact eye over the ground and sky as he searched for something to gaze upon, maybe to find meaning in death, or maybe just to hold onto the world a little longer.

His gaze landed on me and fell to the patch of wooly red hair between my legs. I remembered I was naked from the waist down and placed Dolly in front of my private. In the distance my dress and bloomers waved like a truce flag as I realized they had revealed my whereabouts.

The sight of Dolly over my private seemed to bring the man back to how he came to his present circumstance. He groaned and mumbled in a low angry voice, "I survived Bull Run, Carthage, Yorktown, and I've been kilt by a girl and her doll," he concluded with obvious regret about the lack of glory in his demise. He closed his eyes.

I felt sorry for him. But what was there to do? "Well, sir," I said, "you shouldn't have tried to steal her."

His eye snapped wide open and he studied me. Tears welled and fell. His collapsed, broken face formed a twisted, bizarre smile. A strange sound emerged from him as his body convulsed. I wondered at his strange behavior before I realized he was laughing—howling in a fit of wild hilarity.

I would have liked to laugh too. Yet his gruesome countenance and the fact that I had probably just killed my fourth man filled me with enormous heaviness. For months I had been going back and forth as to whether I was responsible for the deaths of the two card players who had shot each other. Strictly speaking I didn't kill them, they killed each other. Yet I had undeniably killed Uncle Luther. Maybe this one-eyed man wouldn't have hurt me too bad. But he certainly would have stolen Dolly and the ruby necklace. I tried to stay rooted in my righteousness.

He finally stopped laughing and died. I had never seen before and have never since seen someone die laughing. Later, I discovered he was the infamous one-eyed Red Farrell, a hard humorless man, a Confederate deserter, and the indebted henchman to Simon Bamberger, the pawn shop owner who had told me my necklace was fake.

I emptied his pockets and stuffed them with river stones. "I told you I was going to shoot you in the face if you didn't back off. I gave you fair warning and you didn't listen. You didn't believe I'd do it. Well I did it. I did what I said I would and this is your fault for not listening." I kept talking to him, scolding him for his actions, even though he was dead. In his breast pocket where a watch should have been, I found a locket with a tattered picture of a lady. I couldn't tell whether it was his mother, sister, daughter, or sweetheart, but it tugged on my heart strings. I figured any man who carried a picture of a woman in his pocket couldn't be all bad. I asked him about it, but of course he was dead and didn't answer.

All in all he didn't have much of value—just his gun, knife, and those boots he'd been so fond of. I pulled off his boots and discovered an intricate red leather pattern embossed in the cuffs. For a minute I found myself admiring them as he had. I released his gun belt and set it next to his boots. Although he wasn't a big man, as I wrapped my arms around his calves and started dragging him toward the river, I felt his strength and solid stature. I became overheated from the effort of dragging him and stopped to take off my buckskin coat. I had to avert my eyes from his terrible bullet wound. He had been an ugly man to begin with, and the bullet sure hadn't helped. As I dragged him toward the river, his wound and long scraggly hair collected sand and dirt, making him such a mess I couldn't look at all.

The water numbed my legs as I dragged him into the river, which ran high and fast from spring snow melt. With one of my legs wedged behind a boulder so the current wouldn't sweep me away, I pushed him out and let the river take him. I made sure he was good and gone before I scrambled out of the frigid water back onto the riverbank.

I lay belly down on a rock and stuck my face into the water, first drinking and then scrubbing my skin of blood and rouge. The rock had absorbed heat from the sun and it warmed me. I wanted to stay and rest for a while. But I didn't want to be naked anymore, and I was scared someone else would find me. I took my clothes from the tree and dressed.

The man's boots, gun belt, and hat were scattered on the riverbank. Although his dead body had tumbled down the river, his belongings still seemed to contain something of him. I walked over, picked up one of his boots, and pulled it on. It almost fit, so I pulled on the other one. I fastened his gun belt around my waist, then fetched his hat, dusted it off, and placed it on my head.

I paced the riverbank. The water bubbled and tumbled on, never pausing to wonder why. A feeling washed over me and something entered me—his spirit. I had only myself to blame. I should have known better than to put on a dead man's clothes.

The dead are subtle. In real life, they do not moan and drag chains through the night, reaching out for you with skeletal fingers like the ghosts of Charles Dickens's stories. I had tried to conjure my mother and father on several occasions, but I was never visited by their ghosts. All that came were memories. I held those memories, replaying them in my mind so I would not lose them. Luckily, Uncle Luther's ghost never came to me. I tried to forget him. I hoped his spirit was dwelling in outer darkness, or hell, or wherever the damned go. Yet I worried I might meet him there one day.

All I can say of one-eyed Red Farrell is that I felt his spirit in me. I knew then that he wouldn't have killed me. He would have hurt me enough to take Dolly and maybe a little extra for the aggravation, but he was not a murderer of the fairer sex. He had lived in misery with unbearable pains plaguing him for some time, and in death he found relief. Like me, he'd already lost everything and everyone dear to him. What was his life besides pain?

He had loved his new boots and for some reason I felt he wanted me to have them. I never heard his voice. I never saw him. I just knew. In the years to come, he didn't exactly haunt me in the traditional sense. Yet he was sometimes there watching when I wished he wasn't. It was an invasion of privacy, but a small price to pay for killing a man.

TWENTY-THREE

Red Farrell had hitched his mare a little way from the river. That's why he'd been able to sneak up on me. The horse neighed and stared as I approached. The hat, the guns, the boots were all her master's, but she seemed relieved when she discovered I was not him. From her spur scars, I could see that Red Farrell had been harsh. She watched me remove the spurs from the boots and throw them on the ground. She ate the dirty roll from my hand. Then I mounted her without much fuss.

We galloped north out of town through tall timothy grass, past cottonwood trees and scattered homesteads. A large peak loomed to the north like a castle. I later learned it was called Ben Lomond, after a similar mountain in Scotland from where many of the local settlers had emigrated. Bouncing in the saddle with my hair blowing behind me, I felt the power of the mare between my legs, and for the first time I felt strong and free. I wanted to hold that feeling and keep riding forever.

Yet when the homesteads became scarce and thunderclouds stretched ominous dark fingers toward the earth, my freedom turned to dread. Experience had taught me the dangers of the mountains. I wanted to take shelter in a warm log home, and sit down for dinner with my mother, father, and Zeke. But I had no one. And although I had a fortune in the ruby necklace, I had no way to sell it. I turned the mare around and we galloped back, toward Junction City—toward Ogden and Pearl.

★ ★ ★ ★ ★

The railway station, a hastily constructed clapboard structure, was painted a bow-red color so bright I could see it from miles away. It was surrounded by a vast expanse of barren land where tracks had been laid and stockyards built. Telegraph poles had replaced trees and almost all the vegetation had been trampled or eaten by stock.

One tree had been spared. It stood alone a little ways out from the station. Its green blossoms stirred with the breeze. The tree would have been a beautiful reminder of what had been lost except for the grotesque shape of a man hanging from one of its branches. I had seen men hanging, even a woman once. Mother had tried to cover my eyes and turn my head, but I had managed to peek through her fingers.

A posse of men kicked up dust as they made their way from town toward the man in the tree. They were so focused on the hanging man that I slipped past them into town completely unnoticed. Certain no one had seen me, I hitched the mare behind the livery, gave her a goodbye pat, and set out toward the saloon.

Pearl stood on the boardwalk in front of the saloon talking coquettishly with a gentleman. He wasn't like the gentleman in the bakery exactly, but his attire and manner told me he was of a different class from Johnny Dobbs. I walked toward Pearl. She watched me approach and looked perplexed. I must have been a sight with the boots, the hat, and the gun belt. She extricated herself from conversation with the gentleman and walked toward me with her hand covering her mouth.

"What in the world?" she said.

My story about the cursed necklace and the pawn shop tumbled out all jumbled. She looked around, shushed me, and told me to pipe down until we got inside. The saloon was almost empty and, to my relief, there was no sign of Johnny Dobbs. She ushered me to a quiet, corner table and took a seat with her back to the wall so she could see the entrance and everything going on.

I began my story again, starting with the cursed ruby necklace and the pawn shop, but then chaos erupted and a gang of men led by Johnny Dobbs burst through the front door carrying the body of the man who had been hanging from the tree. I lost Pearl's attention. She frowned as they placed the man on the bar.

"Is that man dead?" she asked no one in particular. "Well, that certainly isn't good for business." She stood, marched over to the bar, and spoke to Johnny Dobbs. He gave me a quick glance and then he and three other men, like pallbearers without the convenience of a coffin, removed the body from the bar, carried it through the saloon, and out the back door.

Pearl came back ashen and distracted. She leaned across the table and whispered, "That was the man who made the speech about Thomas Durant and the U.P. last night. He was like a brother to Johnny." She shook her head. "A word against the railroad and the next day you turn up dead. Johnny's hot-headed. He wants revenge. He needs to cool his cannon before he does something stupid. Some things are just too big to fight." She settled into her chair, distracted.

I tried to continue my story, but she shushed me again and told me we needed more privacy. All I wanted was to confess to killing Red Farrell. I was filled with an urgent need to tell someone. When we got to her room, I finally had her attention and told her the whole story, ending with me killing the one-eyed man. Of course, I didn't describe the eerie feeling of his ghost in me because I didn't want her to think I was touched.

She wanted to see his gun, so I handed it over. She inspected it, felt the notches on the handle, and looked down in awe at the boots I wore.

Her eyes were wide and her mouth hung open. She asked,

"Do you know who you killed?" She threw her head back and laughed. "You killed Red Farrell. Johnny and Red have been trying to kill each other for so long I can't even remember what they're feuding about. Oh, my. What a day this is." She handed the gun back to me and then grabbed my wrists in a congratulatory yet possessive gesture. "That should clear the slate with Johnny over your little syphilis prank."

She wanted to see the necklace. I wanted to ask her about my coin purse, if she had taken the money, but I didn't want to insult her and it didn't seem the right time. I fished the ruby necklace out of Dolly and handed it to her. The rubies dangled from her hand. I remembered mother's boney, leathery hand holding them out to me as she lay dying.

"Ruby? Ruby?"

Pearl had been calling me, but I was lost in memories of Mother and had forgotten for a moment that my name was Ruby.

"Ruby, huh? How long you been going by that?" Pearl fingered the necklace in her clean lovely hand so different from my mother's hand hardened from work and withered by sickness. I didn't know what to say.

"No matter," she said and smiled. "This was meant to be."

"So you think they're real? Will you help me sell them?"

She held up the rubies and inspected them. "Of course, they're real. Why else would old Bamberger send Red Farrell out to steal them? Listen, dear, do you have any idea what it means to be cursed? You think your life is bad now? I will not sell them and bring a curse upon you."

Devastated, I choked down my disappointment and tried to suppress tears. She knelt before me. "Now, don't despair. Wait a minute." Her eyes danced with excitement. "I have an idea how we can profit without even selling the necklace."

Her smile was so broad, reassuring, and filled with promise, I couldn't help feeling better. "How?" I asked.

She stood, clapped her hands under her chin, and paced while she spoke. "I've been looking for investors for a business venture. A very wealthy man is interested in backing me, but I don't have any collateral. You see, I need a down payment. If I use the necklace as collateral we can get it back as soon as we start making a profit. Ruby, we can be partners!"

"What kind of business?" I hoped she would say bakery, or dressmaker, or millinery, or even distillery. I wanted to redeem myself for killing, and I didn't want to debase myself or other ladies by selling female favors. But it turned out that was the only kind of business Pearl knew.

"A parlor house," she said.

"What is that?" I asked. "I've never heard of such a thing."

"It isn't a brothel or a bordello even. It's a very fine establishment, a house, where gentlemen, rich gentlemen, visit to be entertained by fine talented ladies, in a discreet yet luxurious atmosphere, with music and dancing, and adult parlor games, and other activities that suit their distinct and unique tastes."

She must have read the look on my face because she said, "Ruby, you must believe me. It's nothing like this place, like the tank. Nothing of that sort will happen to you again, I promise. This is different." She walked toward the window and stared out. "You see, I've been in a fine house, a proper household with a proper family, one of the wealthiest in New York, and I know that the appetites of the men who rule those households aren't any different than those of the lowest horse thief or road agent. They've got the same tastes and perversions, but they smell better. They are clean and rich. And they don't want to be in a lowly brothel. With the railroad, they'll be coming. We can charge them ten times as much as the commoner. Oh, Ruby, I want to make them pay. They humiliated me, took me in and threw me out like a common whore when I was barely grown.

They made it out to be my fault when it was he who came after me—couldn't keep his vile hands off me, bribed me with sweet meats and lollies." She froze in a dark memory, which silenced her.

To fill the awkward silence, I told her about my parents dying and my uncle running Zeke off, and ruining me for marriage. I left out the part about my uncle wanting the necklace, the card game, the three dead men, and also me running off with Samuel Cox. She nodded silently and didn't press me for details. It was a common enough story, I suppose. I was filled with melancholy and resignation, and with kinship for Pearl and all the fallen women. I understood why she wanted to turn the tables on the men who had wronged us. We could not slay them with a swift sword of justice. Such a thing didn't exist for us. We had to be what they'd turned us into and use the only true weapon we had.

Johnny Dobbs could hardly believe I'd killed Red Farrell. If it weren't for the hat, gun, boots, and horse, I don't think he would have believed it. Pearl told him the story, but left out the part about the ruby necklace. She said Red had tried to violate me. She didn't want Johnny to know about her plans for the parlor house.

He was not a forgiving man. It wasn't enough that I'd killed his enemy. He wanted Red's horse, guns, and boots as repayment for my syphilis prank. I negotiated for the boots, pointing out that his feet were way too big for them. I don't know why those boots meant so much to me. It must have been Red's ghost that didn't want Johnny Dobbs to have his boots, and somehow his desire became mine.

J.D. claimed that word had traveled of the beautiful but "spotted" peach who was whoring at his saloon. He said I must publicly declare that I did not have syphilis and then make myself available for inspection. I looked at Pearl. Even though she had influence, he still wore the pants.

"No touching," she said to Johnny and ushered me away by the elbow. For some reason Johnny wasn't fond of me. He always looked at me with a puzzled, suspicious expression. In response to his hostility, I made myself smaller and barely uttered a word in his presence.

Twenty-Four

The dead man's burial, on Monday, May 10, 1869, was completely overshadowed by the driving of the golden spike, which took place out at Promontory Point. And the scandal, which had prevented Thomas Durant from being there on Saturday, was never mentioned again. Many of the nation's newspapers had run stories, and celebrations had even taken place on Saturday as if the spike had been driven as planned. None of them mentioned Durant's kidnapping.

Through industry, temperance, and tightly organized social structures called wards, Mormons had civilized the Great Salt Lake Valley with irrigation, mills, kilns, fine brick buildings, and roads. Yet much of the Utah Territory was still a wild and lawless frontier. Hell-on-wheels towns like Blue Creek and Promontory had sprung up around the railroad and were best avoided. Instead of making the long journey to Promontory, many people celebrated the driving of the golden spike in Ogden, which was rumored to become the junction city, a mandatory stop for anyone crossing the continent by rail.

Pearl feigned grief for Johnny's dead friend, but could hardly contain her excitement over the future parlor house. She pretended to be excited over the railroad, but all day she whispered into my ear new decorating ideas, or small details she thought would make our parlor house perfect. She picked out fine dresses for me from her own wardrobe. Before this I had only worn homespun frocks. Although the new dresses made me look grand, they restricted my breathing and movement.

That day I drank champagne and ate oyster pie for the first time. Johnny, Pearl, and I went to a real restaurant and sat at a table spread with a fine linen cloth. Pearl had gussied me up again and I felt like an entirely different person. She and Johnny weren't too impressed by the oysters. Pearl said she had practically lived on them as a kid. She and Johnny preferred the mutton stew. It was the grandest most plentiful meal I had ever eaten. My body seemed to grow instantly from all the nourishment. Pearl told Johnny I deserved to be treated like a queen since I had killed Red Farrell. I figured it was the rubies and the parlor house she was really happy about. Johnny grumbled over his stew. He opposed Pearl's idea for a parlor house.

At dinner, they spoke about me as if I were not there. This behavior began that night and I never objected. Around Johnny, I tried to be a pretty and empty thing like a vase or a landscape painting. But I listened. I revived my old habit of eavesdropping except it wasn't even necessary to hide.

"I'm not putting up money to fund no fancy fuck house," he said.

"What if I find a way to come up with the money?" Pearl asked.

He just snorted and said, "That'll be the day." He stared at her, hard and dead serious. "I moved the whole operation out here from Corinne on your hunch, Pearl. What if you're wrong? What if Corinne becomes the junction city and we go belly up? You'll be on your back again."

Because she was in such a good humor with the secret of my ruby necklace and her plans for the parlor house, Pearl let Johnny's insult go. But she wouldn't always. Sometimes she'd fight back and things would turn ugly.

After dinner we walked back to the saloon. Pearl and I were giddy from champagne. Johnny walked ahead, subdued and disgruntled. I wasn't sure whether that was his normal disposition, or if he was crabby over the murder of his friend.

Pearl asked me if I was sure this was the life I wanted. I told her I was ruined for marriage and a decent life on account of Uncle Luther violating me. She nodded and told me I wasn't the first. The worst, she said, were the ungodly godlies, who would violate young women and then chastise them for becoming whores. She talked of Venus and Aphrodite. She said we would build a temple of love.

I told her of my strong feelings for Samuel, how I thought it was love, but then he had left me to die. She called him a coward and me a goddess. She said even in my weakness I was strong. She said that men would suck the spirit and strength right through my "glorious hole," and then leave me weakened and hungry. She wanted to build a temple of love where proper patronage would be paid for our gifts. We would call it The Doll House and use the rubies to build it.

When we entered the saloon, I saw the dimpled crate-carrier standing at the bar with a bottle and a glass in front of him. He watched us and smiled broadly. His youthful, clean-shaven smile filled the room with promise and dimples you could get lost in. Most men sported scruffy beards that smelled of axle grease and rotting meat. I figured the crate-carrier was so young his beard hadn't fully come in yet.

He raised his glass and said, "Well now, that's a prettier sight than any sunset I've ever seen. If God has created anything finer than you two ladies, I'd sure like to see it." He took a drink, shook off the whiskey burn, and put down his glass.

Pearl held out her hand. He kissed it and looked at me. "This is my little sister, Ruby," Pearl said. "She'll be staying here with us now."

The crate-carrier took my hand and lifted it to his mouth. His lips lingered for longer than was proper. His hot breath sent a sudden chill through me.

"Why your hair is the color of peaches. I've never seen hair so fine a color." He finally dropped my hand. "My name is Peter, but they call me Whiskey Pete on account of my whiskey wagon."

Pearl smiled at him and looked at me. "He's got a secret still somewhere up there in the mountains, and he graces us Gentiles with his presence by overcharging us for his fine mountain firewater, which we baptize and sell for a profit."

"Aww, now you're flattering me, Miss Pearl."

It appeared he'd been sampling his own stock. His cheeks were flushed. He loosened his collar, shook his head, and took another swallow.

"Pete, we need a man's assistance upstairs. Would you be so kind as to lend us a hand?"

He turned a beet color and looked like he'd been caught with his trousers down.

"You can bring your bottle," Pearl said, smiled, and walked away.

I fell in step behind Pearl aware of the drunk, enthusiastic young lad behind me who seemed just barely to have passed the threshold to manhood. His enthusiasm spread to me. I felt so excited to be alive and to have made his acquaintance, I thought I would burst.

When we entered the exotic sanctuary that was Pearl's bedroom, my excitement changed to awkward discomfort. The last rays of sun imbued the room with forebodings of romance. Pearl lit a gas lamp and pulled the lace curtains shut. The pink sunlight penetrated the lace and shimmered on the wall in an intricate pattern. The sirens' bosoms carved on Pearl's mahogany headboard held Peter's awe-stricken gaze. I could tell from his reaction that he had never been in her bedroom before.

"Now, Peter." Pearl smiled from over the gas lamp, which illuminated her face and golden hair. She guided him into a chair next to a coat rack and gestured for me to sit on the bed. "My sister needs an education, and not the kind you get in a schoolhouse. It's the type of education best given by a handsome young man like you, with a bit of guidance and advice from a lady acquainted with the art of pleasure, like me."

I froze. Pete looked like a lit stick of dynamite was in his pants. He shifted uncomfortably in his chair, loosened his collar some more, took a swig from his bottle, and ran a hand through his thick hair. "Okay," he said and glanced at me. "I'll do my best to oblige." He must have noticed the stricken look on my face because he got out of his chair and knelt before me. He glanced at my hair. "Is this okay with you, Peach?" He must have forgotten my name and not known what to call me. "I won't hurt you."

When I looked into his luminous green eyes and down at his velvet chocolate hair, my breath caught in my throat and I could not speak. The same feeling overcame me as when I had first met Samuel Cox, and I knew it would lead to nothing but trouble. Yet I wanted that trouble—wanted it so badly I began to ache.

I looked at Pearl. She smiled, nodded, and picked up a glass from her bedside table. She poured a half a finger of whiskey. "Here, dear, this will relax you." She handed me the glass. I sipped it and sputtered as the heat burned my throat. Pete looked at Pearl tentatively and she nodded. Pearl poured herself a little glass, then began a passionate speech.

"The realms of pleasure are forbidden to us in the Bible, by preachers and holy men. We cover ourselves with layers of uncomfortable clothes, and try to ignore the pulsing and longing of our most intimate parts. But a long time ago in Greece and Ancient Rome, sex acts were sacred. People made pilgrimages to the temple of the Goddess Aphrodite. They worshipped her and made sacrifices to her—all in the name of pleasure." She looked to each of us. "You must free yourselves from the shackles of shame over copulation and ejaculation. Man must ejaculate. If he carries his seed too long, it turns to poison, and he takes a violent hand." Pearl looked at Peter and gestured to me. "Her ripe body has been cooped up in that dress too long. Free her."

Peter stood behind me and began unfastening my dress. As the fabric fell away, I did feel free—free yet vulnerable. I had heard how far a woman could fall; illegitimate pregnancy, disease. How would Pearl protect me from disaster?

Whiskey Pete required urinary relief. He stood over the chamber pot. Pearl chastised him and told him to go outside. "Fresh urine wafting from the chamber pot makes pleasure tawdry. We are not alley bats!"

During his absence, she briefed me in the technique of fobbing. She said the younger and drunker the man the easier he was to fob, and since Whiskey Pete had both of those balls in his court he'd be easy game. She cautioned me about the appropriate time and place to use this technique.

When Whiskey Pete returned it did not take long for him to become aroused again. I reclined back on the bed and let him kiss me. He pulled his trousers off and tossed them onto the chair. Pearl gave me a signal. As I'd been instructed, I reached down, placed his member between my thighs, and squeezed them together as hard as I could. Sure enough he began a frantic horizontal folk dance on top of me.

An explosion of crashing and yelling erupted from downstairs. Johnny shouted, "Pearl! Pearl! Get down here!" Pearl straightened herself up and flew from the room.

Peter was working hard thrusting himself up and down. My inner thighs felt chafed. I also felt a little guilty for fobbing him. A drop of sweat fell from his forehead and trickled down my cheek into my mouth. It tasted like salty whiskey. Finally, he collapsed on top of me and I felt something wet on my legs. He rolled onto his back and looked up at the ceiling. His muscled chest heaved as he tried to catch his breath.

I began to cover myself by pulling up my new black lace undergarments, but he pulled them back down and stroked my breast, squeezing it in his palm and kneading it like dough.

He looked down at my cooch and smiled. "You are a peach," he said.

I smiled and tried to cover back up so he wouldn't see where his seed had landed and put two and two together.

He jumped out of bed and hollered. "Oh, Peach, that was so good. You are so beautiful. Why, I'd marry you, take you up to my cabin, and put lots of babies in you if . . . if . . ." His smile disappeared.

I propped myself up in bed and stared at him, waiting for the caveat. I silently prayed, *please, please, take me with you. I want to leave this place and live a decent life.* I looked at him with the most innocent but sultry look I could muster and waited for him to continue.

"If . . ." his smile became wistful. "Well, if you weren't an upstairs lady." He looked bashful and somewhat ashamed for what we'd just done.

My insides shattered like a fallen china doll. *An upstairs lady.* That was probably the nicest term for what I'd become. Any chance at real love was lost. After young Whiskey Pete, it would be middle-aged railroad men and newly scrubbed strike-it-rich silver miners. I didn't know if that was his first time with a woman or his hundredth. Since he delivered whiskey to saloons and brothels, it was hard to believe he was a first timer. I wanted to confess my fobbing and ease his sudden shame, but I couldn't utter a sound because I knew I'd fall to pieces.

Perhaps he noticed my wounded look because he walked to

the bed, picked up my hand, and said, "Can I see you again like this next time I'm in town, Peach?"

I nodded. He didn't kiss my hand. He dropped it and then started putting on his trousers. My hand fell like a corpse's. I had no will to move it or any other part of my body. I couldn't focus on anything. In the corner, I sensed Red Farrell's ghost rifling through Whiskey Pete's coat pockets and examining his belongings. Whiskey Pete retrieved his coat from the back of the chair, slid it on, grabbed his hat, tipped it to me, and tiptoed out the door.

"My name's Ophelia," I whispered, wondering if that girl were still alive. I missed my family so much. My brother, Zeke, had always been there with an arm, a look, or a smile. Even though I was now surrounded by people, I was utterly alone without my family. I hoped there was no afterlife so my parents would never know how far I'd fallen. When the door was safely shut, I sobbed into the pillow, sobbed and sobbed until I feared mildew would grow on Pearl's silk pillowcase.

They never did call me Ruby. They called me Peach, Miss Peach, Peach Pie, Peaches and Cream, Peachie. After weeks of strange men, and sometimes even women, performing humiliating syphilis inspections over every inch of my body, I was declared a perfect peach, clean and syphilis-free. The humiliations would have continued, but Pearl finally said, "Enough!" And for the next decade, I was known and addressed as some variation of Peach, formally Miss Peach. I even signed my name *Miss. O. Peach.*

TWENTY-FIVE

Despite the railroad boom, Fifth Street didn't change much during the 1870s. The panic of 1873 and bickering between the Mormon People's Party and the non-Mormon Liberal Party in Corinne slowed construction. The Mormons wanted the junction in Ogden and the capital in Salt Lake. The non-Mormon Liberals had a stronghold in Corinne, and told the federal government that unless state government was located there, the Mormons would take complete control. For many years, uncertainty reigned. As a result, most of the buildings remained timber shanties. The Ogden train depot was an embarrassment. For a few years during the early 1870s, the federal government planned to construct a fancy depot way out in Harrisville, which was the middle of nowhere, and far from a water source. Both parties agreed that was ridiculous. When the panic of '73 struck, those plans were abandoned.

Brigham Young won the battle against the Corinne Gentiles by ceding land around the Ogden railway depot to Union Pacific. Ogden officially became known as Junction City. Pearl's hunch became a reality. With the jewels as collateral, Pearl had secured funds for our parlor house. Johnny Dobbs didn't like it, but there was nothing he could do.

Even though Brigham Young won the battle over the location of Junction City, he could not stop the flood of brothels, saloons, dance halls, and gambling and opium dens that began to prosper on Fifth Street. Hostility grew between the Gentiles and the

Saints because the Saints were allowed to sell all manner of items, even liquor, to the Gentiles, but the Saints were prohibited from patronizing Gentile businesses. While the Saints were appalled by Gentile liquoring and whore-mongering, the Gentiles were equally appalled by polygamy, which they likened to male prostitution. The Mormon newspaper constantly dueled with the Gentile-controlled newspaper over the issues of polygamy and prostitution.

When the morning papers came out, we gathered at the breakfast table over steaming cups and listened as Pearl read the articles. The Mormons claimed that the practice of polygamy rid their society of the evils of prostitution. We all had a good laugh over that because we had plenty of Mormon customers. In fact it was commonly said that Mormon women had the curious habit of "playing dead" when their husbands wanted to bed them. Even polygamists would sometimes patronize brothels so that they could *hook a live one.*

The Doll House was a darling three-story Victorian on Sixth Street just a block south of the White Elephant Saloon on Fifth Street, which locals at the time just referred to as "The Street." Fourth Street was mostly a respectable affair with brick buildings, the Zion Cooperative Mercantile Institution, and two banks: one Mormon owned, and one Gentile.

Johnny and Pearl had bought up a few parcels of land on Fifth Street before the panic of 1873 dried up credit. They were the royal couple of the Junction City underworld, and I was their bastard child. Men would pay a fair sum to ravish the young, orange-haired Miss Peach. It was amazing how many times I could pretend it was the first. Luckily, Pearl chose my patrons and protected me from bullwhackers, buffalo skinners, and other vile types of men, the kind I'd been acquainted with that first night when I was locked in the tank. Those types of men smelled worse than a pigpen. They were usually covered in vermin and months of accumulated sweat, mud, blood, and tobacco juice. Some didn't even have the decency to bathe before seeking a women's comfort. I was thankful to Pearl for sparing me their patronage.

From the time I was very young, my life had been full of physical hardship, from trekking across the Overland Trail, to tending livestock and obstinate crops in the desert. My nails had always been dirty and my hands callused. As long as I could remember, each evening my muscles had ached and my stomach had growled with hunger.

As a strumpet I was well fed. I was well dressed. I had a bath whenever I wanted. And all I had to do was forget everything I'd ever learned about morality, and give myself up for the pleasure of men. It should have been easy. My back didn't ache from labor. My stomach was full. But I harbored a pang, a deep invisible ache inside that split me in two.

I couldn't risk striking out on my own to search the territory for Zeke. But I never stopped praying that we'd be reunited. I had a way of asking all my customers if they'd seen him. I'd start with a compliment to the man's eyes. Depending on the type of man, I might say, "I've never seen such fearsome eyes, or intelligent eyes, or thoughtful eyes, or serious eyes, or mischievous eyes, or bright blue eyes." And then I would say, "The most haunting eyes I ever saw were deep blue eyes on an Indian boy of about seventeen. Isn't that strange? Did you ever see an Indian boy with deep blue eyes like that?"

I figured Zeke's eyes were the one characteristic that really set him apart. I hoped I might hear word of his whereabouts. I got a variety of unhelpful responses. "No place in this world for the half-breed male." Or, "Stay away from them Injuns. A blue-eyed savage is still a savage." Those responses only increased my worry over Zeke's lot.

Each month, I eagerly waited at the parlor window for

Whiskey Pete's mule wagon to arrive. Pearl granted me two free days and one evening to spend with him. In order to forget the shameful truth of our relationship, I fantasized he was a sailor returning from sea, or a soldier returning from battle. In my fantasies we were husband and wife. But in reality, I was a whore and he was a philanderer. We were fallen Saints, apostates, and if the Mormons ever found out, they'd kill us both.

None of that mattered when we were tangled together on the bed up in the attic of the parlor house—my private quarters. With the cozy slanted ceiling sheltering us, we embraced on a bug-free bed under a lavender quilt. Shelves with my favorite books lined the walls and a porcelain basin sat on a table next to a plush upholstered Eastlake platform rocker. On hot summer nights, when the attic air was stifling and unbearable, we'd climb out the window onto a flat spot on the roof to feel the cool air, watch the sun set, and spread a bedroll under the stars. I lived for those times.

For a while, it took a fair amount of ale and spirits to dissolve my embarrassment and the boundaries of my flesh. I finally learned to satisfy my customers without abiding shame. My customers passed through me. But I held Whiskey Pete in my heart. His steady affection kept me from whiskey and laudanum dependence—a dark hole many of the girls fell into. The belief in his love sustained me.

With Whiskey Pete I experienced intense pleasure. It was perhaps a crude, momentary, release, but it helped me understand what my customers were seeking and enabled me to see beyond the sin. Man was born from the sin of desire. I came to see it as natural, much different from the impulse to kill.

One night after sex we lay in bed and Whiskey Pete talked about his wife. He told me about her strong constitution, described the girth of her hips, the fullness of her milk. He told me how she was back in the field only a day after giving birth. "She bears work as well as a mule," he said. "But she closes her eyes and grits her teeth when I bed her. Not like you." He licked my nipple and squeezed my breast in his hand. "She has no nature for pleasure and passion like a woman of your profession."

I told him it was not my profession. It was he alone who aroused my pleasure and passion. I told him with the customers, I had to pretend to like it. I told him it took all my will not to grit my teeth. After hearing him compare his wife to a beast of burden, I was thankful we weren't married. But I wondered about my true nature. Was I born to be a whore?

Pearl was a busy bee. If it weren't for the nature of her business, I think the Saints would have admired her industry. She managed the upstairs girls over the White Elephant Saloon as well as at a few other establishments on The Street. The rumbling trains brought a steady stream of customers wealthy enough to travel by rail. As the trains came and went, whores working The Street close to the station were prodded and pumped with mechanical regularity. In contrast, customers of the Doll House paid more, stayed longer, and took their time.

As the old Indian woman had predicted, the iron horse, which brought previously unknown comforts to the frontier, marked the end of the great buffalo herds and the Indian tribes who depended upon them. Most people saw this as a victory. Not many mourned what was crushed and banished in civilization's westward march. They were only grateful for their comforts and didn't see what was lost.

Thanks to the railroad, during the early 1880s small towns like Ogden began to grow and prosper all across the West. Civilization could not tolerate wilderness. Sadly, by 1882, the buffalo, those immense clumsy looking beasts, had almost completely vanished. Crossing the plains, I'd once seen a whole heard stampede and plunge into a river, so many swimming for their lives with grace and stateliness. I'd also seen countless Indians in their primitive grandeur riding like the wind without saddle or bridle, clinging to their horses as if part of them. Most of their race had been slaughtered like the buffalo, or rounded up and corralled onto reservations.

I didn't know what fate had befallen my beloved brother, Ezekiel. As a half-breed, he walked a thin line between two worlds and didn't belong to either. Was he condemned to wander like the Jew? Where would he find his place in the world?

During the late 1870s, rich men from the east traveled west to hunt buffalo. They were not like the mountain men and buffalo skinners of the previous age who had killed the beasts for income and survival. They were industrialists who killed only for sport. After their conquests, they came to the Doll House where they boasted of their exploits. Meanwhile buffalo carcasses and bones littered the land. These men's hands were as soft as ladies' hands, and I doubted many of them could even ride a mount with enough skill to hunt. They shot from the top of slow-moving railroad cars, which pulled up alongside the herds. Even though they sickened me, I smiled and provided pleasure.

By 1881, a network of canary wires began to crisscross Fifth Street. City officials planned to build a mechanized streetcar like the one that ran in San Francisco. The depression had ended, and speculation on Fifth Street led to another real estate boom. A whole block of timber-frame shanties was torn down and construction of the illustrious Broom Hotel began. The Street, however, was still dirt. Both children and small dogs could drown in its giant mud puddles.

My private sanctuary in the attic of the Doll House kept me sane. The world I created there had nothing to do with the

Ogden underworld in which I operated. When Pearl and Johnny Dobbs weren't working, they lived on a small farm on Washington Street north of town where they had stables and some livestock. The livery near Fifth Street was usually full and fairly expensive. In addition to her place on the farm with Johnny, Pearl also kept a private room at the Doll House.

Beyond a single strand of costume pearls hanging elegantly from the front door of the Doll House, and some cupid statues in the garden, there was nothing to mark the establishment. We employed a doorman who doubled as a bouncer. Customers came by invitation only and were required to check their weapons at the door. I don't know how Pearl recruited our customers. Most of them were regulars. We never lacked business, and Pearl boasted of a long waiting list. Exclusivity built mystique and bred demand.

In the back of the house we had a small kitchen garden. I tried tending it for a while, but I couldn't make anything grow. Once I'd seen a man walking down the street who had the same black hair as Ezekiel had. With great hope, I followed him for several blocks until he turned, and I realized it wasn't him. I began to doubt I'd ever find him. I tried my best to forget him. Yet I couldn't give up the hope that one day we'd be reunited.

When I painted my face for the evening, I saw tiny little lines forming at the corners of my eyes and mouth. I wondered how long men would continue to pay for my favors. I stayed out of the sun, always wore a bonnet, and used copious amounts of powder and rouge. But I knew one day I'd be too old and withered to turn a head. Pearl planned for that day. As the years went by, she spent more time at her desk squinting and scribbling in ledgers. She stashed away money, bought property, and invested in other businesses.

I had more possessions and comfort than I'd ever dreamt of—fine dresses and bonnets, jewels, money, property, servants, even a bank account in my name. Yet I'd never forget my early life of poverty—the hunger and scarcity, which had forced me to eat Dolly's stuffing. Before I was orphaned, I'd been rich in my family's company. Since I'd become a whore and murderess, I'd be excluded from celestial reunion with them. And so I was truly damned. I felt empty and lonely. Each morning, I'd wake up terrified.

Pearl and Johnny were my only family. I counted myself lucky to have resembled Pearl's dead sister. I became her chosen one and a true object of her affection. Sometimes she slipped and called me Annie, but I never corrected her. She saw the other girls only as a means to make money. The more money they earned, the better she treated them, and so a jealous hierarchy developed. Even though I was ashamed by her behavior, I never protested. The fact that she treated everyone else poorly increased my stature. I learned to be what other people wanted me to be, to take the shape of their desires, like a play-actor on an intimate stage. I shifted form so much, I'd lost track of my true self and my own desires.

TWENTY-SIX

I thought I was the only one Pearl truly loved until one Sunday morning in April of 1881 when I awoke to some noise coming from the kitchen. It was so early the cock had not yet crowed. Dawn was a thin line waiting to crack. I heard a series of high-spirited shushes and giggles coming from Pearl at an hour I'd never before seen her even remotely awake.

I tiptoed downstairs and caught her rummaging around in the icebox, putting leftover ham into a picnic basket. A hunting rifle and a shotgun lay on the kitchen table. She was with a mannish-looking woman who wore trousers and sported a hunting jacket. The woman looked bashful but defiant.

"Oh, sorry, Peach," Pearl whispered. "I didn't mean to wake you." She flicked her fingers at me. "Go back to bed."

Without moving an inch, I studied the woman in man's clothes standing next to Pearl. Pearl looked at the woman and explained. "This is my good friend Emily Browning. We're going hunting."

I didn't know Pearl had any friends. She hardly ventured outside, especially during the day, never mind the wee hours of the morning. She could barely contain her enthusiasm for this outing. It was absurd—Pearl hunting?

"It's nice to make your acquaintance, Emily Browning. Oh, are you related to the gunsmith?" I asked.

She smiled tiredly as if this were a frequent question. "My father started that business. He died a couple of years ago. One of my brothers has taken over. I'm just one of his twenty-two offspring." She touched Pearl's elbow.

"*You're* going hunting?" I said to Pearl emphasizing the word *you're* so Emily might understand what she was in for with Pearl along.

"Yes." Pearl answered impatiently.

"For quail," Emily chimed in, her voice strong and confident. Pearl continued packing the picnic basket, and Emily picked up the shotgun.

A wistful longing came over me as I recalled my hunting days with Zeke. I swallowed. "Can I come?" I was ashamed of my pathetic pleading tone. Pearl hesitated and looked at Emily, who shrugged and nodded.

Pearl shouted, "Hurry! Go get ready. We were just about to leave."

I started up the stairs and overheard her say to Emily, "She knows a thing or two about guns." I halted in my tracks, spun around, and looked at Pearl. She smiled and winked. I turned and ran up the stairs.

"Wear an outdoor dress or some trousers if you have any!" she called after me.

"I know!" I sang.

It had been about six months since Whiskey Pete had been to see me. I'd once spied a look at his first wife when I saw them together at the mercantile. Her dour face and dowdy build gave me confidence. But he had amassed some savings and proved to the church he was worthy to take a second wife. I'd heard she was fifteen years old and as beautiful and fragile as an orchid. Enamored by her youth and beauty, he must have forgotten all about me. I'd fallen into deep despair over losing him. The prospect of a Sunday outing filled me with joy.

The weather was fine and we had a grand time. Emily was impressed with my marksmanship and amused by Pearl's excited ladylike handling of the assorted rifles and shotguns. I'd never seen this side of Pearl. She laughed like a schoolgirl and looked at Emily with such esteem and admiration, I felt jealous and fearful that Emily would replace me. Pearl's affection toward me had been mostly sisterly. I felt something different between her and Emily, something almost romantic.

Pearl and Johnny's relations had always been turbulent and filled with nasty rows. Yet Johnny had managed to hold back and never unleash his full fury upon her, until one Sunday morning not long after the hunting outing. Part of Johnny's vicious reputation around Ogden was built on the false rumor that he had killed Red Farrell. If I hadn't felt so guilty about it, I would have found my status as a secret killer amusing. I was a multiple murderess, and they treated me as if I were a prized poodle.

My manner had changed over the years from a spirited, defiant, red-headed tomboy to an exotic flower with a demure ladylike façade. I cultivated subtle yet sultry mannerisms to attract wealthy patrons. I sometimes sang in public and was known for my sweet, melodious voice. Once in a while Pearl and I drank a little too much and ended up spending the night in a dance hall, not for the money, just for fun.

Pearl loved to dance. She glided over the dance floor as if she had wings. If she didn't have to keep up the lofty parlor house reputation, I bet she would have done the can-can. Unfortunately since my fall from the cliff, I'd been plagued with leg aches and a slight limp. I disguised my affliction the best I could, but dancing aggravated my old injury.

I'd spent every holiday and ate most Sunday dinners at Pearl and Johnny's farmhouse along with other assorted characters who came and went over the years. Although Johnny didn't seem to actively despise me, he never did warm up to me. It was like he still harbored that beating he never got to give me. Sometimes I wished he'd just have whipped me over that syphilis prank because his prolonged silent aggression unsettled me for over a decade.

It all came to a head that April morning when I awoke to crashing noises and Johnny hurling expletives. He blasted all manner of filthy names, some I'd never even heard, at Pearl. His voice quivered with rage. A trail of blood led under the bed where Pearl hid like a whimpering bitch. I ran to my room, retrieved my six-shooter from the bedside table, ran back, and trained the gun on Johnny, who by that time looked more like a wild beast than a man.

"I shot Red Farrel!" I yelled. "And I will shoot you if you don't get the hell out of here right now." Red's ghost stepped into me. It was the moment he'd been waiting for, the reason he'd been haunting me all those years. I fought between our opposing wills, trying not to pull the trigger and kill Johnny outright as Red so desperately wanted.

Pearl's voice came from under the bed. "Peach, don't do it. They'll hang you. There's bad blood between me and the sheriff right now."

I locked gazes with Johnny Dobbs. Hate burned in me so hot, I thought I could incinerate him. I said, "Well, that's just fine, Pearl. It would save me the trouble of hanging myself." The words came out with a force and truth that surprised and saddened me. Until I uttered those words, I had not realized the depths of my despair.

On his way out, Johnny Dobbs broke every precious vase, lamp, and painting that adorned our elegant parlor house. Pearl crawled out from under the bed and mooned over each object, ignoring her own wounds. "He'll pay for this," she hissed.

Red Farrell's ghost was angry and disappointed that I didn't kill Johnny. He didn't throw dishes or slam doors. There was nothing much left to break. I felt him in me. I can't explain it. He wanted me to pull the trigger so bad, I almost did. The only thing that stopped me was the thought of Johnny Dobbs's ghost haunting me too. Hanging would have been a relief—an end to my misery. I thought that then, but who knows what my feelings would have been with the hangman's noose around my neck.

We closed the Doll House for a few days and cleaned the place. Pearl packed a trunk and said she had some business in New York City. She left me in charge and boarded a train that would take her right across the territories all the way to the Atlantic Ocean! Oh, how I begged to go with her and visit the Great Metropolis. But Pearl said no. Her mission could be dangerous, and someone needed to oversee the parlor house. She gave me detailed instructions about what to do should she not return. I pressed her for details. She wouldn't tell me anything. I was terrified of losing her and being left alone in the world, especially with Johnny Dobbs as an enemy. She said not to worry; if things went according to plan, we'd be rid of Johnny Dobbs and only richer for his riddance.

TWENTY-SEVEN

When I went to the Union Pacific Station to welcome Pearl back home, she was accompanied by a Pinkerton detective, Charles Sirringo, whom she affectionately introduced as "Charlie." Johnny Dobbs was promptly arrested for a murder and a bank robbery, which he'd committed in Gotham during the early 'sixties before he and Pearl came west. He had used the robbery money to buy whores, and increased it by following the construction of the railroad and pimping sex to the laborers all the way to Ogden. He then built a small empire of gambling dens, saloons, and some of the nastiest back-alley cribs known to man.

All of Johnny Dobbs's money and property were confiscated by the Pinkertons. Charles Sirringo arrested him and extradited him to NYC for trial, where he was found guilty and sentenced to hang at Sing Sing. Pearl did not collect a fee for the information she provided about Johnny, but she was granted immunity for her association with him, because she'd been a minor at the time of the crime. At first, she feared one of Johnny Dobbs's men might try to avenge him. Instead, all of his underlings and associates fought amongst themselves and clambered to replace him.

As the date of Johnny's execution grew closer, Pearl became anxious and full of regret. She said that Johnny had saved her. He had loved her. What would she have become without him? I reminded her that he had also beaten her to a pulp and shattered all her cherished belongings.

"That was because of Emily," she whispered.

I couldn't believe Johnny was jealous of Pearl's friend, Emily Browning, the tomboy from the hunting outing. I didn't comprehend. After all the men whom Pearl had pleasured, why would Johnny fly into a rage over Pearl's friend Emily?

"It's because I loved her," Pearl said. "In a way that I could never love him."

And then I understood. Johnny only had access to the part of Pearl that she sold and bartered. The part of Pearl he really wanted, her true love and compassion, was locked away from him.

Emily Browning married a respectable Mormon and was forbidden by her family to ever associate with the likes of Pearl Kelly again. Pearl was devastated. When Detective Sirringo arrested Johnny and extradited him to New York for trial, Pearl had at first seemed relieved, as if a great heaviness had been lifted from her. Although Johnny had once provided Pearl with protection, financial support, and doting affection, over the years he had grown to resent Pearl's prosperity and independence. He tried harder to control her, often with physical force. But their fight over Emily was the breaking point from which she could not return.

Over time, Pearl had developed age lines, and her girlish figure turned more matronly. With the help of cosmetics, she was still a beauty. Moreover, she had an easy, confident way with men, a quick wit, and a sense of humor that made her the life of the party. When Pearl heard Johnny would face the gallows, everything changed. She became sullen and distracted, forgot all his meanness, and berated herself for treachery. She couldn't think of anything else but Johnny's pending execution. I didn't think Pearl was capable of such guilt because being

Pearl meant that you moved ahead without regret or reproach.

She wrote letter after letter to Johnny at Sing Sing Prison begging for his forgiveness. None of her letters were answered. Finally they were returned with a short note that said the prisoner had been executed. Soon after that, Pearl contracted a terrible disease. I don't know if it was a mere coincidence, or if somehow she had made herself sick with all her mooning and guilt. Either way, she became seriously ill.

Of course, I wasn't a doctor, but I could tell, the sores, the fevers, the burning eyes and headaches, were not phantoms of her imagination. She stayed in a dark room most of the day and only went out in the evening and at night. As sores festered on her body, high-necked blouses replaced the low-cut bodices that had once shown off her cleavage.

When the sores spread to her face, she remained indoors except for walks with a veil. We permanently closed the parlor house. Pearl didn't want any rumors about her illness to get out, so we let go of all the girls and staff. The new owner of Johnny's place had tossed Old Nell onto the street, so we hired her to help. Pearl knew no one listened to Old Nell because she was half-blind and three-quarters demented. She not only helped me nurse Pearl, but also performed most of the housekeeping and cooking duties. Old Nell knew herbal remedies. She came from a long line of prostitutes who'd passed down these remedies, probably dating all the way back to ancient Egypt, for all I knew. But since she was touched and losing her memory, I often feared we'd end up poisoning Pearl instead of healing her.

The autumn Pearl fell sick, all my energy was spent keeping deterioration and disorder at bay. As soon as I tended to one thing, be it soiled laundry, a torn stocking, or a cracked dish, something else broke. Death and decay consumed everything.

Pearl's pain was horrific, and yet she refused to see the doctor. There were many types of pox. I couldn't recognize one type of pox from the other. Pearl feared the shame and humiliation we'd face if anyone found out she was ill. Because she was a madam, they'd say it was the French pox or cupid's curse. She refused the doctor because she said he was greedy, and I'd be paying for his silence long after she was buried. The disease destroyed Pearl's vanity. But it didn't take her pride.

She did not want to try the mercury cure, which was a common treatment for pox. It was often said to be worse than the disease. Pearl just wanted morphine. She said she didn't have the will to fight her death because she believed it was inevitable and she deserved it.

I was scared that Pearl's illness would spread to me and I would suffer as she did. Yet as I continued to care for her, I witnessed a remarkable transformation. Pearl's beauty was consumed by ugly painful sores, and her outward appearance changed from that of a beautiful swan to a rotting river rat. Yet her soul filled with radiance.

Truthfully, Pearl had not been a nice person. She had been charming and witty, yet manipulatively cruel to almost everyone but me. She saw others not for who they were but how she could profit from them. Although she gave generously to the orphans, she did not spend time with them, or care for them, or even dare to place her lovely, jewel-laden hand on one of their lousy heads.

All the same, I admired Pearl. During a period of economic decline, she had risen from the gutters to build, if not an empire, at least a comfortable kingdom over which she presided. She had managed to become literate after a brief internment with a wealthy family and had further educated herself in the classics and business. Her intellect was keen and discerning. I could forgive the fact that she prospered from the backs of her sisters. What other labor could have brought such fortune to a woman?

At least she had encouraged the men to use *French Preventatives* by offering discounts. She never exploited children. At seventeen, I was the youngest girl she'd ever employed. Although many girls, including Pearl, had no idea of their birth dates and could only guess at their ages.

Pearl's disposition toward men had ranged from amused disdain to maternal kindness. Although she profited from and exploited men's weakness for female flesh, she instructed her whores to show customers only affection. Men who wanted to be flogged flocked to Pearl. She understood their need for punishment and never judged them as evil or perverse. She had said women are vessels for both pleasure and pain, for the sacred and profane. She told us that we must lose ourselves in the rapture of both and claimed that was the only way women could be one with the divine. That was what she had said on the rare occasions she waxed philosophical. Most of the time, she was figuring profits.

I never saw her soul at peace except when she suffered with the disease ravaging her body. In life she had clung to her beauty as if it was all she was. Only near death, when the burden of her beauty had deteriorated, could the radiance of her spirit finally shine.

After Johnny was arrested, Pearl had her bed with the beautifully carved mahogany headboard moved from their farmhouse into her bedroom at the Doll House. I leaned over her beautiful bed and plumped the pillows as she gazed at the intricately carved sirens with wonder. "Johnny and I will be together in hell," she mused. Her smile turned to a pain-filled grimace.

I couldn't think of a response. She had no reprieve or respite from agony, except for a few hours after morphine. Death did not come easily or fast. Yet even though the fight and light were gone from her eyes, she clung to her existence. I watched her suffer as I'd watched my mother and father suffer, although without morphine I'd been helpless to relieve their pain. But even though Pearl had morphine, her suffering seemed greater, her disease fiercer, and yet slower to take her life.

I went to a den on Fifth Street to purchase opium and a pipe. The chasing-dragon girl lay naked on a cot in the back room like a ghost, her eyes glazed over, every one of her bones visible. I couldn't believe she had lasted this long. I returned to Pearl's bedside, held the pipe out to her, and begged her to try it. Pearl had disdained opium eaters. She saw them as lazy and lacking in willpower.

"Please," I said. "Do it for me. I can no longer abide the pain in your eyes. I'd rather you look like a euphoric, glassy-eyed hookah-sucker then see you in such agony."

She took the pipe, inhaled, lay back, and asked me to sing.

Pearl, the rock of my world, was crumbling. Dust thickened on the furniture like morning frost, paint peeled, soot covered the walls. The fire went out for no reason at all. October turned to November. The last bright gold and red leaves fell. With nowhere to hide, birds flitted about on skeletal branches in naked trees, which seemed to me dead rather than dormant. Pearl became smaller and closer to death. Outside our house, the world was lifeless and frozen. Only a few thin rays of light graced the earth each day. I was afraid.

Two weeks before Christmas Pearl called me to her bedside. She extended an arm toward me. In her sore-covered, jaundiced hand, the rubies of my ruin sparkled like everlasting life. They were as shiny and new as the day, over a decade ago, that my mother had held them out to me from her dying hand. They seemed the only thing in the world that wasn't subject to death and decay.

I tried to stay strong for Pearl, but the sight of those rubies broke me. I saw my mother dying. I saw my father dying. I saw

Zeke riding away. Worst of all was the memory of being bent over the table and that critical moment when I refused to give up the necklace. My whole life I'd been replaying that moment and berating myself. Why had I stayed silent and let Uncle Luther violate me? Why had I chosen the rubies over my honor? Was I born to be a whore?

I couldn't bring any more pain upon Pearl, and so I pretended my tears were of joy not anguish. "Oh, Pearl." I took them gently from her withered hand. "You still have them. And all this time I thought we were cursed."

Pearl croaked, "All my debts are settled. Everything I have goes to you. You are still young. Be free. Be happy. You will be very wealthy. But Peach, be careful, this town is full of wolves."

I put the jewels down on the bedside table, pulled up her bed sheets, tucked them around her, and smoothed back her hair. Taking care of Pearl helped me stop ruminating on my own misery and all the memories that had flooded back at the sight of the necklace. Still I felt its presence on the table like a coiled venomous snake.

"Peach, what is your real name?"

Except when she slipped and called me Annie, Pearl had taken to calling me Peach like everyone else. I never corrected her. I couldn't use my real name, so what did it really matter? We knew each other so well and yet we didn't know each other at all. I had not uttered my real name in a long time.

"My real name is Ophelia," I whispered. "Ophelia Oatman. I'm wanted in four states and three territories. My crimes and misdeeds are so numerous they can't even be printed on a handbill."

"Ophelia Oatman." Pearl smiled. "A dangerous outlaw."

"And you thought I was just a whore."

"I never thought you were just a whore."

"You thought I was Annie."

"I needed you to be Annie. But I knew you weren't. Thanks for pretending."

She seemed at peace. The opium had taken effect.

"What's your real name?" I whispered.

"Mary Rose O'Brien." Her eyes glazed over and she slipped from the room to a faraway place.

"Nice to meet you, Mary Rose. Get some rest now."

I left the rubies on the bedside table and tiptoed out of the room. Mary Rose O'Brien smiled and closed her eyes for the last time.

TWENTY-EIGHT

I envied Pearl's death and transformation, for I was left to suffer alone through the cold dark winter. The cat, which we called Miss Havisham, and Old Nell were the only signs of life at the Doll House. Miss Havisham caught mice, slinked from room to room, and quietly rested in front of the fire. Old Nell never rested. I suppose it was her way of mourning. She shuffled from room to room or went outside, chopped wood, and poked at the frozen ground with a spade. She barely uttered a word. When she did it was an incomprehensible rant that would leave me pining for the mute.

No longer the object of men's desires, I felt lost with neither identity nor purpose. I'd thought about inviting some of the girls around for Christmas dinner, but the house was too sad, and I didn't have the will to take any action, so it ended as only a thought.

On Christmas Eve, I sat by the fire with the novel *A Christmas Carol* on my lap. Miss Havisham was curled up by my feet. Old Nell was already in bed. Although the book was open, the words failed to mean anything. I stopped reading and stared into the fire.

I remembered the Christmases out at J.D. and Pearl's farmhouse north of town. They'd always had big festive dinners with a few of the regulars from Johnny's place along with an assortment of misfits who came and went over the years. It wasn't a holy affair, but someone always said a prayer before dinner, and the occasions were filled with merriment. When there was snow we'd take sleigh rides and build snowmen and sometimes have snowball fights. It was usually a good time except for the one year a brawl broke out and someone got shot. After that Pearl reined in the tomfoolery so things wouldn't get out of hand again.

Besides crazy Old Nell and Miss Havisham, I was utterly alone that Christmas. As there was a shortage of accommodations in Ogden, I resolved to turn the Doll House into a wholesome boarding house. That would not only bring income, but also company.

Miss Havisham sensed a disturbance and raised her head. Her eyes searched the room in alarm, and those big cat pupils rolled from side to side like marbles. She turned her attention toward the entryway. Seconds later, someone was banging on the front door. I grabbed a small derringer from a drawer and went to the window. Hidden behind the drapes, I spied a look onto the porch.

Whiskey Pete stood with his head bowed. Next to him, a bearded man of about forty grasped a *Book of Mormon* firmly in his ungloved hand as if it were a weapon. Snowflakes swirled around them. The two men didn't seem affected by the weather.

I knew why they had come. I shouldn't have answered the door. I should have pretended no one was home. But the gas lamp and the smoke from the fireplace gave me away. I placed the derringer on a small table and opened the door a crack. "May I help you?" I said addressing the older man. He pushed the door open, thrust Peter in by his collar, and slammed the door shut.

He pointed the book at me. "You are a sinner and a whore. Satan lives in you and has used you as an instrument to tempt Brother Peter away from the Lord."

He pushed Peter onto his knees. Peter kept his head hanging

and did not look at me.

The man put his hand on Peter's shoulder and held the *Book of Mormon* over his head. "Lord, help me cast Satan from Brother Peter so that he might find salvation. This woman is the devil's handmaiden." He commanded, "Look at her, Peter!" Whiskey Pete finally looked up at me.

"Her face is the face of evil. Her body is Satan's fruit. Partake of it and you will be cast into a fiery lake of brimstone to suffer for eternity. Renounce her! Cast her spell from your soul!"

Peter and the man closed their eyes and began their incantation, a verse they had memorized and rehearsed. Their horrible voices filled our sad house, and I feared Old Nell would awake. She was blind but not deaf. When they finished, Peter, still on his knees, panted from the effort. The elder unsheathed his Bowie knife and held it to Peter's throat.

"Now your blood *should be spilled,* so that you might gain the salvation you desire!"

Blood atonement. I feared he would slit Whiskey Pete's throat. I glanced at the derringer on the table. Peter looked at the elder, confused and surprised. He shook his head. "Brother, I—"

The elder put his knife back in its sheath. "No! The Lord does not dwell in a house of assignation. Your ashes will not rise to him from here." He pulled a bottle of whiskey from his pocket, and opened it. "This is the fire water, which weakened your will. These spirits are forbidden to women and the weak among us." He drew a long gulp from the bottle, perhaps to show that he was not among the weak. "Brother Peter, you are forbidden this drink. You are forbidden to sell it to your brethren. If the profits from your sales to Gentiles are henceforth given to the Prophet, perhaps we can spare your blood." He poured some of the whiskey over Peter's head and slipped the bottle back into his coat pocket.

The older man looked at me. "Sister, will you repent? Will you accept the teachings of Joseph Smith, join the Saints in the one true religion, and save yourself from eternal damnation? I can cast the devil from you now if you permit me."

I thought of mother and father. Of how they'd been devoted to Joseph Smith. But of how they questioned polygamy and then Brigham Young when he sent them into the barren desert to grow cotton. The elder before me did not know that I was an apostate, a daughter of perdition. If he had known, he would have slit my throat with the sharp blade of his Bowie. I remembered how I had doted over the Prophet Joseph Smith. How I'd stared at his picture and longed to be one of his wives. His youngest wife had been just fourteen years old. Now that I knew what it meant to be a wife, I was disgusted.

The elder's leg must have smelled of fish or fowl because Miss Havisham, who normally didn't take to strangers, began circling and rubbing against him. His legs became entangled in his attempts to discourage her. He gave her a sharp kick. The sickening thud of his boot cracking her bone filled the room. She let out an awful yowl, flew across the room, and took cover under the divan.

I let out a shocked cry and covered my mouth with my hands. I shook my head, lowered my hands, and yelled, "You self-righteous son of a—"

The kitchen door burst open and Nell stood there training a shotgun on the elder as best she could with her one good eye. Peter was still on his knees. I stepped back and grabbed my derringer. The elder reached inside his coat.

"Put your hands in the air," Old Nell said with menacing authority. "We will all face our maker in the afterlife. Maybe you'll find out youse been wrong all along, worshipping false prophets! Don't you come around here and play God with us, or I'll shoot you in the bollocks."

In the past ten years, Nell hadn't said anything that made a lick of sense. That Christmas she was my miracle. I hoped that maybe she had come to her senses and would be right for some conversation and companionship. But after that night she turned back into a living ghost, never saying a word, just drifting from room to room.

If the elder who came to exorcise Satan from Peter hadn't kicked Miss Havisham across the room, perhaps I would have given myself up for salvation. It was one of those moments when I felt myself falling toward a destiny that was not mine. The whole encounter made my heart and soul heavy with fear and anguish. I'd never forget the look in Peter's eyes. Did he really believe I was the face of evil? Or was it blood atonement he feared? We had all heard stories of apostates killed by the Danites for the glorious cause of their own salvation. The Saints were at their best in times of trouble when they had to rally together and build something or fight an enemy. With idle hands, they'd nothing better to do than condemn their brothers.

Twenty-Nine

I lived in a finely built house and had plenty of money. Yet the emptiness of life without struggle, of opulence and no love, weakened my will to live. The devil no more resided in me than he did in a loaf of bread. Still, a dark heaviness descended upon me. The fierce winter wind penetrated the brick walls and windowpanes, leaving me with a constant chill. I looked forward to spring for light and guidance.

Spring finally came, but my despair did not lift. Even the delicate purple crocus emerging from the newly thawed earth failed to cheer me. I felt discarded, worthless, unloved. I ventured into town only to be met with scornful glares from decent folks and lewd invitations from the ruffians. Dressed plainly, I still could not escape my reputation or the orange hair that marked me as a strumpet. Without the confident Pearl by my side, I didn't know how to conduct myself, and so I averted my eyes and hung my head.

By Easter Sunday, when life returned to the valley, I still found no salvation, only loneliness. I had traded the jewel of my chastity for a ruby necklace, and I couldn't forgive myself or forget that I had chosen my fate. I was the evil temptress, the seductress, responsible for the fall of man from paradise and all of the greed and misdeeds that followed.

I decided no one would miss me if I was gone. Late in the afternoon on Easter Sunday, while children and families were strolling in Lester Park after Easter egg hunts and big dinners, I put on my black mourning dress and adorned myself with the sparkling ruby necklace. I rode to the eastern foothills, left my mare unhitched by a stream, and gave her a goodbye pat. As I clambered up a steep, eroded hill to the cliff, balsa flowers waved their cheerful yellow heads among a chorus of sage. My chest tightened and my eyes burned. The irresistible rocky cliff pulled me like a magnet, for my misery had always drawn me to great heights.

A cliff had always been like an altar to me, where I'd sit on the edge and contemplate my insignificance. On that day, it would be an altar of sacrifice, not a place to sooth my soul. Yet I never did know for sure. The edge always lured me. Usually I found a reason to resist.

I scrambled over jagged rocks to the edge of the cliff and sat against a rock. The sky was a flag striped with pastel pink and violet, the Salt Lake a calm blue blanket tucked into the earth's curvature. The beauty only tightened the pain in my heart, and grief poured out of me with the unstoppable energy of spring snow melt flooding a mountain stream. I cried for all the people I had lost. I cried for the unrequited love of Samuel Cox and Whiskey Pete, the look in his petrified eyes as he realized I was the face of evil. I was terrified of being alone.

I stood, walked to the edge, closed my eyes, and felt the empty space below me. The breeze lifted my hair. Birds chirped and crickets sang in a frantic, life-affirming stanza. I gave my grief to the silky air, and wrapped the empty space around me like a shawl. I wanted to dissolve into the soft spring sky and free myself of anguish.

A breeze blew in from the north and the air changed. It felt cold and empty. It chilled me and filled me with uncertainty. The image of my brother flooded my mind. I fingered the rubies at my throat. I was overcome with a strong feeling that my brother was still alive, and that I was meant to find him. He was alone too. I snapped out of my indulgent despair and wracked my brain for ideas. I stepped back from the edge and opened my eyes as if reborn by this spark of an idea. I saw things then that were obscured to me when no possibility of love was in my heart.

It had never occurred to me that with my wealth, I had power. I could hire people and make things happen. I remembered the detective Charles Sirringo, who had accompanied Pearl back from New York. I could hire him to find my brother. This new purpose brought me back to life. On the way down the hill, I began to mentally compose the letter I would write to Charles Sirringo.

Back at the parlor house I riffled through Pearl's desk and found a calling card for Mr. Sirringo. To my pleasant surprise, his address was in Denver. I vowed that after I wrote to Mr. Sirringo, I'd attend to all the papers and ledgers on Pearl's old desk. After I wrote the letter, I decided a telegram would be faster and I could certainly afford it. On Monday morning I raced down to the telegraph office.

I couldn't believe it. Charles Sirringo immediately sent a telegram back saying he would be on the next train to Ogden. On the day he was scheduled to arrive, I went to meet his train at Union Station. First, I stopped for scones at the Chicago Bakery next to the ticket office. Then I secured a hack to wait for us out front. I had only met him briefly that one day with Pearl before he got busy arresting Johnny Dobbs. Yet he'd made a strong impression on me, and I figured I'd recognize him.

The usual chaotic jumble of travelers dragging luggage and stumbling over trunks cluttered the station platform. Merchants competing to be heard above the hubbub and chugging engines called out the day's specials in loud, obnoxious voices. I jostled through the crowd and searched the station for Mr. Sirringo,

ignoring the sidelong glances I received for being an unaccompanied female.

Finally, a train pulled out of the station and took most of the
mob with it, clearing the platform. Mr. Sirringo spotted me and
approached, carrying a medium-sized carpet bag in one hand
and an ornately carved cane in the other. He didn't lean too
heavily on the cane. But as he approached I saw the strain in his
eyes. I placed him in his thirties and figured he limped from
injury rather than age.

He put his bag down and lifted his hat. "Miss Peach? How
do you do?"

I nodded, "Very well. And how are you? Tired from your
journey, I expect."

"I'm fine. I slept most of the way. My condolences about
Pearl, I had no idea she was ill. She seemed so full of life."

I nodded and we began walking through the station together.
"Yes, it was quite sudden. Perhaps she contracted an illness
while traveling." An awkward silence passed between us. "I have
a carriage waiting," I said and led the way.

We traveled over the muddy streets in a comfortable coach.
"The Doll House," I explained, "is just a lodging house now."
Because he was a detective, I assumed he knew all there was to
know about Pearl and the Doll House. He probably knew more
about Pearl than I did. "I trust you will be comfortable there."

"That's a pity. Pearl spoke very highly of the Doll House and
you too, actually. It sounded like some establishment."

I smiled and wondered what he was getting at. "Anything you
need or desire, please let me know and I will arrange it. Upstairs
girls are starving all over town, thanks to the social reformers.
I'm certainly glad to be out of that business. Pearl put every
waking moment into the house. It was her life's ambition to
operate a swanky establishment. But really, Mr. Sirringo,
underneath all the glamour, it was just a dressed-up bordello."

He looked straight at me with big amused brown eyes. Those eyes drank in everything and put my soul on trial. After three blocks, the carriage stopped in front of the house.

"That was a short ride. I have a bad leg, but I certainly could have walked," he said.

"Yes, but the streets are atrocious. There's knee-deep mud this time of year."

He grabbed his cane. The handle was carved into a mallard's head. I gently put my hand over his and looked into his eyes. "I just want you to know how grateful I am that you came on such short notice. I hope it is not a hardship on your family."

His stare was unnerving, yet kind. "I have no family, Miss Peach. It would have been cruel to subject a lady to the hardship and loneliness that comes from marrying a man in my line of work." He stepped out of the carriage and held the door open for me. "Or maybe I was just born to be a bachelor."

I stepped down. We stood next to the white gate leading to the Doll House's front garden. Red and white tulips bordered the path. Yellow daffodils, hyacinth, and iris clustered around two ivy-covered cupid statues, which I'd forgotten to remove.

"I have many fond memories of time spent at bordellos." Mr. Sirringo smiled wistfully as he gazed at the house.

"Well then, our history won't bother you." I opened the gate and led him down the path to the front door.

"I don't think I've ever seen a brothel quite like this. It could be inhabited by cherubs and gingerbread people, it looks so charming and innocent."

I laughed. "It isn't a brothel anymore, Mr. Sirringo. It's just a boarding house now."

I told him I'd have Nell put out tea and scones for him in the parlor. We agreed to discuss business later over supper in the dining room.

I spent the hours between tea and supper trying to make

sense of the papers and ledgers on Pearl's desk. I wanted to get a hold of the finances, and I didn't want to appear a vacant-headed idiot in front of Detective Sirringo. As far as I could tell from the ledgers, we'd been very wealthy for quite some time. I couldn't help but wonder why Pearl had me see customers for so long. Soon, she always said; soon we'll have enough.

Rheumy-eyed Nell cooked a light supper and set the table. Only one other lodger boarded at the time. He had taken supper in the kitchen and then went out. Old Nell slept on a cot in the pantry, tended the garden, and helped with the housework. I'd grown accustomed to her ghastly looks, but she frightened the lodgers, so I often served the meals. It was hard to believe she'd once been a queen, more beautiful than Pearl. Her presence reminded me of what I could become with age, sickness, and the misfortune of having an angry man gouge out one of my eyes.

Detective Sirringo was clearly not the type of man to be frightened by an ugly old woman, so I didn't try to hide Nell. We sat across from each other in the respectably decorated dining room. All traces of the phallic and erotic art Pearl had collected and displayed had been destroyed in Johnny Dobbs's tirade and never replaced. The house had a cozy, folksy feel with no traces of the brothel it had once been. Yet I continually had to remind myself that I was there to talk business with Detective Sirringo and not seduce him. Seduction had become a force of habit.

I'd been in the business of men long enough to be a cool expert. Detective Sirringo didn't have chiseled or pretty-boy features like those of Samuel Cox or Whiskey Pete. I'd fallen hard for their good looks and charm. I told myself never again. No, Charles Sirringo wasn't dashing or even particularly charming, but something about him gave me the butterfly stomach.

"So, Mr. Sirringo, tell me, how did you get into detective

work?" I wanted us to become acquainted before we discussed the business of finding Ezekiel.

He finished chewing and wiped his mustache with a linen napkin. "I've been in this business since I was a young man." He took a sip of wine, put his glass down, and looked straight into my eyes in that unnerving manner of his. I relaxed when he finally looked off into the corner. I took a tiny, careful sip of my wine and warned myself not to drink too much.

"When I was about nineteen, a peddler came through my little hometown of Matagorda, Texas. He was selling the latest tonics, tinctures, cure-alls, snake oil, that sort of thing. He sweet-talked my sister and got her to go to the river with him. I found her there beaten and abused. She was engaged at the time. When her fiancé found out she'd been violated, he called off the engagement. My sister couldn't live with the shame. She killed herself." He spoke matter-of-factly, without emotion.

I looked at my plate and held a napkin over my mouth to hide my quivering lip.

He continued. "By the time I realized what had happened, the peddler was long gone. I hunted him through four counties, most of it Indian Territory. Once I had his scent, I couldn't let it go. It took me three months, but I finally caught him. I've been hunting men ever since, first for bounty, and then for the Pinkertons. I got a letter of introduction from James Garret because I helped him infiltrate an outlaw gang. After I passed the detective exam, I worked for the Pinkerton Agency for almost a decade. Now I'm independent again."

"What happened to him?" I asked.

"Who?"

"The peddler."

"I killed him. Sometimes that's all you can do. I don't know how many young girls' lives he'd ruined, but for me one was enough." He cleared his throat and pushed his plate to the side a little. "The funny thing is, I was at a phrenology demonstration once, and I volunteered to go up on stage and let this famous doctor examine my head. I swear he didn't know anything about me, and he said based on my skull shape that I'd make an excellent detective. So perhaps it was my destiny."

I smiled tightly, remembering the doctor who had told me that I had the cranium of a whore.

"So how did you get into your line of work?" he blurted.

I blushed and hesitated to answer.

He stumbled. "Oh, I spoke without thinking. Excuse my rudeness, Miss Peach." He raised his brows in honest sincerity.

"No. It is all right. You shared your story, so I'll share mine." I took big swallow of wine and breathed deeply before I began. "I lived in Grafton, which is way down in the southwest part of the territory. We were Saints. Can you believe that? I was a Saint once, Mr. Sirringo. But then my parents died. My uncle came all the way from Missouri, and I thought he was going to help us. Truth is, I would have been married off to one of the old men in Grafton and I didn't want that. It turned out my uncle didn't come to help us. He came looking for some ruby necklace he said my mother stole. He framed my brother, Ezekiel, for giving information to the Utes. See, my brother was a half-breed. He barely escaped hanging. I was left alone with my uncle, and . . . well, he ruined me for marriage and a decent life. I thought of killing myself too, but I ran away instead. I was poor and desperate when I met Pearl. She took me in and treated me like her sister." I left out many details because I was scared of him finding out too much about me.

He didn't say anything. But he kept staring into my eyes. The flickering candle light danced in his. They were both cool and warm at the same time. I had no idea what he was thinking.

"Now that Pearl is dead, I have no one. My whole life, I've

dreamt of finding my brother. I have this strong feeling he is alive and he needs me. Do you think you could find him? I'll pay you a king's ransom."

As solid as stone, he stared at me without emotion and said, "If there is anyone on earth who can find your brother, it is me. If need be, I will spend the rest of my days searching. But I don't think it will take that long."

The force of his conviction brought me to tears. "Thank you. Thank you so much. I will pay you everything I have. I will even pay you with a fine ruby necklace if you'll take it." I dabbed my eyes with my napkin and tried to compose myself.

He handed me his handkerchief and interrupted my blubbering. "Now, now, Miss Peach, I don't want all your money." He was flustered. "This is an unusual situation. In all my years, I've never worked for a—a lady."

I felt foolish. "I'm sorry I came apart. That won't happen again."

"No need to apologize. Your life has been full of hardship and loss. Pay me what you will, but please allow me one small favor."

"What's that?" I asked

"While I'm searching for your brother, I'd also like to settle the score with your uncle."

"What do you mean?" I asked.

He raised his eyebrows and tilted his head.

"Oh, that won't be necessary. I just want to find my brother."

"It would be my pleasure."

Mr. Sirringo was one of the country's best detectives, and I feared my secrets would eventually be revealed. So I told him that I shot my uncle while he was playing cards. I didn't tell him that I could have saved myself from rape if I had just given up the damned ruby necklace. When I described what transpired during the poker game, he roared with laughter.

"Mr. Sirringo! What about those two innocent souls who

died in ensuing chaos?"

"Oh, right." He cleared his throat. "In my experience there's no such thing as an innocent man. Ahhh," he sighed and downed the rest of his wine. Then he leaned back in his chair and asked, "Is that it? Is that your biggest secret?"

"No. Actually it's not." I told him how I tried to hock the ruby necklace to a local pawnbroker. In fact I told him the whole story of what happened with Red Farrell and Dolly. When I got to the point where Red Farrell died laughing, and I was standing there with Dolly over my twat, Detective Sirringo burst out laughing again. This time he laughed so hard, I thought he'd fall out of his chair. I felt Red Farrell then, standing in the corner with his arms crossed, watching the detective have a good belly roll at his expense.

"Mr. Sirringo." I tried to interrupt his fit of laughter, but it made him laugh even harder. "Detective Sirringo!" I couldn't help the smile in my voice. "Sir, I felt very bad for taking the life of Red Farrell. It really isn't funny." I stifled a giggle.

He finally composed himself. "Listen, Red Farrell was one of the vilest men to walk God's green earth. Every bounty hunter west of the Mississippi would have been right overjoyed to put a bullet in him and collect the reward."

Red Farrell's ghost moved closer to the detective and tried to stare him down. Of course, Mr. Sirringo was blind to his presence.

"Still, I don't think he aimed to kill me, just steal the jewels."

"I wouldn't bet on it. You know how you stay alive in my business? You don't give them the chance. If you think they're fixing to shoot, you shoot first. These are outlaws we're talking about, Miss Peach. You think they have any scruples?"

I looked at Red Farrell's ghost and he looked caught out, like he'd been duping me all this time into thinking he wasn't so bad. He slipped out of the room, and I never saw him or felt his presence again.

Mr. Sirringo shook his head and chuckled. "On the train ride back from New York, Pearl told me you were a dangerous woman. When I met you I couldn't imagine what she meant. But I've been dying to find out. I like a lady with spunk and a strong backbone." He fished in his pocket for something.

"We can retire to the parlor if you'd like to smoke or drink spirits."

I rang a bell, and Nell came out to clear the table.

In the parlor, the detective stood by the fireplace and lit a pipe as I retrieved a jewelry box containing the ruby necklace from a locked table drawer. I sat in a chair with the box in my lap.

"Mr. Sirringo—"

"Please, call me Charlie or Chas."

"Are you superstitious?"

"No, not at all. I'm a man of science. To be honest with you, I view most religion as elaborate superstition." He sucked on his pipe.

I opened the jewel box, picked up the ruby necklace, stood up, walked over to him, and extended my hand. "That's good, because I wish to pay you with this."

He looked at the jewels and then at me, perplexed. He held the pipe in one hand, took the ruby necklace in the other, and inspected it.

I explained. "That necklace is real. However, I believe it is cursed. Would you take it as payment?"

As he inspected it, he became transfixed by the rubies. "You don't have to tell me these are real rubies. I can tell. Are you certain you want to pay me with them? They are worth far more than my fees. I could become a man of leisure. Then what would I do with myself?"

"I'm absolutely sure. In fact, you will be doing me a favor by taking them. I'm also sure you will find some interesting way to spend your time, Detective."

"Please, call me Chas. And what shall I call you? I certainly can't keep calling you after a piece of fruit."

THIRTY

His question stumped me. I'd been called some variation of Peach for so long that I wasn't sure Ophelia still existed. I'd told him most everything about myself, so why not my name? I wasn't trying to please him or be someone other than myself. He still seemed to like me—Ophelia Oatman.

"I was once Ophelia Oatman. But I haven't been her for a long time."

"Who have you been?"

"Miss Peach."

"Pearl's peach?"

"Everyone's peach, or at least anyone who paid to pluck me."

"And you closed the Doll House brothel, why? Don't you want to be Miss Peach anymore?" He handed me the necklace.

I took the necklace and held it in my palm. "I have enough money now. Besides, Miss Peach is rotten inside. She is the fruit of my ruin."

Detective Sirringo watched closely as I put the necklace back in its box and locked it in the table drawer.

I looked at him and smiled. "Anyway, times are changing. I met with the mayor and we couldn't come to an agreement." I didn't describe my degrading meeting with the mayor, how he'd called me a juicy peach in front of a group of pompous men, how they'd laughed, how he'd locked his door and tried to show me his terms. "I don't know how Pearl dealt with all those sorts of men, but she seemed to have them in her pocket."

His eyes widened. He put his hand to the corner of his mouth like he was telling me a secret. "She may have had them in more than just her pocket."

I laughed. The detective sure had a sense of humor.

He pointed to the drawer where I'd locked the jewels. "Are you really keeping a priceless ruby necklace in that flimsy table drawer?" His mustache hid his lips, but his eyes smiled.

"It may be the safest place. After all who would suspect it?"

The next morning we met in the study after breakfast to discuss the search for Ezekiel. With an air of confidence and authority, Detective Sirringo spread a map of the Utah Territory across Pearl's old desk. He stood behind her desk, leaned over, and studied it. Sunlight from the window behind him danced on a slice of the map and filled me with hopeful anticipation.

The ray of light disappeared. Overcome by doubt, I panicked. "Detective Sirringo, I must be able to trust you. Last night, I told you things about myself, for which I could be hung. How can I ensure that you will be loyal to me, and that I can trust you? Is the ruby necklace adequate payment?"

He looked up from the map. "The ruby necklace is more than adequate payment. But I'll need money for expenses. I'm not a lawman, Miss Oatman." He stood to his full height and addressed me. "By virtue of being my employer, you have my unwavering loyalty. Believe me, despite your past occupation, this is a more honorable assignment than most of the ones I had for the Pinkerton Agency."

"Pearl once told me never to trust a Pinkerton."

"She was right. A Pinkerton takes an oath and his only allegiance is to the Pinkerton Agency. But I am no longer a Pinkerton, Miss Oatman. I work for you now. Would you like me to take an oath and pledge my allegiance to you?"

"That won't be necessary. I thank you for your patience. I've had many unfortunate experiences with men. Trust is difficult."

He looked down at the map. "There's a lot of righteousness in this world but not much right. Neither the Anarchists nor the Pinkertons have any respect for the law, man's law or God's law." He looked up at me. "Now let's get down to the business of finding your brother, shall we? Come look at this map and show me where you grew up, some places you traveled, and where you think your brother was most likely to go."

"Okay. But it was ten years ago. What do you think the chances are he's anywhere near there?"

"People are like pigeons. They've got built-in homing devices. Even if they wander far, they often return to their roots."

I stood next to Charlie and pointed out Grafton on the map. While standing so close to him, I felt a spark between us and tried to will it away. I could not jeopardize the search for Zeke. And I would not subject myself to yet another disastrous affair. I stepped away. "Uncle Luther came during the Ute War. He wanted to get rid of Zeke. Even though Zeke wasn't quite a man, he was tall and mighty fierce. He was a threat, so Uncle Luther framed him for trading secrets to Black Hawk. A posse of Mormons chased Zeke out of town." The memories of the night Zeke ran away trickled back. "I stalled them the best I could because I was almost certain they wanted to hang him. They already hated him for being a half-breed. I don't know. After the dust settled, I think Zeke would've tried to find a Gentile settlement, like a railroad or mining camp. He would have steered cleared of Mormons the best he could."

"Gentile? What exactly does that mean?" He screwed up his face in confusion and distaste.

"The Mormons call themselves Saints and everyone else, even the Jews, they call Gentiles."

"I see. Well you'd make a good detective, Ophelia. That's exactly what I was thinking. After a period of hiding, I think he would have tried to find work in the mines or on the railroad. Most of the railroad laborers have been let go, so I'd say he's most likely in a mining camp. Now look at this. See this place here?" He pointed to an area on the map south of Grafton and north of Saint George. "This place used to be called Rockpile. Then there was a silver stampede and now it's a full-fledged town called Silver Reef. There's an active mine and a population of about fifteen hundred residents. I had a brief assignment there. It's one of the only non-Mormon settlements around, and it's also the only place in the country where they've ever found silver in sandstone." He hesitated and looked at the map. "There's also this here boomtown, Frisco." He pointed to an area south of Chicken Creek. "This is a wild and dangerous place. I can take the rail right there and start snooping around. If I don't find anything there, I'll buy a horse and ride over to Silver Reef. What do you think about that plan?"

"I think it's a fine plan, and I would be pleased if you could start as soon as possible. We can go to the bank, see to your rail ticket, and make sure you have everything you need to depart tomorrow."

The spring sun had hardened the muddy streets, so we decided to walk downtown. I held my head up and felt confident walking with Charlie down Fifth Street. I didn't have to endure the catcalls and propositions, which I was subjected to when unaccompanied. Anyone who had disrespected Pearl would have found himself pulled into an alley and beaten. She always kept a ruffian in her pocket who enjoyed that kind of work. When we closed the Doll House, we dismissed all of our men.

The social reformers hadn't changed anything on Fifth Street. Pimps and the proprietors of gambling dens ushered those in the know through narrow doorways leading to tunnels, which opened into opium and gambling dens, cribs, and illicit saloons. Most of the activities that had taken place on street level were now underground. You name it and you could find it down there. Because it was all underground, those who had formerly feared being seen in a saloon or house of ill repute could now visit in relative anonymity. I'd always known about the tunnels, although as a parlor house girl I'd been spared the seediest elements of The Street.

Detective Sirringo confessed he'd spent so much time living undercover with outlaws that he was uncomfortable in polite society. We had that in common. But we really didn't fit into the rough demimonde either. We were both misfits.

We went to the bank on Fourth Street and I withdrew an ample amount of cash for his expenses. Having enough wealth to hire a man made me feel powerful. For it had always been the other way around. Yet the cynical side of me feared I would never see him again. What recourse would I have if he took off with the money? I hoped the promise of the ruby necklace would keep him honest.

On the walk back to the house, Charlie told me that although he'd never worked for a woman, he was honored to be on my case. My cynicism melted, and I believed he sincerely wanted to help me. In some respects he seemed as lonely and as lost as I was.

That evening I ate dinner in the kitchen rather than in the dining room with Charlie. I did not want to seem rude, but I feared we were becoming too familiar. When I was going up to my room in the attic to retire for the night, we nearly collided in the hallway. He looked from me to the narrow attic stairs puzzled. "Where are you going?"

"My private chambers are in the attic."

He gestured to the many empty bedrooms on the second floor. "You have so many spacious rooms here. Why do you live in the attic?"

I looked at the doors to the bedrooms. I didn't want to

remember what had happened in those rooms. I smiled tightly and was careful with my words. "Yes, well, I'm just a creature of habit, I suppose. Sleep well, Mr. Sirringo." In reality, Pearl and the ghosts of the customers haunted the house.

"Sweet dreams, Ophelia."

As I climbed the stairs to the attic, I sensed his gaze and the small smile hiding under his mustache. I could not sleep that night. I had no use for lustful feelings toward him, and yet I couldn't seem to keep them at bay. Perhaps it was my nature, caused by red hair and a misshapen cranium.

THIRTY-ONE

On May 2, 1883, Detective Sirringo took the Utah Central to Salt Lake where he would take the Southern train to the end of the line at Frisco. Before he left, he told me about his childhood on a cattle ranch in southwest Texas. When he was twelve, his parents were killed in a minor Civil War skirmish. At the time of his parents' death, he was already roping and breaking mustangs, so he became an apprentice drover. He was as comfortable in the saddle and sleeping on the ground as he was riding in coaches and staying in hotels. He considered himself a cowboy detective, not like the flat-footed eastern greenhorns he loved to ridicule.

An eternity of two and a half weeks passed before I received a telegram from him. My hands shook as I held the envelope, which he had sent via the Wells Fargo telegraph office in Silver Reef. The telegraph said:

Complications arise. I believe I have found your brother. He is armed and dangerous. If I approach, I'm afraid only one of us will be left standing. It's possible I have been recognized and he believes I'm a Pinkerton. Please advise.

"What! Oh, no. Wait!" I yelled at the telegram delivery boy. He was in the street and already had one leg over his early-model safety bicycle. He stopped and looked at me.

"Stay right there!" I grabbed my money purse and ran down the front path toward him.

"This is urgent. I need a ride to the telegraph office."

"Uh, sorry, miss, I don't think I should do that."

"A dollar and I'll jump off before anyone sees me. I don't weigh that much."

"A dollar! Okay, sure, jump on."

I hopped on the front of his bicycle and held on for dear life. It was a wobbly five-minute ride. But the boy was pleased to earn a dollar. I ran into the telegraph office and began to fill out a form. How could I be so close to finding my brother only to lose him? What was wrong with Detective Sirringo? Why couldn't he approach a man without killing him? It was a good thing that telegrams charge by the letter, or I would have unleashed a windy diatribe.

Leave S.R. at once. I will board next train to Frisco. Meet me there with a horse. Will bring my own saddle. From Frisco will travel to S.R. where I will approach Z. Quite certain he won't shoot me.

Zeke had never been a dangerous man, and I had never been a dangerous woman. Our lives had made us that way. To the annoyance of the telegraph operator, I paced the telegraph office for one hour and ten minutes until I received a telegram back from the detective:

I will depart S.R. today and ride through the night. Disembark train at Milford NOT Frisco. Will wait at station for you with horse.

I began walking at a fast clip back home. The delivery boy rode up and offered me a lift at no extra charge. Sweet thing, he said that he didn't want to take advantage of me, and a dollar was worth a round trip.

Nell stared at me as I pulled out a trunk from Pearl's room and started looking through her old wardrobe for a travel dress. I threw several items into the trunk before I abandoned it for a medium-sized carpet bag.

"Where you going, Miss Peach?"

The catatonic vulnerability in her voice reminded me that she'd be on her own, and although she was as tough as rubber boots, she depended on me.

I continued to pack as I spoke. "Just a short trip by rail and horse." I stopped and looked at her. "I will be back. Mr. Greene is our only boarder. He's a nice gentleman with simple needs and he's settled in here. See to his needs. But if anyone else inquires about a room, just tell them we're full."

"We've got rooms."

I let out a heavy sigh and put my hands on my hips. "I know that, Nell, but tell them we're full. Make things easy for yourself while I'm away."

She nodded. I felt guilty for being short with her, but I was in such a frantic state. I finally settled on a cornflower blue traveling dress and my riding habit. I searched for my boots and came across the boots of Red Farrell. I picked up one of the boots and stared at it. The leather was soft now, even though they'd scarcely been worn. Trying to remember when I'd worn them over the years, I wondered how they could possibly look so worn. They seemed to have a life of their own. They would be far more practical, yet much less fashionable, than the ladies boots I planned to wear. Without thinking I slipped them on just to see how they felt. I grabbed a few other necessities, only what would fit in the carpet bag. Forgetting about the boots, I went downstairs, unlocked the sideboard drawer, took out the ruby necklace, and called Nell to help me.

We stood in front of the hall mirror. I held up my hair while she fumbled with the clasp of the necklace. I looked at Old Nell, and myself, and the rubies. In time I'd be old and haggard like Nell. But the rubies would never age. They reminded me of everyone and everything I'd lost. Finally I would be rid of them. I'd give them to the detective and get Ezekiel in return. I was transfixed with the image of the three of us in the mirror. The rubies were more than just jewels to me. After Nell fastened the clasp, I tucked them out of sight under the collar of my dress where I thought they would be safe. And so I would begin the journey to find Ezekiel, laden with my past: the cursed rubies, and Red Farrell's boots.

I waited for my train on the platform at Union Station. I'd been in such a rush to get there that I forgot to take off Red Farrell's boots. I looked down and noticed them just as the ground began shaking and the air rumbling from the approaching train. My heart raced. I looked like a fool. But it was too late to do anything about it. Tension from longing, fear, and excitement filled my body, and I could hardly wait to board the train and take my seat. The steam engine's eerie whistle pierced the rumbling and filled me with a sudden dread because it sounded like a lamentation. For almost a decade, I had heard the whistle cry over and over with its high notes of promise and low tones of loss. My train finally arrived and I climbed the stairs to begin another journey.

The Utah Central took me from Ogden to Salt Lake City. Then I took the Utah Southern to Milford, which was the last stop before the end of the line in Frisco. During all my years earning money from trysts with railroad passengers who passed through Ogden, I had only been a passenger on a railcar twice. Both times I had only traveled as far as Salt Lake City. When Pearl went to the great metropolis of New York City, I had wanted so badly to accompany her. Then I could say I'd truly been somewhere.

Detective Sirringo had told me of his travels all over the western frontier. He had also been to most of the big eastern cities. He'd even once taken a ship around the tip of South America and up to San Francisco. I looked out the train window at the rushing meadows and remembered traveling the roads before the march of progress had trampled the fields and replaced them with railroad tracks. I remembered traveling with my family to Grafton all full of purpose and a higher calling. We had believed we were blessed by the Heavenly Father. Looking back on all that had happened to us, it seemed a presumptuous and naïve belief.

I tried to compose what I would say to Detective Sirringo. I'd been rattled and irritated by his telegram insinuating that he might have to kill my brother. Although I appreciated that he'd found Zeke and was willing to accompany me on the one-hundred-mile trip from Milford to Silver Reef, I didn't understand why things had taken a violent turn.

At Milford I disembarked to a small desolate depot with more cattle and sheep than people. The train continued southwest to Frisco. I wondered why Charlie told me to get off at Milord instead of Frisco. It took me a few minutes to spot him amongst the stockmen herding cattle onto railcars. Dressed in the getup of a Texas stockman, he blended with the rest of them. In Ogden, he had donned city clothes and blended in as a gentleman traveler. With his stockman's hat and boots, he seemed taller than his five foot, eight inches. As the son of an Irish mother and an Italian father, he'd had a pleasant complexion that was neither dark nor pale. But exposure to sun on his journey had darkened his skin, and the sides of his mustache had grown long, drooping past his mouth, making it difficult to recognize him as the man I'd met in Ogden.

I had the impression that he was chewing tobacco, but as I approached I saw it was the end of his mustache. I later found out he had chewed tobacco for a long time and had managed to kick that habit only to replace it with the embarrassing habit of chewing on his own mustache. He averted his eyes as he relieved me of my bag and saddle.

"I apologize." He stared at me intently. "My telegram must have startled you."

"Detective Sirringo, I hired you to find my brother, not kill him."

"Yes. I believe I have found your brother. Although I could not confirm it because if I had approached the man in question, it most likely would have resulted in a gunfight."

"I see. Well, you did the right thing to back down and send a telegram. Thank you for your discretion."

At the words *back down,* he straightened. "I'm not known to be a man who backs down. In the past, I've had the authority to arrest and apprehend. Or I'd call in the local authorities. I've never hunted a man so I could bear him good news. I did not realize it would be so difficult."

"Well, I'm here now. Just lead me to Ezekiel. As soon as he sees me, he'll recognize me and there will be no problems."

A worried look crossed his face. He changed the subject. "No coach for you, just a horse! You're my kind of gal. I had forgotten you were a pioneer, Miss Oatman." He looked around for other luggage. "Is this all you have?"

"No sense weighing down the horses with anything I don't need. A true pioneer where I'm from would have walked. Perhaps we can purchase a hand-cart and pull it to Silver Reef just for fun. What do you say, Detective?"

He laughed at my joke. "I'm sure glad you wanted to ride horseback rather than coach. Gilmer and Salisbury run a daily between Milford and Silver Reef, but they're targets for road agents and thieves. Anyway, wait till you see your mount."

She was a perfectly civilized white pony. Detective Sirringo had secured himself a rather uncivilized bronco. It seemed the challenge of riding a brute took his mind off the long monotonous stretches of sand and sage. He said he'd never traveled the country with a lady in tow. I rolled my eyes and reminded him of my youth, the days before I became a painted lady outfitted with fancy dresses and fashionable boots and bonnets. Secretly,

I worried. I'd lived in comfort for so long, I'd turned green.

He asked me if I wanted to get a good night's sleep and a square meal before we hit the trail. I told him that I wanted to get going as soon as possible.

"That is good," he said. "My identity may be known, and if Ezekiel thinks a Pinkerton is trailing him, there's a chance he'll skip town."

"What? You mean after being so close, we could lose him?"

He looked to the horizon and sighed. "I shouldn't have said anything. There's a possibility it's not even him." He spread a small blanket over my pony's back, hoisted the saddle onto her, and began fastening it.

"Is he a wanted man? Why would he run?"

"I don't know. But he seems to have a guilty conscience."

I wanted to get going so we could arrive in Silver Reef before the man who might be Zeke left. Unfortunately, we had to stop at the mercantile and purchase additional supplies. I needed two canteens and a bedroll. We also bought dried elk, hard tack, beans, and Johnny cakes, all kinds of things I hadn't eaten since I was a kid. I urged him to hurry. But he took his sweet time and meticulously packed our saddlebags. I paced back and forth with all the dignity of a child who needs to use the privy.

"I'm not trying to dawdle or irritate you, Miss Oatman. Trust me, we will pay later if we don't take the time to pack correctly now."

I grabbed my carpet bag. "Don't watch me. I'm going to change my clothes over there." I pointed to a thicket of sage and pinon pine. He looked at me, surprised, went back to packing, and failed to suppress a smirk. Barely concealed by the pinion pines, I stripped off my cornflower blue traveling dress and took out my riding clothes; a chemise and jacket, and a custom tailored split-riding skirt so I could ride astride. There was freedom in not having a reputation to defend. When I returned he looked at my boots and smirked.

"I took these off the body of Red Farrell after I shot him."

He raised his brows, nodded, and continued readying our mounts.

"I suppose I am a dangerous woman. I've never claimed to be a lady. I certainly have no intention of riding sidesaddle for one hundred miles. I don't care what anyone thinks of me or my boots."

He looked at me and smiled. "Truth be told, I've never had much use or patience for ladies."

He had packed all our supplies in the saddlebags and strapped a shotgun across the back of my saddle. A rifle lay across the back of his saddle, and he wore two colts on his person. We began riding.

He looked at me sideways. "Did you know they arrested a woman in Montana for riding into town sidesaddle? That is a shameful waste of a lawman's time." He shook his head in disgust.

On the trail, he told me story after story of his days as a cowboy: breaking broncos, and going undercover trying to infiltrate outlaw gangs and break up anarchists. Riding on the open range brought out the storyteller in him. From his stories, he sounded like a hero in a dime novel. He'd narrowly escaped death several times, including a mine explosion, which blew the hands and face off a man standing next to him. I didn't know if he was vain, or if he was trying to impress me, or both. His head seemed as big as Texas. I supposed he'd earned his reputation as a crack shot. If his legend was as big as he made out, no wonder why they'd recognized him in Silver Reef.

I had worked for over a decade as a painted lady in one of the territory's roughest towns, so I had a few stories of my own to tell. But I held my tongue. Most of my stories were lewd, and although I tried to get over my shame, I didn't want to wave my petticoat flag and continually remind Detective Sirringo of what I'd been. He might get it into his mind that I was up for that business again.

After riding for fifteen miles over relatively flat land, we reached the small town of Minersville. He said since it was the last outpost until Cedar City, we had to stop. We filled our canteens and had an early supper. After Minersville, we rode another grueling thirty miles. As the twilight disappeared and darkness descended, the road became increasingly rough. I was scared and saddle sore. He said we could continue riding in the dark because he knew where to water the horses and make camp.

"I know exactly where we're going," he assured me.

"That's good," I said. "Because I sure don't. I've never known where I was going."

A sliver of moon finally came out, but it wasn't enough to see by. It was late night by the time we stopped riding. Luckily his word was true. We came upon the exact spot he had slept the previous night. The ground was still flattened from his bedroll. We saw to the horses but were too exhausted to do anything else. We collapsed onto our bedrolls and fell into deep sleep.

When I awoke the next morning a coffee pot already sat percolating over a small fire. I helped him tend the horses. We drank our coffee and ate bacon and Johnny cakes in relative silence. I braided my hair and decided to keep it that way for the rest of our journey. As the day wore on, he began to talk more and more. We rode across a range, then through a valley into Cedar City. We restocked and revived. Charlie asked if I wanted to find lodging, but I insisted we press on.

At sunset we found a nice place with some rock shelter to make camp. While he went after some quail, I gathered wood, started a fire, and dug up some sego root and prickly pear. I was cutting the spines out of the prickly pear when he returned swinging a plump pair of quail.

He held the birds up by their feet. "I snuck up and caught 'em in the act."

The male's plume dangled like a sagging upside-down question mark.

"It's mating time, Detective. Did you at least let them finish?"

He laughed off my question, although I hadn't been joking.

"What are you doing with that cactus?" he asked.

"A little green to go with the meat. Don't you Texas boys eat vegetables, or are you strictly the flesh-eating kind?"

"Well, I try and eat greens when I can. But I never ate a cactus, that's for sure."

At dinner, he was surprised and pleased that the cactus was palatable, and I was happy that I could teach him something. After we ate, he pulled out a harmonica. We both stretched out on our bedrolls by the fire. He played and I sang. First, "Oh! Susanna," then "When Johnny Comes Marching Home." We ended with "Amazing Grace." He played well. I supposed it was a skill perfected on lonely nights traveling the west in search of train robbers and outlaws. While he played, his hands obscured his mouth, but his large eyes filled with sentiment as he looked at me singing across the fire.

I had sung to Pearl on her deathbed, and I had sung in smoky saloons and dance halls. I had sung sultry tunes at the Doll House with the aim to seduce. Yet only under the stars in the cool night air, did my voice feel clean and free. When we finished "Amazing Grace," warm tears rolled down my dusty cheeks. I smiled and hoped that he would know I was happy and that he didn't have to worry about his blubbering fair-sexed companion. With wet glistening eyes, he hollered a rebel-yell and slapped his knee.

"Ophelia!" He looked at me and smiled wide, "We make a

good pair!" A coyote filled the following silence with one lonely howl followed by a discordant chorus.

"The coyotes think so too, Detective Sirringo."

"Please call me Charlie." He smiled. "You sing like an angel."

I laughed and sighed. "Too bad they don't let whores into heaven."

"Awww, who wants to go there anyway? Full of temperance ladies, reformers, and preachers—sounds more like hell."

"You know, if you were Mormon, you could be the ruler of your own eternal kingdom."

He snorted. "What would I want with that? Texas is big enough for me."

I nodded and smiled. "Charlie," I began again, "what do you think the chances are that this man is my brother?"

"Well . . ." He absentmindedly chewed on the side of his mustache. "I'm almost positive."

"How are you so sure?"

"Although he's a half-breed Indian, in some way that I can't really put my finger on, he looks like you. Also, he goes by the name of Eli."

"That was my father's name!"

"I know."

"How did you know that?" I asked.

"Miss Oatman —"

"Please, call me Ophelia."

He grinned. "Ophelia, remember I'm not just a Texas cow drover who plays mouth organ to the stars. I'm also a former Pinkerton, and Pinkertons is arguably the best detective agency in the country, maybe the world."

I thought of Scotland Yard, but didn't say anything. Perhaps all of Charlie's tall tales were real. But a larger than life character from the pages of a dime-store novel was too good to be true. I wondered what his flaw was.

He stood up, raised his fists to the sky, and cracked his neck from side to side. His dark fire-lit shadow stretched long on the sand behind him. He retrieved a bottle of spirits from his saddlebag and then sat down by the fire again. "Just a little nightcap." He uncorked the bottle. "I regret that I don't have a glass. Would you like some?" He carefully wiped the rim with his kerchief and handed the bottle to me.

I took a sip, bracing for the usual gut-rot whiskey. The smooth orangey taste was surprisingly pleasant. I looked at the unmarked bottle and took another sip. "Mmmm, that's good. What is it?"

"French brandywine."

"I think I've had something like this before." I took another sip and handed it back. "It's delicious. Thank you."

"Have more, please." He held out the bottle to me.

"No, thank you. I don't want to take it all."

"I normally liquor myself on something a little stronger, Miss—Ophelia. I brought this along for you."

"That was very thoughtful. Let's save it for later. You never know when we'll have to hunker down from a storm."

"Good thinking, best to hit the hay and get an early start." He stood up and put the bottle away. When he came back, he paced in front of the fire and looked at where I had laid out my bedroll far away from his on the other side of the fire. He stroked his chin and chewed on his mustache again. "I don't mean to sound improper, but can I make a suggestion?"

"What's that?"

"Just in case of danger, I think we ought to sleep close together." He patted one of his six-shooters. "With this at my side and a Winchester pillow, I can protect us from anything or anyone that tries to sneak up in the night."

I didn't know what to do or think. After a day's riding, then making music and drinking brandywine, I could feel an unwanted affection growing between us. I'd felt it from the day he got off the train, and it was growing stronger. I tried to suppress my lustful nature. After I'd spent nearly ten years working as an upstairs girl, a proper romance was impossible. My mission was to find Zeke, not to have a tryst with a mustache-chewing cowboy detective.

"For safety?" I asked.

He held his hands in the air. "As your employee, I feel the duty to protect you." He put his hands behind his back and said, "I'll keep my hands to myself, promise."

"Okay." I began walking away from camp so I could relieve myself before bed. I called to him over my shoulder. "You really ought to stop chewing on your mustache. A habit like that can mark a man."

"Was I doing that again?"

"Yes." I turned and smiled.

"Where you going?"

"Just the privy, I'll be all right. I'm a pioneer girl." I squatted in the bushes, remembering a story about a little pioneer girl who'd been dragged away by Indians when she wandered off to pick flowers. The frontier was a dangerous place.

When I returned, he'd moved our bedrolls close together. He sat against a boulder with his drover's coat over him and his boots still on. His Winchester sat right next to him. He had taken off his hat and placed it between the back of his head and the rock. He smiled at me in the moonlight.

I lowered myself to the ground, got comfortable on the bedroll, and looked up at the night sky. An awkward silence stretched between us. I was aware of my every breath. Charlie's eyes closed and his head drooped. I remembered having romantic relations outside with Whiskey Pete and Samuel Cox. Some of the whores were forced to work outdoors in alleys and pens. I'd never had to stoop that low. I had enjoyed sex under the stars. Those nights had been magical. If Samuel Cox and Peter hadn't betrayed me, they would have been good memories.

The possibility that Detective Sirringo was full of bull crossed my mind. Perhaps he was a charlatan detective who would lead me on a wild goose chase and take the ruby necklace despite his failure. Perhaps he was a bad man, the kind who liked to cut up whores. Perhaps he would rape and kill me, or gouge out my eyes.

I looked over at him. He'd awakened and looked up, contemplating the stars as innocent as a baby watching a mechanical toy.

He looked down at me. "Are you comfortable?" He squinted in the dark. "You look distressed."

"I was just thinking."

"Don't think, sleep." He closed his eyes again.

And I wished I could. But sleep did not come easily that night. Soon enough he was snoring. He was a deep sleeper. His mouth hung open so wide I imagined a spider or scorpion crawling into it. I marveled that one of his enemies hadn't already killed him in his sleep. The night became colder, and I caught a chill. I moved closer to Charlie, snuggled under his coat, and finally fell asleep with his warmth on my back.

Sometime in the middle of the night or maybe the early morning before sunrise, I felt a stabbing pain in my stomach. The agony crippled me. I couldn't stand or walk, so I crawled away from where we slept. I vomited onto the sand, gagging and retching over and over until I yearned for a bullet in the head. I must have passed out, because the next morning sun tickled my eyelids and I awoke in Charlie's arms with his coat over me. I felt drained, and weak, and embarrassed.

He held a canteen to my lips. "See if you can hold down some water."

"No. I'm okay. We have to get going. We have to find Ezekiel."

"You're in no condition to ride."

"I must. We can't risk losing him."

Charlie got up and gently guided me into a sitting position. He tucked his coat around me to protect me from the morning chill. "Ride on the back of my horse until you recover some strength. If you fall off your horse and injure yourself, things will get a lot worse." He began packing up camp. "I don't suppose you want anything to eat?"

I shook my head and squinted. It was difficult to keep my eyes open.

"Who's Samuel?" Charlie asked as he saddled the horses.

I looked at him surprised. "Samuel? Why do you ask?"

"You were delirious. You kept yelling, 'Samuel, don't leave me. Please don't leave me.' I kept telling you I wasn't Samuel and I wasn't going to leave you. But I couldn't get any sense into you."

"I'm sorry. I've been such a burden. Thank you for staying and caring for me. I'm not usually like this. I'll be better soon."

"I wouldn't leave any lady out here, even if I wasn't working for her. I don't know who Samuel was, or what he did, but I'm not like him. You can trust me, Ophelia."

As we rode that day, it took all the strength I had just to hold on to Charlie. We trailed my pony and went at a slow pace. But at least we were moving forward, getting closer to Silver Reef and Ezekiel. We stopped at noon. I drank some water and had a nibble of a Johnny cake.

"I haven't eaten game for a long while. It could have been the quail."

Charlie nodded. "That could do it. How are you feeling?"

"I'm feeling a little stronger. I think I can ride."

We left behind snow-capped peaks and descended into a warmer, arid climate filled with sand and sage. Parched throats and the heat evaporated our conversations. Even Charlie's stories eventually dried up. A giant sandstone reef appeared, stretched as far as the eye could see. It reminded me of my childhood—my family. Our lives and struggles had transpired in a gigantic amphitheater of strange magnificent rocks. "Are we close?"

"Very close." Charlie stopped and let his horse drink from the creek. He squinted into the distance ahead and grimaced. "I'm not so sure it's a good idea that you meet your brother. I don't think he's the same person you remember."

There was something about Ezekiel that Charlie didn't want to tell me. "I'm hardly the same person either. I wasn't a whore when we were children."

"Stop!" He looked at me sternly.

I wondered if he'd spoken to any of his male employers with such impunity.

"Don't talk about yourself like that. It's in the past. Put it behind you. Keep it dry."

I got off my pony and let her drink. "Eventually, I will have to tell my brother." I snapped sage leaves from a bush and crushed them between my fingers. "What makes Ezekiel so dangerous that you couldn't approach him?"

"There's been trouble in Silver Reef: labor riots, people disappearing, arson, all sorts of things. I think he's involved. Ezekiel goes by Eli Black now. But some people call him Chinese Red."

"Chinese Red? What does that mean?"

"He worked as a blackleg in the silver mine during a strike. They would never employ him for white wages, so he worked for Celestial wages. Some people say he looks like he's half Chinaman."

I shook my head and felt sad for Zeke. Curse of the half-breed: no race or tribe would accept you. You might belong to any, but none wanted to claim you. I would accept him. I couldn't wait to embrace him. "He's half Indian, not a Celestial."

"All the whites hate him for being a blackleg. Finally he quit, but it was too late. Now he works for Mr. Gee."

"What's a blackleg and who is Mr. Gee?"

"A blackleg is a strikebreaker. Mr. Gee controls the Chinese lottery, opium trade, and a whole lot of Celestial prostitutes in Silver Reef, including a handful of white girls. Silver Reef residents hate the Celestials for taking miners' jobs. Yet many of the whites are hooked on Celestial habits, opium, lottery, and even their girls. A mob tried to burn out Gee, but he just used the opportunity to rebuild bigger and better. Some say he's the richest man in town."

"Silver Reef doesn't sound too different from any other mining town. I'm sure at heart Zeke is still the same. He's just trying to survive."

Charlie nodded, but his eyes told me there was something else. "Silver Reef is the only place in the whole country they ever found silver in sandstone."

I looked at the sandstone reef. "I love being back in red rock country, especially in spring. Summer just about melts the flesh from your bones. I'm sure you've experienced that."

"Have I told you about the desert turtle drive?" Charlie asked. He began telling me a silly story about hard-up drovers trying to herd desert tortoises.

At sunset we stopped riding and made camp. The next day I found out we'd only been about fifteen miles from Silver Reef. Charlie seemed reluctant to leave the wilderness and go into town.

"Would you like to be my sister or my wife?" Charlie asked as he saw to the horses.

After that long in the saddle my brain was addled and my

behind felt like blistered mush. I didn't know what to say, so I just looked at him cockeyed.

Charlie explained. "We don't want to attract scandal or unwanted solicitations, so we should establish false identities."

"Right. A whore traveling with a former Pinkerton in search of a half-breed turned Celestial's henchman is indeed scandalous. What do you want, Charlie? Do you want me to be your wife or your sister?"

"I think we should be married. We'll draw less attention if we're married. I've changed my getup, so hopefully I won't be recognized. Of course, this is just for the purpose of finding Ezekiel."

I smiled. "Of course, I understand. And why are we visiting Silver Reef?"

"We're in the cattle business, just passing through, on our way to Los Angeles. Whatever you do, do not mention to anyone that I'm a detective, especially a former Pinkerton."

I began collecting kindling for the fire. "So what do we want with Zeke?"

Charlie watched me with his hands on his hips. "Remember his name is Eli. Call him Eli. It's okay to tell people we are looking for him as long as no one discovers our true identities. We can say he worked for us once. You should have a fairly brief reunion, and then we should leave Silver Reef. It has the feeling of a town about to explode. I suspect Gee is planning some sort of retaliation. I've been in the middle of riots, and they are no place for the fairer sex." A worried look crossed his face. He lost track of the task he'd been doing and began pacing.

"Come on, Charlie, I'm no owl afraid of the woods. Don't you think Ezekiel will come with us?"

Charlie stopped in his tracks and looked at me. "What do you mean?"

"I wasn't planning on finding my brother just to say a brief

'How do you do?' I want to take him home."

Charlie looked troubled. "Ophelia, you need to meet him first. He's hardly a kitten. It's also possible he's indebted to Mr. Gee. Seems half of the town is."

"Well, I can pay off his debts."

"Perhaps, but not with opium."

We ate salt pork and beans with the rest of the Johnny cakes. I was pretty sure the quail had made me sick. After dinner we sat around the fire. Charlie took out the bottle of brandywine and handed it to me first.

I held the bottle up in a toast and took a little sip. The fire warmed my front, but I felt the cool night air bite my back. The liquor warmed me all over. I warned myself not to drink too much as it always made me overly affectionate. I handed the bottle back to Charlie. "Thank you. Pearl said never to trust sheriffs or Pinkertons. But so far you are all right."

Charlie raised his brows. "Now that's the pot calling the kettle black! I'd no more trust Pearl than a bull in a China shop. Look what she did to you. How old did you say you were when she so kindly took you in?"

"No one did anything to me. I chose my life. Maybe it's just what I am. What I was born to be. The feelings I sometimes have are not natural for a lady."

Charlie scoffed and shook his head. "Ha! Ladies don't act natural. They are the furthest thing from it. Nature knows nothing of ladies and gentlemen, of society and civilization. Here in the wilderness ladies and gentlemen would perish. Real men and women do whatever's necessary to survive. They can't afford pretentions."

I slept well that night. The novelty of Charlie had worn off, and I relaxed in his presence.

THIRTY-TWO

We dawdled the next morning. By the time we arrived in Silver Reef the next day, it was close to candle-lighting time. We were saddle sore, covered with dust, and stank to high heaven. Charlie secured lodging at the Cosmopolitan Hotel. They brought me up a steaming bath. While I bathed in the room, Charlie walked down to the bathhouse. After cleaning ourselves up, we took a late supper at the Cosmopolitan restaurant next to the hotel. With no rail service in Silver Reef, I don't know how they secured such fresh food and fancy English crockery, but the establishment exceeded my expectations.

We took a stroll after dinner. Even though it was late, the town was hopping with all kinds of people, mostly miners, carrying on in the saloons and drabs. The main street sported both clapboard shanties as well as sturdier structures constructed of adobe bricks and stones. A jaunty violin tune drifted from The Elkhorn Saloon competing with the music of a player piano from The Exchange Saloon. A painted lady stood on the porch to The Cabinet Saloon. Tobacco, grilled meat, and the smell of horse dung hung in the air. I urged Charlie into each one of the saloons.

He hesitated and muttered, "A nice married couple wouldn't be poking around in all these saloons."

"Who cares?" I said. "I want to find Zeke." I clutched his elbow and nudged him into the Pioneer Billiard Hall. The sandstone silver mine must have been productive to support the saloons, three breweries, countless tobacco shops, and a huge mercantile. I marveled at how they transported so many goods to a place with no rail service.

Charlie was right. All cleaned up and with a proper dress, I attracted much unwanted attention from the men in the saloons. As in most other mining towns, there was a severe shortage of women in Silver Reef. I didn't want trouble, or for Charlie to get in a scuffle trying to protect my nonexistent honor, so I finally suggested we retire and find Zeke the next day.

Our room at the Cosmopolitan Hotel had two small beds, a sitting area, a wash basin, a mirror, and a writing desk. After three nights on the trail with Charlie, I thought most of the awkwardness between us had dissolved. Yet when we found ourselves alone in candlelit quarters after posing as husband and wife all evening, I felt an arousing uneasiness between us. The room grew smaller. I became intensely aware of each movement and breath.

In the desert, Charlie had slept with his boots on. But in the hotel room he took them off, set his six-shooter on the table, and reclined on the bed. He moaned. "As much as I like sleeping in plain air, I do appreciate a bath and a bed. How do you fare, Miss Ophelia? It sure is nice to see you refreshed."

I rinsed my hands and face in the wash basin. It was easy to get my skin clean since I had stopped painting my face. "Yes, it is quite nice. But I mustn't grow too accustomed as we still have a long journey back."

"How does it feel to be my wife?"

I rattled on while I washed. "It's nice to finally have a man in my employment rather than the other way around. Pearl always said there isn't much difference in becoming someone's wife or being a whore. You either sell yourself to the one or many. At least as whores we got to keep our own money. Pearl hired a few men over the years, but mostly they were rogues. Not the types of men you'd cross the river with, that's for sure." I sat on the bed and bent over to unlace my boots.

Charlie sat up and looked at me, astonished. He hopped out of bed, knelt down, and began to unlace my boots. "And you believed Pearl? She was saying all that to trick you. You poor girl, she took advantage of you, Ophelia."

He stopped unlacing my boot and looked up at me.

I stared at him and tried to control my temper. "She left everything to me. Doesn't that redeem her? Without Pearl, I wouldn't be here about to be reunited with my brother."

He didn't answer. He shook his head and went back to unlacing my boot. "Let me do this. You must be tired. I don't treat you well just because you're my employer. You are a fine and beautiful lady." He stopped and stared into my eyes.

"Charlie!" I shook my head, pulled my foot away, and began to protest. A terrible sadness came over me with the realization that after working ten years as a strumpet, I was ruined for real love. "Don't do this. You know I'm not a lady. Don't pretend you don't know my past. And don't get a notion that I'll give you my favors. We should get a separate room."

He abandoned my boot and sat next to me on the bed. "That's not the way it is. Don't you understand? I have real feelings for you, Ophelia. In all my days, I've never felt this way for anyone." He took my jaw in his hand and forced me to look at him. "It doesn't matter what you were. That's not what you were meant to be." He tried to kiss me. I turned my head.

He persisted. "Just one kiss."

I glanced at him. The end of his mustache had found its way into his mouth, and he was absentmindedly chewing on it—a peculiar habit for such a strong, confident man. He realized what I was looking at, stopped chewing his mustache, took his hand from my jaw, and slumped on the bed, defeated.

I had a weakness for downtrodden men. "I'll give you one

kiss, but only if you promise to stop chewing on your mustache."

He ignited and took my face into his strong hands again. "A kiss is not a violin. There are no strings attached."

I melted under the tenderness of his touch. No one had ever held me like that. He kissed me and I felt almighty warmth. I didn't know if I could stop the torrent of passion that coursed through our hungry bodies and the overwhelming longing, which sprang from our lonely souls.

To my great relief and surprise, I didn't have to. Besides the kiss and the tender removal of my boots, Charlie Sirringo was a gentleman. Being so familiar with the nature of male passion and the strong bodily urge to relieve itself, I knew the willpower Charlie must have had to exert in order to stop at one passionate kiss. He wasn't a gentleman, and I certainly wasn't a lady, but we both put on a good show for each other. Despite his tall tales and self-admiration, I had developed trust and fondness for the detective.

The next day I tried to forget the strong feelings from the previous night and the passionate embrace in which we momentarily found ourselves entangled. The mission of my trip was to find my lost brother, Ezekiel, and on the cusp of that endeavor, I did not want my mind and heart clouded by a torrid love affair that could only lead to disaster, as they all had in the past.

Charlie had been tailing Zeke long enough to know his comings and goings. Unfortunately, Zeke had noticed Charlie tailing him and had already threatened him at least once. I was glad Charlie hadn't tried to confront Zeke.

From a safe distance, we watched the man Charlie believed was Zeke walk into and out of various merchants, collecting for Mr. Gee's Chinese lottery. With his head down, he focused on the lottery tickets and did not notice us watching him. I don't know if I would ever have recognized him if Charlie hadn't pointed him out from across the street. His black hair was longer than I remembered. He was both thicker and taller. He looked up. I gasped at his hardened scowl and the vertical scar on the right side of his face. He adorned himself with a curious mixture of Indian and Chinese talismans, but wore a white man's jacket and a brocade vest. If I hadn't believed he was my brother, I would never have approached him. Charlie hung back while I followed him. Two or three men loitering watched.

"Sir. Excuse me, sir," I called from behind him.

"What do you want?" he yelled without looking back. He continued walking.

I shouted, "I'm looking for my brother, Ezekiel."

He stopped in his tracks and turned slowly around. I noticed a strange tattoo on his neck. He looked at my hair and my face. Our eyes met, and I knew it was him.

"I'll be damned!" he said.

He ran over and picked me up. My feet left the ground. We embraced for a long time. "Little O! I've looked for you everywhere," he whispered into my ear. He put me down and brushed my tears away with his large rough thumb.

A few men had gathered in front of the tobacco store. They started jeering. "Get your hands of that white lady, you red Chink!" someone shouted. Fury flashed in Zeke's eyes. His hand rested on his gun.

I grabbed his wrist. "Ignore them," I pleaded.

Charlie walked over to the group of men and appeared to be smoothing things out. Zeke stared at Charlie.

"Who is that? Is that your husband?"

"No. We're just pretending he is for now so we don't blow his cover. He's a detective," I whispered. "I hired him to find you."

"Well, I almost shot him last week. That dang fool's been tailing me everywhere, as if I hadn't noticed him."

I almost defended Charlie and his reputation. Instead I said,

"Oh, Zeke, let's sit and have tea somewhere. We have ten years to catch up on."

He looked at the papers in his hand. Uncertainty crossed his face. "Of course, a quick cup," he said. "Then I must finish these rounds, or Mr. Gee will have me roasted. I can meet you again as soon as I'm done. Then I'll be all yours." He smiled and laughed. "Little O! All grown up! I never thought I'd see you again." He shoved the papers into his pocket, put his arm around me, and led me down Main Street.

He escorted me all the way to the end of Main Street into China Town. We went into a teahouse and sat at a rickety table.

"No one will bother us here." He looked around and shook his head. "I'm half white. I was raised by whites. The Chinese ways are as foreign to me as feathers to a fish, but they accept me and the whites do not. Hungry ghosts, is what Mr. Gee calls them." He motioned to an ancient Chinese woman. She nodded and brought tea.

An old Chinese man with a long gray braid emerged from the back room and pulled a ragged curtain shut behind him. The curtain hid the opium eaters from sight, but it didn't stop the sweetly scented smoke from filling the room. The smell reminded me of Pearl's last days.

I wanted to tell Zeke he looked well. But he did not. I saw behind the scar. I saw the happy handsome boy he'd once been. Other people would not see him that way.

The familiar and somewhat deferential way they treated Ezekiel in the tea shop led me to believe he frequented the establishment. He seemed comfortable there in a way he hadn't been on the street. Still he was unsettled, as if I was keeping him from some urgent business.

He told me after going into hiding for a while, he tried to return to Grafton to find me, but was chased out again. He said he almost didn't make it out alive. He said everywhere he went, he tried to find me, just in case I'd run away. He admitted that he'd finally given up. He didn't tell me how he came by the scar on his face.

"When I got to Silver Reef, I fell on hard times. But becoming a blackleg only made things worse. I became an opium addict. Mr. Gee helped me. If it weren't for him, I doubt I'd be alive to see you today. I'm indebted to him."

I leaned across our steaming cups of tea and whispered. "Zeke, I can help. I know I don't look it now, but I have money. Lots of money. I can pay your debts. Come home with me and start over. I own a boarding house in Ogden. I could really use a man to help."

He sat back and furrowed his brow. "I'm happy for you. But Ophelia, how did you come into such wealth?"

I froze. I looked him in the eyes but could not speak the truth. "Well, it's a long story and one I'm not too proud of. What matters is that I've found you, and we can be together again. You are my only family."

Zeke swallowed, looked at the floor, and then up at me. "The problem is I'm indebted to Gee for more than just money, Little O."

"Maybe, but everyone has their price."

"Did you marry a wealthy man?"

"No, I'm not married."

The door to the teahouse opened. Charlie saw us, nodded at me, and took a seat at a small table by the front door.

Ezekiel sighed, shook his head, and shifted in his chair. "Can we lose him now? I already have a shadow."

Charlie tried to act casual, but he couldn't help constantly looking over at me. I wished he would wait outside. The kiss had changed something between us. I feared his presence would scare Zeke away. I smiled at Charlie, nodded my head a few times, gave him the okay sign with my fingers, and then jerked my head and eyes toward the door. That should have given him the clue to go away. But he stayed and stared at me with the intense, unbroken loyalty of a guard dog.

Zeke stared daggers across the room at Charlie. I could see why Charlie thought he was formidable, and I was glad he hadn't decided to approach him without me.

I talked low so Charlie wouldn't hear. "I'll ask him to leave."

I got up, walked over to Charlie, and put my hand gently on his shoulder. "Thank you so much. I'm very happy. You've done a wonderful job. You really are the world's best detective. We're okay now. You can go." My eyes motioned to the door. He made no move to go.

"You want me to leave?" His intense brown eyes cut right through me.

"Your presence makes Ezekiel a little nervous. I may have better luck convincing him to leave Silver Reef if I'm alone. I'll meet you back at the hotel a little later, okay?"

Reluctantly Charlie got up. He kept his eyes on Zeke until he was half out the door. "Be careful." He shot me a stern look and hesitated to leave.

"Charlie, he's my brother," I whispered.

When Charlie left, the tension in the tea shop instantly diminished. I sat back down, looking forward to a nice long chat with my brother.

He took my hands in his and looked at me. "O, I hate to leave you so soon after we've been reunited. I can't tell you how happy I am to see you. But I must finish some business now. After I'm done, I'll never let you out of my sight again. I'll be finished in two or three hours. Where can I find you?"

"I'm staying at the Cosmopolitan Hotel. There's a bench on the front porch. I'll wait for you there."

He stood, leaned over, and kissed me on the cheek. "I'll be there."

"Zeke," I looked up at him, "Can I go and see Mr. Gee? Talk to him about paying your debt?"

"No, Ophelia, don't do that. We'll talk about it later. Look, I'd walk you back to your hotel, but I suspect that puppy dog of yours is waiting outside."

"Zeke, he's not my pet. He's a detective!" I grinned because we sounded like kids again.

"Whatever you say, Little O." He smiled, tipped his hat to me, and went out the door with a big, brotherly smirk on his face.

THIRTY-THREE

Charlie fell in step beside me as soon as I left the teahouse. I wanted to walk alone and relish my reunion with Ezekiel. I was overjoyed but anxious. As we walked, silence settled between Charlie and me like a thick drapery. He waited for me to say something. I said nothing. His I-told-you-so expression irritated me. Charlie couldn't see Zeke the boy, my brother. He saw a dangerous hardened man, a half-savage criminal.

"Well?" he finally said.

Even though May in the desert was moister than the rest of the year, a wagon sped down the road like greased lightning and raised a thick cloud of dust. People scurried out of the way before they were killed or lost a limb. Charlie threw himself in front of me. After it had passed, he still held me protectively by the elbow. Several men hurled expletives and pumped fists at the disappearing wagon. One drunk started shooting at it, an obvious waste of lead. Charlie shook his head and handed me his hankie.

"Thank you." I wiped the grit from my eyes.

"What do you think?" he asked.

"About what?"

"About him?"

It bothered me that he didn't call Ezekiel by name or refer to him as my brother.

"I am right overjoyed to be reunited with my brother, Ezekiel. I owe you a world of gratitude, but I trust your compensation is adequate." I handed him back his hankie and began fumbling with the clasp of the ruby necklace.

He took the hankie and placed it back in his pocket, watching quietly without offering any assistance as I struggled to undo the necklace. The clasp finally came undone and I pulled the ruby necklace from my neck. I held it out to him. His face registered shock, hurt, confusion, then turned hard and stony.

"Here are the rubies I promised."

Without extending a hand to take them he said, "I will see you safely back home to Ogden first."

I continued holding them out to him. "There is no need. I'm afraid it may take awhile before Ezekiel is able to depart."

Charlie shook his head and protested. "I will wait with you then. I can't leave you alone here in this town. It is only proper that I see you safely home."

"Proper!" I scoffed. "Charlie, please. I'm a soiled dove, a strumpet, a painted lady, a whore, a jezebel, a hooker, a harlot, a tramp . . ." A few men stopped and appeared to be listening although they pretended not to be.

Charlie threw the onlookers an irritated glance. "Please, stop," he said, quiet but firm.

"Proper? Do you realize I've sold my every orifice to anyone willing to pay? I've performed every perverted, indecent sex act you can imagine and probably some you can't. I'm probably destined to die of cupid's curse. I—"

"Miss Oatman! That is enough!" His explosive outburst startled me. He grabbed my elbow and led me away from the gawkers to the alley.

I pulled my elbow from his grasp. "Yes, Detective Sirringo, it is enough. In fact it's too much. It's too much for you, and it's too much for me. You have completed your assignment. Your services are no longer needed, thank you!" I held the necklace out to him one last time. He refused to take it. I threw it onto the ground next to his boot. Then I hitched my skirt, turned, and ran down the alley away from him, away from the town, away from the silver mine, and into the desert.

The desert doesn't offer shelter. The burning sun, the sand, the sheer openness simultaneously amplifies and reduces you. I ran and stumbled trying to find shade until my bad leg ached and, exhausted, I sat on the sand against a rock. The unbearable heat forced me to crawl between two leaning rocks into a small slice of shade. There I spent the better part of two hours crying like an abandoned baby. After my conniption fit subsided, I realized that not only had my hot-headed outburst chased away a truly good man, but also that I could be keeping company with rattlers and scorpions. I wiped the snot and sand from my face, crawled out from between the rocks, and wandered back into town.

The sun had dropped out of sight, and the desert sky had softened to soft pink infused with fiery red. Soot-covered men streamed tiredly from the mines into town for supper. They didn't bother to wash before they ate, so great was their hunger and fatigue. While passing open café doors, I saw them slumped over bowls, shoveling stew into their mouths as if their stomachs were as deep as the mines they descended.

Those miners were only a few rungs above the bullwhackers and beasts of burden who pulled freight wagons. They performed backbreaking labor all day, paid inflated rates for tools at the company store, and ate and drank what little was left of their wages at night. When the silver dried up, they'd have nothing to show for all their backbreaking labor. They'd wander to the next boomtown, living off the land as they went. And every bonanza mining settlement would eventually become a ghost town.

The Cosmopolitan Hotel was quiet when I returned. I expected most people were out eating or drinking somewhere. I climbed the stairs to our room. The door was locked. I unlocked it and found the room completely empty except for my belongings. Charlie was gone. In my heart, I had hoped he'd be there ready to mend things. I looked at the empty room and realized I'd gone too far. I threw myself onto his bed and wept over the lingering scents of tobacco, leather, sage, and his unique musk, which I feared I'd never smell again.

I soon realized it was time to meet Zeke. I pinched my cheeks, brushed my hair, and pinned it up. Since the sun was down, I decided not to wear a bonnet. I stood at the mirror, ready to apply lip rouge out of habit. I realized what I was doing, stopped, and threw it into my carpet bag with the rest of my belongings. With the bag in one hand, I trumped down the stairs and went outside to sit on the front porch and wait for Ezekiel. About twenty minutes passed before I came to the dreadful realization that either he hadn't shown up, or I had missed him. I squinted at the beautiful sunset and tried to stay calm.

The beefy mutton-chopped innkeeper strolled onto the porch in his silly checkered trousers. He propped one leg on the railing, struck a match against his boot, lit a cigarette, and looked at me. "Your husband already left."

I stared straight ahead. "Yes, I'm aware of that."

The innkeeper waited for me to explain. I didn't offer any explanation. He stood there smoking and contemplating me.

I sighed and hugged my bag to my chest. "Did anyone call for me?"

"No. Who were you expecting?"

"Never mind that." I stood up and smoothed my skirt. "Do you happen to know where I might find a Mr. Gee?"

"What do you want to see that Chink for?"

"Never mind that. Do you know where I can find him?"

"Sure, everyone knows where Gee lives. Come here." He

walked to the edge of the porch and pointed west. "Right there in that stone house. But listen, if you're in some kind of trouble, I can tell you someone else to call on. Do not go to that Celestial."

"I am not in trouble. The man who left was not my husband. He was a detective, my employee! And as a matter of fact, Mr. Gee is a relation of mine!" I stuck my chin in the air defiantly.

"A relation of yours? Well, now, that's funny because you don't look at all Chinese. Well, if I had known that, I wouldn't have let you stay in my hotel. I've seen a lot of things in my day, but I never did see no red-headed Chinese."

THIRTY-FOUR

I fetched my pony from the livery and rode to Mr. Gee's. He was home and agreed to see me even though it was past calling hours. I entered his opulent study and found a much younger man than I'd expected. His hairless face showed no signs of even the slightest whisker. He was so impeccably dressed and clean, I found myself taking stock of my own appearance and attire. His body was trim. He had not cultivated the portliness common in wealthy men.

Under the spell cast by incredibly handsome men and women, I was lowered by Mr. Gee's presence. I pulled at a ragged thread on my sleeve and nervously fingered a loose button at my collar. He assessed me with a confidence I found unnerving. I tucked a piece of stray hair behind my ear. Instead of looking at him, I studied the guns and swords adorning his walls, the most precious of them protected by glass cases. He was a collector, a connoisseur of precious artifacts. I couldn't help think that, what with Pearl's fancy chalices and his precious blades, they would have made a fine pair.

Before I could formally introduce myself, Ezekiel walked by the open door and saw me.

"Ophelia!" he said, surprised. He entered the room and looked at us inquisitively. His eyes questioned me, but he addressed Mr. Gee. "Mr. Gee, this is my sister, Ophelia. We've been separated for some time, and she has just arrived in Silver Reef."

Mr. Gee stepped closer and studied my face until I worried over every imperfection and freckle. I looked at Zeke. He nodded almost imperceptibly. At first I was surprised that Zeke would show deference to a younger man. But then I understood. Mr. Gee had a formidable way.

"Sister, you say?"

"Half-sister."

He squinted and studied me further. "Ah, yes. I see it. Very interesting. May I offer you a drink? We have an arsenal of beverages, and I'm sure there's something to suit your tastes. Wine or cider perhaps?"

He was charming and had such manners it put me off guard. "That would be lovely, thank you. I'll have cider."

"Eli," he said to Zeke.

I silently reminded myself to call Zeke "Eli" by thinking of our father, although they bore no resemblance to each other.

"Please tell Lu to bring a glass of cider for your sister. And there's a quick bit of business I'd like you to attend to. Lu will tell you the details. It won't take long." Mr. Gee grinned like a viper. "Now I hope you will trust me alone with your lovely sister. I hear she has some business to discuss with me."

Zeke hesitated and raised his brows, "I suppose I trust you, Mr. Gee. But should trust fail, her guard dog has her tail." Zeke grinned at his joke and winked at me.

No longer, I thought.

Mr. Gee smiled sideways. "Always good to have reinforcements, but I'm not the enemy."

"Watch out," Zeke warned me. "He's a sly one. I'll be back soon, Little O." Zeke gave me a reassuring look and left the room.

When I was certain Zeke was out of earshot I turned to Mr. Gee. "Thank you, Mr. Gee, for employing my brother. You gave him a chance when no one else would."

"He is a great asset. Besides, I have a soft spot for those of mixed races."

I looked closer at his features and understood. "Mr. Gee, my brother and I have been separated for some time. I hired a private detective to track him down."

"Ah, yes, the guard dog."

"I would like to pay his debt to you and take him home."

Mr. Gee frowned and studied me.

"I have the means to pay you," I said.

He studied my plain clothes, shook his head, and wore a pained expression. "Really? Eli is very valuable to me. In fact, I'd say his services are almost priceless."

"Surely, everyone has a price, Mr. Gee."

He nodded in agreement. "True enough. And what is your price?"

"Tell me how much you want, and I will pay it."

He moved closer to me. "I don't believe you have the means to pay what he is worth. I have enough money. Truth is there's not much worth buying in this vile town. Good men are hard to come by, as are women. You see, I collect both."

He gently twisted a lose strand of my hair around his finger. I felt his breath on my neck. "Pay me with your favors," he whispered.

A knock interrupted the awkward moment. A flustered-looking old Chinese man carrying a glass of cider entered the room, followed by Charlie. The old man apologized. "Sorry, sir, he bahged in. Says he has ahgent biness."

Charlie narrowed his eyes and looked from me to Mr. Gee. He took off his hat and stared at me. "Sorry to interrupt. I rode all the way back into town because I forgot to give you these." He fished in his pocket and pulled out the strand of rubies. "Your necklace."

The ruby necklace hung sparkling from Charlie's hand, and

drew Mr. Gee's attention away from me like a magnet. Transfixed, Mr. Gee gaped at the rubies.

Charlie smiled. "How can you possibly pay your brother's debt when I'm still holding onto these precious rubies? So sorry. I hope you didn't think I'd stolen them."

Our eyes locked. "Thank you for your honesty, Mr. Sirringo. Your timing is impeccable. I was just trying to convince Mr. Gee here that a plainly dressed woman, such as I, has something worth offering him."

Charlie held the rubies out to Mr. Gee, who held them close to the flickering gas lamp and inspected them.

"They are genuine," I said.

"I know," said Mr. Gee. "They are exquisite."

Zeke burst into the room. With his hands on his knees he doubled over and tried to catch his breath. "Hey, Pinkerton." His chest heaved as he tried to get the words out. "You and Ophelia have to get out of town now. Don't go back to your hotel. Get on your horses and go. Hurry! No time to waste. There's an angry mob gathering."

"But . . ." I looked at Mr. Gee.

"These will do." He held the rubies and nodded.

As Zeke ushered Charlie and me out of the room, he shot a confused look at Gee and the necklace.

"You're free," I said. "Come with us. I'll die if I lose you again."

Zeke looked puzzled. "I'll catch up with you on the trail. If I don't, wait for me at Garden of the Gods. Remember that place, east of Rockville? Can you find it?"

I nodded.

"Okay then, go!" he shouted.

Charlie and I galloped out of town until the exhausted horses failed to keep pace. It seemed no one was tailing us, so we slowed down to save the horses. Neither of us knew what we were running from, but it felt good to be together. Charlie knew the way to Rockville. I prayed I could find the Garden of the Gods from there.

We kept riding. I smelled smoke and looked back toward Silver Reef. A giant blaze glowed orange in the black night. We stopped and stared. Hooves pounded the earth. Charlie trained his gun in the direction of the sound. Ezekiel burst out of the darkness and rode toward us. "Come on!" He galloped past and didn't stop to explain.

As we followed Ezekiel, I sensed Charlie's discomfort. He was a man who liked to go his own way. Zeke knew the country and led us through a maze of rocks and canyons until we were safely lost from even the best tracker or Indian scout. We arrived at a small creek, hitched the horses, set up camp, and did not speak. I gathered kindling and made a fire ring.

Ezekiel shook his head. "I don't think we should light a fire tonight. The smoke could lead them here."

We sat on the ground in the dark. A few stars had come out, but it wasn't late enough for starlight to illuminate the night sky.

"Who is after you? And why do they want to harm Ophelia and me?" asked Charlie.

"Mr. Gee saved me," said Zeke. "I owed him one last favor."

"Oh, Jesus." Charlie took a bottle of whiskey from his saddlebag and shook his head. "I did not hear that!"

"Saved you from what, from whom?" I asked.

"From opium addiction. I had reached rock bottom," said Zeke.

"Hang on." Charlie walked back to the fire and sat down. "Isn't Gee the one importing and selling that stuff?"

"Yes, but he forbids anyone who works for him to partake. Once I started working for him, I kicked the habit. It wasn't easy. I had to let go of longing and regret." He looked at me when he said *regret*. "I had to find the middle way, the Tao."

"That sounds suspicious, like some kind of Oriental philosophy." Charlie drained the last bit of whiskey from the bottle.

Zeke stared at Charlie. "It is Oriental philosophy. And yet it helped me more than fire and brimstone ever did."

Charlie stood up, picked up the empty bottle, and placed it on a rock five-hundred yards away. He walked back toward us, took out his six-shooter, and aimed for the target.

I wondered how much whiskey he'd already drunk and when. "Charlie, are you crazy? The sound of gunfire could attract whoever's hunting us!"

"True enough." He slipped his six-shooter back in the holster. He looked at Zeke. "So tell us, what is this all about?"

"Your cover is blown. You see, Pinkertons aren't too popular with the miners. A drunken angry mob had formed and was looking for you. They'll probably forget what it was all about by morning. But no telling what they would've done tonight."

Charlie rummaged through his saddlebag and retrieved another bottle of whiskey. "I'm not a Pinkerton anymore, haven't been for a while."

"Well, you must have had some reputation, because someone recognized you there. I'd say your days of working undercover are over."

Charlie looked stunned and disappointed. He sat back down with the new bottle between his hands. I couldn't stop staring at his hands.

"So what does that have to do with Ophelia? You said we were both in danger. What do they have against her?"

Zeke sighed and looked perplexed. "Well, that's the odd thing. Somehow a rumor got out that she's a red-headed Chinese woman and a relative of Mr. Gee's. I don't know if they just wanted to see her, or if they'd actually hurt her. But it's best not to find out."

Charlie screwed up his face. I looked at the ground.

Zeke continued. "They were looking for her and saying things that are unrepeatable. You must know when a mob of drunken men get an idea, there's no telling what they'll do. I think it will all blow over. They really want me because—"

Charlie interrupted him. "Don't tell us anything about your crimes. That is absurd. Any idiot can tell Ophelia isn't a Celestial."

Charlie uncorked the bottle, took a drink, and handed it to Zeke. He took a sip and passed it to me. The whiskey burn warmed me and loosened my tongue.

"I told the innkeeper that I was Chinese and a relation of Mr. Gee's." I looked at Charlie. "It's also possible I mentioned that you're a detective."

Zeke and Charlie exchanged looks. Charlie knitted his brow and stared at the unlit fire. I felt chilled and wished we could light it.

Zeke shook his head in amused exasperation. "You were always a strange one, Little O." He fished in his pocket. "Oh, I almost forgot this." He pulled out the ruby necklace, leaned across the unlit fire, and handed it to me. "You can't buy me, O. I'm not a slave. What was between me and Mr. Gee was about more than just money."

I tucked my hands under my armpits and imagined the fire was lit. "The rubies belong to Charlie."

Charlie smiled at me. "I think they'd look better on you, Ophelia. Why don't you wear them and I'll admire them on you."

I looked at him. "Charlie, you take those jewels and sell them. Get what they're worth. You won't have to worry about money or going undercover. You can write that book you were talking about."

Charlie laughed. "I never did see a woman try so hard to get rid of a priceless necklace. Tell me, Ophelia, what did those jewels ever do to you?"

He meant it as a joke, but his words tore me right open. I felt a flood of memory and emotion release. Tears poured forth. Without looking, I felt both Ezekiel's and Charlie's quiet concerned looks. Their kindness broke me. Zeke came over and put his arm around me. His body warmed and comforted me. I tucked my head into his chest and cried until I felt better. We didn't even have to speak. It had always been that way between us.

"She's freezing," Zeke said. "Let's take a chance and light that fire."

Charlie lit the fire. "I'm sorry I said that, Ophelia. Sometimes I ask tough questions that break people. Too many years as a crack-shot investigator I guess."

Zeke rolled his eyes. The fire smoked and ignited. I held my hands out to the flames.

"It's not your fault, Charlie. I do have a bad history with those jewels, and it's about time you both knew." Zeke still had his arm around me. I looked up at him. "Ma gave me that ruby necklace in secret when she was dying. She told me not to tell anyone about it. Uncle Luther was looking for it. I think that was the real reason he came to Grafton, not to take care of us. I had the necklace hidden real good, sewn inside Dolly, where no one would ever think to look. But I told him Ma had sold it. He would have stopped. He wouldn't have . . . violated me if, if I'd given the necklace to him. But I didn't. I kept it hidden. I wouldn't give it up. I don't know why. I must have been a whore all along to let him do that to me, so I could keep a ruby necklace." I covered my face with my hands to hide my shame and tears.

Zeke held me by the shoulders and turned me toward him. "Ophelia, I knew what you were, and it wasn't a whore. We were just kids. You were just a girl." He let go, took his hat off, and ran his hands through his long black hair. "Listen, you couldn't trust that old swine. Even if you had given him the necklace, he probably would have violated you anyway. And what would have happened to you when Uncle Luther left town with the necklace? You probably would have become Elder Thompson's fourth wife, remember him?" Zeke made a funny face and mimicked Elder Thompson's goofy toothless smile. Ezekiel always had a way of making me laugh even in the worst of times. "You wanted to keep that necklace because it was your ticket to freedom. And it was all you had left of Ma."

"Freedom?" I looked at the flames. "Do you know what happened to me? I became a soiled dove. I used the ruby necklace to open a parlor house."

Zeke looked across the fire at Charlie. "Let he who is without sin cast the first stone."

Charlie nodded in agreement. "No man can condemn you. Let bygones be bygones."

Zeke put a hand on my back. "You ran a business, not much different from a saloon, a gambling house, or an opium den. Hey, I would have been better off at a parlor house than an opium den. But shoot, I never could afford those fancy ladies." He tousled my hair like I was a pup. "You did all right. After all, what could you do?"

Charlie chimed in. "All right? She did more than all right! She's got so much money she hasn't even bothered to count it." Charlie winked at me from across the fire.

I smiled. "You're just a pair of boys walking around in men's bodies. And I love you both." I looked at Charlie and he looked at me. "But neither of you understand women."

"No one does," said Charlie. Zeke nodded in agreement.

"That's right," I agreed. "Not even me, and I am one."

Charlie took a couple of tin coffee mugs from his saddlebag.

He poured whiskey into them and handed one to Zeke and me. "We've all sinned. Let's toast our sins and then put them behind us." He held up the bottle.

We held up our mugs. "Is this how they repent in Texas?" Zeke asked.

"Hell, yes," said Charlie.

"To our sins," we said in unison.

"Now go and sin no more," I quickly added before we drank.

Thirty-Five

The Grafton graveyard had not changed much. The town looked like it had gone through a short period of growth and then decline. Several abandoned homesteads littered the hillsides. We didn't see a soul as we rode past the meeting house. Although the flimsy white crosses over our parents' graves were weather-beaten, they were still there, fluttering in the breeze.

Ezekiel shook his head. "We never did get a chance to make them a proper headstone."

"No, we didn't." I answered. We stood with our heads bowed.

Charlie paced the cemetery and read all the headstones while chewing on his mustache. Graveyards made him anxious.

The dress of a bonnet-clad woman swung like a church bell as she ran from town toward the cemetery. Ezekiel turned from her approaching figure and walked to the farthest corner of the graveyard.

She opened the gate, closed it behind her, and rushed toward me. "Ophelia Oatman! I would recognize that hair anywhere. Why child, we figured you for dead!"

"Yes, well, hello, Mrs. Thompson, I'm grateful to be among the living."

Mrs. Thompson looked around the graveyard nervously. "Well, you're not, dear," she said, gesturing to the graves. "Except of course for those two men, now tell me, who are they? Is one of them your husband? How on earth did you survive your kidnapping? I want to know everything? Does your uncle know you are alive?"

"My uncle?"

"Yes, your Uncle Luther, poor soul, shot in the arm, would have bled to death if widow May Belle Hopkins didn't find him and nurse him back to life." Mrs. Thompson smiled demurely. "You know all this, don't you? Surely, you've been reunited with your Uncle Luther already. Why, he's been scouring the territory for you."

Charlie had overheard. He came over and listened with his arms crossed against his chest. I almost fainted, but Charlie put his arm around me just in time. I couldn't speak.

"No, ma'am, this is the first my wife and I have heard of this. We thought all her relations were dead. Please, go on."

"After the shooting, May Belle Hopkins nursed Luther back to health. They fell in love. Luther converted and they got married. Why, Ophelia, your Uncle Luther is a Saint now!" The thrill in her voice filled the desolate graveyard. She smiled a tight smile and looked at Charlie. Then she glanced over at Zeke, who stood at the edge of the graveyard with his back to us. She spoke in a low solemn tone. "Why, you are still a Saint, aren't you?"

From the corner of the graveyard Ezekiel turned toward me. Our eyes met. He had heard. I looked from Zeke to Charlie.

We returned to Ogden. Ezekiel and Charlie didn't have too much in common. They disagreed on many issues and argued about many things. Yet they both had restless spirits. And they agreed that Uncle Luther deserved to die. They argued over which one of them had the right to kill him. I don't know why I spent so much of my time and energy trying to talk them out of killing a man who'd caused me so much suffering. I suppose, like my past, I just wanted to put him behind me.

Charlie started an autobiography about his life as a Texas

cowboy and Pinkerton detective. I helped him with the writing and editing. I anonymously donated money to build Ogden's first orphanage. In the early days of Ogden, before Belle London and Kate Flint, two infamous madams, Pearl Kelly and Miss Peach, ruled Fifth Street. I have kept my story secret until now.

ABOUT THE AUTHOR

Alison L. McLennan was born and raised in Quincy, Massachusetts, until she moved to Utah in search of outdoor adventure. Her debut novel, *Falling for Johnny,* won an honorable mention in the 2012 Utah Original Writing Contest and the 2013 Inkubate Literary Blockbuster Challenge. Johnny was inspired by the infamous James "Whitey" Bulger. McLennan provided commentary on radio, TV, and print during Bulger's trial. She earned a Bachelor of University Studies Degree in Expressive Therapy with a minor in creative writing from the University of Utah and an MFA from the Solstice program where she was awarded the Dennis Lehane Fellowship for Fiction. She was once stranded in the Yukon Territory with only one shoe. She currently lives in Ogden, Utah, and is working on a sequel to *Ophelia's War.*